I0779384

ii

SECRETS DARK AND DEEP

Sherri Stewart

Chapter One

"Three may keep a secret, if two of them are dead."

~ Benjamin Franklin

Maddie Caldecott froze two feet from her desk. Bright pink lilies circled and overwhelmed a single, diminutive red rose in a dark green glass vase. Who put them in her office?

Her eyes darted around the newsroom common area at the skeleton weekend crew who was busy preparing for the six o'clock newscast. A few chatted, but no one was watching her. At least, they didn't appear to be watching. Still, it wouldn't be their first prank. Her penchant for neatness gave them plenty of fodder for juvenile behavior. Their favorite trick—moving things around on her desk—usually hit its mark, especially if she was focused on digging into a case. Didn't they know a tidy desk signified a life in control?

This time she would not react, although a few drops of water had spilled from the vase, marring her monthly desk calendar. She reached for a tissue to blot it dry, but stopped. It was better not to play into their hands. Instead, she approached the desk and lifted the vase to see if there was a note attached.

"I wouldn't do that if I were you."

Her arm froze midair. She spun toward Page Grisham, who stood in the doorway, a box of files posted on her hip. "What do you mean?"

The associate producer's freckled face, turned-up nose, and orange hair always carried a sense of whimsy but not now. "Those pink ones are poisonous. You're not even supposed to touch them." She pushed her glasses up the bridge of her nose. "Spider lilies? *Lycoris Radiata*. The flowers of death?"

"What do you mean—flowers of death?" She cast another glance at the faces of the staff members in the room. This prank was going way too far.

Page joined her at the edge of the desk and peered over her horn-rimmed glasses at the flowers, then backed up. "Could be a silly legend, but then again it could be true. I learned about them in botany class in college. The bulbs are poisonous if you eat them. Of course, most people don't eat flowers, but touching them could give you a rash, and you don't want that before you go on air. Where did you get them?"

"They were here when I arrived. Maybe one of the other anchors left them over the weekend." Maddie quickly put the vase down, then she took a step back, her eyes landing on a folded piece of paper sitting next to her phone. "There's a note." Something about the nefarious thing made her pick it up by the corner. She rounded the desk to her swivel chair and sat, her eyes glued on the paper. "Guess we'll know the truth in a second." She opened it with the tips of her fingers and read it aloud.

Madeleine,
When your eyes change from cerulean blue to stormy red, I see both heaven and hell, but they can't hide your secrets. Past secrets. Dark secrets.
It won't be long, my love. Remember, a kiss from a rose.

Absalom

She flicked the note across the desk, then moved it to a 90-degree angle with the edge of her pen. "I don't understand. Secrets? What do you think it means?" She edged the note toward the associate producer with her pen.

Page peered at the note over her glasses. "Looks like you have a fan. Wonder how the vase got on your desk? I didn't see anyone walk by, and I'm pretty observant."

Maddie's nose scrunched up. "Cerulean—I mean, really? Maybe it's from one of them." She gestured with her chin toward the rows of desks. "A not very funny joke. I don't know anybody by the name of Absalom. Wasn't he one of David's sons in the Bible? The one with the long hair?" Her arms encircled her chest, her fingernails digging into her skin until she made herself stop. "I don't like solving mysteries when they're personal." Opening the middle drawer, she took out a pair of tweezers and picked up the note by its corner, then she strode out of the office and approached the nearest desk to her office door.

Blythe Marchand, the weekend assignment editor, was on her cell phone. "Okay, so Chopper 5 is sending in a video. Yeah, I got it. Breaking news. I'll add it to the preliminary rundown. 10-4." When Blythe hung up, she noticed Maddie for the first time and reached up to hug her, which Maddie allowed with her eyes squeezed tight. "Hey, girl, you look spent. What's going on?"

Maddie held up the note. "Did you see anyone deliver flowers to my desk?"

Yawning, Blythe shook her head as if to shake the sleep away. She had probably been here since four in the morning. "Sorry. Wait, now I remember. The receptionist brought them back a couple hours ago. Are they from Gregory?"

She snickered. "Gregory doesn't send me flowers. The note said Absalom sent them. That's what I'm trying to find out." *Obviously, or I wouldn't be asking.* Maddie twirled a strand of her red hair.

"We need to meet later to go over the rundown and the length of each feature."

"Fine. I'll be back shortly to meet with you and Page about the script, so she can get it to the control room." Maddie headed to the lobby, surprised that the front office was open on a Saturday. She waited for Dana to finish dealing with someone who appeared to be a college student—judging from his bright eyes, suit, and tie. He was probably here for an internship interview. She offered him a smile that came out askew, since the last thing she wanted to do was smile.

Dana held up a manicured finger in her direction. "I'll be right with you." She picked up her phone and pressed a button. "Your 4:45 is here…right, thank you." Then she turned to Maddie and reached up to give her a hug. Two in a matter of minutes? "Hey, Mad. We never see you up here, except when you rush in from the parking lot. What can I do for you? By the way, I like your sweater. It matches your green eyes."

"It gets so cold back there. The weekend producer keeps the temperature in the low sixties." She rubbed her arm to confirm her words. "But that's not why I'm here. I received a flower arrangement with this strange note attached." She held it up by its corner. "The person's name was Absalom." She spelled it out. "Did you happen to see who delivered it—like maybe a guy wearing a toga?" She snickered at her biblical joke.

Dana didn't seem to get it. "Weird name. Sorry, I didn't see anyone. The flowers showed up while I was in the restroom. I was only in there for five minutes tops. Really strange flowers—those lilies kind of looked like claws around that rose. I didn't read the note except to glance at your name."

"Hmm. They didn't come from a florist?" At her shrug, Maddie frowned. "Strange. The guy's probably a fan—or a stalker." When she noticed the puzzled eyes of the receptionist, she clarified, "'The person said, It won't be long, my love.'"

Dana backed up in her rolling seat. "Yikes. Sure sounds more like a stalker than a fan. Maybe you should call the police. I mean, think about it. He—and I'm making an assumption here—waited until I was away from the desk to bring them in. That shows premeditation." She rubbed her arms. "Ew, that means someone was watching me. It gives me the willies."

Waving a dismissive hand, Maddie stepped away. "My apologies. It's just someone's idea of a sick joke. Thanks for the information."

"Keep me posted, Maddie. It might be a good idea to show the note to security just in case."

"Good idea," she said. Maybe they'd caught the guy's image on the security camera outside. With a wave, Maddie hurried back to her area, checking the time on her phone before heading toward the security office, although she doubted anyone would be in the office today. Usually only a single security guard did the rounds outside on weekends. The flowers were off-putting by themselves, but the note was even more so. Well, enough of that. She needed her wits about her as she prepared to anchor the weekend news, and she still had to meet with the producer, go over her notes, and do something with this hair that turned into a bundle of ringlets in Orlando's humidity. What she didn't have was time to waste.

Just then her phone played "Misty," her signal that Gregory Lucas was on the line. Why she had chosen that old song was beyond her. It's not as if she 'got misty the moment he was near.' Gregory was safe. He didn't get too close. She liked that.

"Hey, babe. I almost hung up. Are you at work?"

She winced at his name for her. It's not like she was a teenager from the 50s. "I'm just preparing to meet with

Blythe, Page, and the tech director about tonight's telecast."
Now was not the time to tell him about the flowers or the
note. Gregory didn't need or want to know. It would just
make him upset, and he needed a cool head. "What are you
doing?"

"I'm meeting with my publicist and speech writer in a
few minutes. Don't forget the shindig at the art museum at
eight. Lots of possible donors there. Do you have time to go
to your place and change into that navy blue sheath before
meeting me at the museum? You look great in it."

Her eyes squeezed shut for a moment, then she pivoted
and headed in the opposite direction from the security office.
She'd forgotten about the charity function at the museum.
Somehow, she'd make it work—she had to. Gregory was
counting on her. "I'll do my best to be there on time, sheath
on body." Back in her office, she stuffed the flowers in the
bottom drawer of the file cabinet, so they wouldn't be a
distraction as she finished her work for the broadcast.

This was what life would be like with Gregory Lucas—
maybe even worse as election time drew closer. It had all
seemed exciting when he'd told her after their third date that
he was directing his romantic interests solely on her.
Directing his romantic interests—that's how he'd put it. As
if it was something to be determined like an agenda item.

When he'd told her of his romantic interest, unease had
been her first reaction. Why? And how should she respond?
Yes, Gregory was dashing—that was the most fitting
adjective for him. A man of action, determined, principled,
and all the parts fit together well. But he made her feel a bit
like an item on a checklist. Gregory needed someone on his
arm for the plethora of social engagements he had to attend
to garner votes. Basically, that's what it came down to.

Tonight would be date number seven. Why she kept
count, she didn't know. Maybe it was because she knew their
days were numbered. Her head still clouded with the fact that
her life couldn't be real with Gregory. Everything had to

pass muster with his election committee. That's not how she wanted to live. And for sure she couldn't tell him about the flowers she'd received. All right, two anxiety-provoking events were too much to handle at the moment. Like Gregory, she couldn't let her personal life affect her work, so all thoughts of flowers and political boyfriends went into a file in her brain to be opened later.

Somehow, she made it through the newscast. Another teen killed in a drive-by shooting. Fires in California, the birth of a new virus, threats of war in Somalia —the daily news always caused a hollow dread in her core. Viewers always asked her why she and her colleagues didn't report good news. Journalism 101—"bad news sells"—was her answer early on in her career, but now it just sounded glib. The murders, accidents, and wars affected each of them long past the airings. Something akin to PTSD clung to each and every journalist after the newscast was over. The sobbing mother who'd lost her only child. The teenager who'd killed himself after being bullied in the school restroom. Journalists could report, but they couldn't provide solutions.

Two things worked for her whenever the heavy, dark blanket of anguish weighed against her. First, order. A neat desk and a thorough check of her notes and facts kept the darkness at bay, since she was in control. But sometimes, when the news was overwhelming and order wasn't enough, she recited psalms she'd memorized. "Thou wilt keep in perfect peace whose mind is stayed on Thee," she often chanted during commercials. King James worked the best for her—it sounded more regal.

Others found their remedy against the darkness in a bottle or a pillbox. Some never found a cure and left to find a job they didn't have to take home with them. Gallows humor and salty repartee were common in the studio. Eugene Michaels, the meteorologist, always made her cringe with his colorful but inappropriate jokes. At first, she didn't hide the fact that her colleagues' salty language bothered her, and the rest of the crew even used to tease her about it. But when she listened more deeply, she realized that quips and oaths were elixirs for those trying to cope, whether in newsrooms, police stations, or emergency rooms.

Bad news or not, this was the career she'd chosen way back in high school when she worked on a video-broadcasting team. From the beginning, she believed that accurately reporting the news was like keeping a tidy house. Provide accurate reporting, and the community would choose order over chaos. Despite the dark blanket, she drew energy from every minute of her work and threw herself into every story she covered.

As she left the building, the drawer of her brain opened, and the message played in her mind: someone, "Absalom," was coming for her. Furtive eyes scanned the area for anyone that looked out of place, but she saw no one. It wasn't dark yet—the thought gave her comfort; still she scurried to her car and jumped in as soon as the door opened. From now on, instead of leaving her car in the visitors' parking lot, which was a lot more practical, she'd park in the fenced-in lot. With the note hot in her purse, it reminded her that her life was not her own. He could be watching her right now. Would he follow her home? Would he be waiting for her when she took Rory to the park?

It was then she saw a new note held in place by the windshield wiper.

Chapter Two

"Man is not what he thinks he is, he is what he hides."

~ André Malraux

Her body took over by reflex. Locking the doors, shaky fingers shoved the key in the ignition, then put the car in reverse, and her feet took over, stomping the accelerator and causing the car to bolt backward. If hcr pursuer was watching, the effect of the note flapping in her windshield would be apparent by the wheelie her foot had managed.

Breathing through her lips, she thought about driving straight to the local police department. Let them pull the note from its place, so they could see she wasn't some hysterical female. She was hysterical, though—at least her heart was beating faster than normal. Cases like this often went awry. That's what she'd learned when doing that investigative report on women being stalked. Maybe this Absalom was somehow connected with that report, but that was years ago and for a different station. The writer of the note could be any of the myriad of suspects she'd reported on.

Veering into a Wawa gas station, she pulled into one of the aisles. She didn't need gas; what she needed was to collect herself. Not seeing anyone suspicious, she stepped out of the car with one leg, leaned forward, and seized the note, freeing the single rose and lilies hidden beneath it.

There was no doubt this was the same guy. She stuffed the note into her purse, not giving it a second glance. The museum event loomed ahead in less than a half hour, and Gregory wouldn't be happy if she was late. There'd be time later tonight to deal with it. Right now, she needed to become the suitable woman Gregory required.

Pulling into her single-car garage, she stayed in the car until the garage door was down, then hurried into her condo, turning on every light she found on the way to her bedroom closet. With no time for a shower—which was fine, since who wants to take a shower when one's being stalked—she shrugged into the blue dress Gregory suggested she wear. She slipped into matching shoes, which cramped her feet, so she forced them off and decided on her old, go-to sandals.

In the bathroom, she dabbed at the smears under her eyes with a damp cloth, flossed, applied lip gloss, and gathered her mop of curls and snarls into a messy bun. It would have to do.

Rory barked. The dog. In her haste, she'd forgotten to take the dog out. She rushed into the bedroom, where the shih tzu lay on the bed. Her tail started wagging when Maddie kissed her on the head. "I'm so sorry, baby. Just a little walk because I'm late." Who knew if the guy had followed her home?

Attaching Rory's leash, she opened the front door and steered the dog toward the shrubs that lined the living-room window. Of course, Rory pulled on the leash wanting to sniff at everything. "C'mon, Rory, I'm in a hurry. I'll make it up to you tomorrow. Gregory will be mad if I'm late."

A female voice mere feet away made both her and Rory jump. Her neighbor, Mrs. Eldridge, appeared around the myrtle bush. "Sorry to scare you. I was just out pulling some weeds when I heard your voice. How are you, dear? You looked so pretty on the news today."

When Maddie regained her voice, she thanked the white-haired widow. "Well, I need to hurry to an event. It's nice seeing you, Mrs. Eldridge. Maybe we can have tea sometime." She winced. Tea? With a wave, she hurried into the house, grabbed her keys, and dashed to the garage.

She hadn't been to the museum in years, but Siri would get her there. On the way she prayed, Lord, You know who's doing this. Make it stop. Help me to be…suitable tonight. Amen. Suitable? It was the only word she could think of, but it fit.

A song played on the radio, a ballad with no words at first, just violins, then a man's haunting voice broke in. The minute she heard his voice, Maddie pressed the off button multiple times to make it stop. Why had she done that? She was probably just a bit off tonight.

Once in the museum parking lot, Maddie parked as close as she could to patrons who were arriving at the same time. She hooked on to a group of silver-haired women and their husbands who were chatting about other social events they'd been to around the state. Luckily, they didn't seem to notice her following them. Maddie had learned the trick of hooking onto the back of a group of people when she was working in Manhattan. It had kept her safe.

Waiting just inside the entrance stood Gregory. Was he checking his watch? Well, she'd made it. That's what he wanted. When she joined him just inside the lobby, his eyes traveled up and down her frame, and he nodded his approval. "You never disappoint, Madeleine."

"Thank you. As I told you before, call me Maddie, please. My full name always makes me think I've done something wrong." She offered a smile, weak as it felt from her end. When he offered his arm, she took it and let him lead her into the exhibition hall. Clusters of people gathered around art displays, all impeccably dressed, all holding cocktails or glasses of wine.

Tuxedoed caterers meandered among the guests, offering hors d'oeuvres or replacing empty glasses with full ones. A string quartet added appropriate background music to the undertone of chatter. As the patrons passed them, they smiled at Gregory and tried to get his attention. Many recognized her as well and nodded her way.

"How was your day?" Gregory was looking at her when she glanced up at him. She was tall, at 5 foot 8, but Gregory beat her by three inches.

"I'm sorry?"

"I said, how was your day?" His eyes softened, and she debated telling him about her new "fan," but just as she began, a middle-aged woman with a pince-nez and purple-tinged, coiffed hair tapped his other arm.

"There you are. I wanted to talk to about the appropriation committee's de—"

And the moment passed. It was just as well. He had more important things to concentrate on. But it would be nice if, just once, Gregory wanted to know more than how her day went. They'd never had a deep conversation about what was important in life, just superficial information that anyone could find out with a few questions.

As the woman kept a firm grip on his arm and attention, Maddie stepped away to peruse a glass cubicle housing an indigo vase patterned with storks. The plaque indicated it hailed from Honduras, 500 CE. After all these years, it amazed her that ancient art could be so well-preserved. More so than humans—with this stalker, would she even make it to her next birthday?

The spiky leaves surrounding the birds reminded Maddie of the flowers on her desk and windshield, and the new note, still unread in her clutch. A glimpse behind her showed Gregory deep in conversation with a trio of men and the same woman, laughing at something he'd just said. With all those people around, no one would notice if she read it. Circling the vase display, she opened her purse and pulled out the note, then remembered that the mere touch of the accompanying lilies might be poisonous, so she left the flashy pink blossom in the opposite corner from her lipstick and car keys.

Turning her back on the vase, she summoned a strengthening breath and unfolded the note.

Madeleine,
No doubt you've shared my gift to you with your colleagues. Please don't. What we have becomes tawdry when too many eyes see it. It's obvious you don't remember me. Maybe this will jog your memory.

> *"I sometimes think that never blows so red*
> *The Rose as where some buried Caesar bled;*
> *That every Hyacinth the Garden wears*
> *Dropt in her Lap from some once lovely Head."*

Absalom

What? What was this disturbing poem supposed to mean? "Some buried Caesar bled"? Was that some kind of metaphor? The words had a threatening tone, linking a flower to death—just like the spider lilies. Why would someone write these horrid words? What had she ever done to warrant this behavior? Maddie swallowed, which engendered a spasm of coughing. No amount of self-talk stopped it. Why hadn't she packed a bottle of water? Answer, because her purse couldn't hold a thimble, much less a bottle. Now her eyes were tearing up, and she was becoming a wet, muddled mess.

No restroom sign was anywhere close, and she certainly wasn't going to return to Gregory in her present condition. Focusing, she forced herself to breathe to fight the cough. When it subsided for a minute, she cast a quick glance around the side of the display, hoping nobody had noticed her outburst. Good, Gregory was still engaged in a conversation with the same woman and three men. He'd be awhile.

She'd been foolish to read the note at a social function like this. Should she have read it when she was alone in her condo? Who was this Absalom? Maybe it was an anagram. Molslamb, Amslomb, lambmos, blomsam. None of them made sense; neither did the poem, which had something to do with the flowers she'd received. Add to that the warning that Absalom, whoever he was, was coming soon. She had to discover who this person was, so she could protect herself. If not, he could be here at this exhibition or looking in her condo windows or in the parking lot at work. How was she going to take Rory outside to do her business three times a day?

Summoning a breath, she clicked on her phone and typed the first line of the poem into Google. She didn't remember the poem; maybe she'd studied it in college or high school, which meant Absalom was from her past. In an instant, a dozen results appeared.

She scrolled through the list to find a commentary on what it meant. An analysis of the poem appeared on the twelfth result down. Clicking on it, Maddie scanned the long explanation, trying to grab anything she could hold on to for the notes she'd received.

The verses came from quatrain 19 of The Rubaiyat by Omar Khayyam. She'd studied at least part of that poem in eleventh grade World Lit, her favorite class in high school. They'd lit candles, one of the guys in the class had brought his guitar and provided background music as, one by one, they'd recorded themselves reading the poem. It had been a very pleasant experience, but she didn't remember much about the poem itself.

With a side-glance at Gregory, who was still busy, she hurriedly typed 'commentary' next to the title. Only a few results appeared, most from bloggers. She clicked on one. It said the rose was a symbol of the blood Julius Caesar had shed when his friends betrayed him. Had she in some way betrayed the writer of this note? Was he seeking revenge? She'd never been thoughtless. Distracted, yes, but not thoughtless.

A touch to her elbow sent her purse and her phone flying in a quick arc to the ground. She whipped around to see Gregory, his head tilted, his eyes narrowed.

"What are you doing over here?"

"Just—" She bent to retrieve the items that had spewed from her purse. Her lipstick had rolled six feet away. The letter, her wallet, and her grandmother's cloth handkerchief sat at her feet. As she skittered to retrieve her lipstick, Gregory knelt and now held the flower that looked even more sinister in its wilted state.

"You didn't answer my question. Why are you over here? We have a lot of people to meet. Personal contact is a more effective way of garnering votes than any other means."

"Sorry." She lowered her eyes to avoid his stormy glare. This was important to him, and she'd disappointed him. Once everything was back in her purse except for the flowers, she rose to a standing position.

He stared at the flowers on the ground. "Madeleine, what in the world?" He picked up the flowers and brought them to his nose—

"Don't. They may be poisonous."

His hand released them, and they fell again to the floor. The two of them stared at what had fallen for a few moments. He was waiting for her to explain. She tried to think of a suitable reason that didn't border on a lie.

When he finally spoke, his voice was low. "What do you mean—poisonous?"

"It's nothing." Maddie bent again, opened her purse to retrieve the handkerchief, and used it to pick up the flowers and stow them in her purse. "A fan left them on my windshield with a note. That's all." She deliberated telling him about the note, but now was not the time. With a poor excuse of a smile, she offered her arm and apologized again.

He shrugged. "It's time to go find our seats for the banquet. I hope we won't be late."

Banquet. She'd forgotten all about the banquet. That meant hours and hours of listening to speakers and making small talk with the other guests at the table who'd paid extra to sit with Gregory. Sometimes, she felt less like a companion and more like a trained seal or a pink poodle.

When they reached table number eight, two seats remained, and they weren't adjacent. Their delay was her fault, so she'd do her penance by sitting between two strangers for the next several hours.

After Gregory had pulled out her chair and returned to his own, she smiled at the man next to her who nodded in her direction as he swilled his cocktail. From the flush of his face, particularly his nose, this wasn't his first drink. On the other side sat a woman of a certain age whose fingernails tapped on her bread plate with each point she made to the woman on the other side of her.

Gregory was already delighting the four people closest to him with one of his anecdotes. He was a natural schmoozer, and soon the whole table fell under his sway. This freed her up to think about what she should do with the note and the flower that hopefully weren't burning a hole through her purse.

She wished she could take the paper out and study the words. Maybe they'd evoke a memory or a link between her and the man. With nods and smiles in Gregory's direction every time their eyes met, she reviewed the details in her mind.

The stalker had been at her place of work twice that day. The thought sent a spiral of shivers through her. Instead of freaking out, I need to make a plan. Tomorrow she'd go in early and ask the security department to go through the videos of the lobby and the front parking lot. Second, the flowers were distinctive enough that it shouldn't be difficult to find out where he'd purchased them. A Google search should reveal where one could buy them. Third, the guy definitely held a grudge from the past, but she had grown up and gone to school in New Jersey. The link with Absalom probably didn't go that far back. It must be a local person.

Which left one possibility. Something she'd reported on—either as an anchor or as a reporter—had elicited a deadly reaction from the stalker. He wanted her dead, and he was giving her fair warning.

She glanced up to see everyone looking at her. What now? While everyone at the table held amused expressions, Gregory's eyebrows pointed into a V as if he was sending her a reprimand. He nodded toward her plate. She looked down to see her bread plate turned upside-down as the hub of a tableware wheel with each piece of silverware acting as the spokes. When and why and how had she done that?

Her knuckles covered her lips as she started giggling of all things. Until she glanced up at fourteen eyes studying her as if she were a lab specimen. "Sorry. I'll take care of it." Their eyes were still on her. Flipping the bread plate, she rearranged the spoons, forks, and knives, to the left and right of her plate. "Salad fork on the far left, and work your way in. Bread knife at twelve o'clock. Spoons protect the knives," she recited. Okay, they were still staring at her. She swallowed and managed her best apologetic expression. "There, everything's back in its proper place. You were saying—" She inclined her head toward Gregory because he was most likely speaking when he was so rudely interrupted.

His face was unreadable—was that a word? "Gregory, why don't you tell them about your recent trip to San Francisco when there was that mix-up?" Anything to move the attention away from her very warm face. All eyes turned to him. Good.

He leaned back, a pert smile playing on his lips. Gregory loved to tell this story. "Well, I checked into a hotel before heading over to a political caucus meeting. Imagine my surprise when I opened the door to the penthouse. Fresh fruit. A bottle of Champagne with a small box of chocolates. Suffice it to say, I was suitably impressed. We lowly senate candidates don't usually merit suites, much less chocolates."

Everyone chuckled, and he looked pleased. "Anyway, there was a knock at the door. I opened to a valet standing there, one arm holding a large manila envelope and a clipboard, his other arm behind his back.

"'For you, Mr. Lucas,' he said and handed me the envelope. As I wasn't expecting any correspondence, I was eager to see what was inside the envelope, but the valet stood there. Then it occurred to me he was waiting for a tip. So, I fished in my pockets for some money, knowing I didn't have much cash, if any.

"Just then, the man said, 'I need you to sign for the document, Mr. Lucas.' Then he turned the clipboard around and pointed at the line where I should sign. I glanced at the name to the left, and it all made sense. It read George Lucas." Everyone burst out in laughter.

"So, what did you do, Gregory?" the women sitting next to him fingered the pearls of her necklace.

"I told the valet there had been a mistake and beat a hasty retreat out of the room. The man at the check-in desk apologized and comped me a different room. So, it all worked out, although it wasn't as grand, and there were no chocolates."

The servers arrived on cue, placing beautifully presented salads in front of each guest and refilling water glasses as they asked each diner to choose chicken, salmon, or pasta.

Maddie picked at her greens, moving the olives around with her fork, separating the vegetables from the condiments. Should the grape tomatoes stay with the greens or sit by themselves in the fruit pile? She'd disappointed Gregory. Their eyes had met when everyone else was focused on their food, and she'd read disapproval. Just because she'd rearranged her plate and silverware? Maybe if she explained why she was distracted, he'd understand. He would, in his own way. It was not as if his eyes read, "Madeleine, you wait until your dad gets home"—the line her mother always issued because it worked. The thought almost brought a giggle, but she stifled it, not wanting to evoke more disappointment.

For the rest of the evening, Maddie was the perfect companion. She laughed on cue, nodded at the right moments, and fielded questions about her work at the station. Then the speakers started, all party leaders lauding Gregory with their support, and the crowd roared their agreement.

Then it was Gregory's turn. He was in his element, telling stories about different big donors in the room, talking about the programs he supported or planned to establish. Gregory evoked trust—he was their golden boy—and as Maddie scanned the faces in the room, she could tell he had their support, both moral and financial. But that was to be expected. The debates would bring a more moderate result, but these events buoyed up his foundation. Even if she felt like a trophy sometimes, Maddie enjoyed some of the venues he took her to. This museum would be one, had she not made an idiot of herself.

After shaking the hands of many of his supporters, he returned to the table, circled to where she was sitting, and whispered that it was time to leave. As she grabbed her wrap, he spoke to each person sitting at the table, shook their hands, and thanked them for their support. He helped her put on her wrap, and his hand remained on the small of her back as they made their departure.

Night had fallen while they sat at their tables, and a slight shiver descended her spine as she stepped outside. Yes, it was a bit chilly, but it was more than that. Her breaths came in quick succession as she waved goodbye to Gregory, then hesitated before she took the first few steps toward her car.

"Do you want me to walk you to your car?"

What? "Oh, no. That's not necessary." Maddie spun around toward him. It surprised her. She'd expected the kiss on the cheek, as he waited under the porte-cochère for the valet to bring his car. But rare was the time when he walked her to the car. He was always in a hurry. "I mean, would you?"

Looking toward the underground parking lot, he said, "Sure, it will be a few minutes before they bring the car around." He stuffed his hands in his pockets, and they set off. The parking lot was devoid of people since they'd left early, so there was no group to tail onto. Their footsteps and a distant car honk were the only sounds, so she searched for something smart or witty to say, but then he spoke first.

"What's going on with you?"

Odd. "Nothing. I'm fine."

"Madeleine," he said in a tone that didn't bode well. "Help me understand why you were hiding behind that art exhibit, and what you were thinking, building sandcastles with your dishes?"

"What?" Oh, now she understood. This walk to her car had nothing to do with chivalry and everything to do with a reprimand. Memories flitted back. The time she was called into the principal's office for cutting class. The talk before the grounding her father gave her after a family friend had told him she'd seen her at the movies instead of the library. Yes, she'd been a bit of a "sneaky snake," as her grandmother called Maddie when she'd hit puberty. She'd deserved those reprovals. Now she waited for him to finish talking about how bad it looked for her not to be engaged in the conversation at hand.

"I'm sorry. There's a lot going on right now, and I haven't had time to process it today. Somebody is stalking me, and the two notes he left—one on my desk and the other on my windshield—were disturbing, as were the flowers."

The car was just ahead. Good. She doubted there would be a date number eight.

They reached her car. He took her key fob from her hand and opened the door for her. "I'm sorry as well." He checked the windshield. "Good. No note. Looks like you're safe. You can talk to me any time at all if you have a problem. I'll always make time for you. You know that, right?" He nudged her chin with his index finger.

Maddie fought the urge to jerk away. She'd didn't need someone to "make time for her." Yeah, he'd pencil her in between meeting with his publicist and going to the gym. He was waiting for an answer. "I know." Maddie slid into her car, tossed her purse on the passenger seat, and started to close the door when he blocked it with his hip, then reached down and kissed her head instead of her cheek.

"I care about you, Madeleine." He turned to leave without waiting for a response.

All she could do was nod. Closing the door, she murmured, "And it's Maddie, Greg." Besides Gregory, her parents were the only ones that called her Madeleine. Her mother had named her after the little French orphan in the children's book—the one who never followed the rules, but everyone loved her except for the nuns who ran the orphanage. Unlike her namesake in the children's book, and the Maddie of her teenage years, adult Maddie always followed the rules. Rules made everything go according to plan; chaos ensued when rules were not followed.

She pulled out of the parking space and drove toward the exit, glancing in the rear-view mirror to see if he was standing there, wounded by her nonresponse, but Gregory was long gone.

Another boyfriend bit the dust. Not that there had been many others. Somehow, it brought a bit of relief. When she reached a red light, she checked to make sure she had her purse. More than a few times, she'd left it next to her chair at work or at the movie theatre. Would it be so hard to design dresses with pockets big enough to hold keys and a phone? A pat on the seat next to her brought momentary relief— quashed the next moment by the rustle of paper. Had the note fallen out of her purse? The clasp on the purse was closed. The light changed, and so did the modicum of calm inside her.

She accelerated, suddenly feeling vulnerable. With her right hand, she felt for what would confirm her worst nightmare, and her fingers landed on the crepey texture of the petals that hadn't been there before she left the car. She quickly drew her hand away. In one day, Absalom had invaded her office, left a note on her windshield, and now he had broken into her car. Dread filled her. Leaving flowers at her office was one thing, but now he'd penetrated her locked car. This wasn't just an office gag. Her hands trembled, and she glanced in her rear-view mirror. Was he following her, the darkness hiding his identity? What would the note sitting next to her say? Was it safe to go home?

Chapter Three

"We dance round in a ring and suppose, but the secret sits
in the middle and knows."

~ Robert Frost, The Secret Sits

Maddie rubbed her fingers against the goose bumps
forming on her arms. Her wrap didn't provide much warmth.
The plastic chair couldn't be more uncomfortable. Maybe
that's why waiting rooms were full of uncomfortable
chairs—so people wouldn't want to stay. The tick of a clock
and the detective's taps on the keyboard were the only
sounds in this cramped office. And the smell. Didn't—she
checked the name tag on his rumpled shirt—Detective Brody
Messner know that spearmint gum didn't mix well with the
onions from the hamburger sitting on his desk? How long
had it been sitting there? She resisted the urge to throw the
greasy hamburger and its wrapper in the trash.

He rubbed his hand over a day's growth of stubble,
which sounded like razor blades scratching a chalkboard,
then he peered up at her over his glasses. "Okay, Ms.
Caldecott, I have all your information. Now you said this
person named—" He peered at his screen—"Absalom left
three notes. I have two here. Where is the third one?"

Maddie lifted the plastic rain hat containing the note
from her car and the flower blossom. "Sorry, I didn't want

to contaminate the note if it had his fingerprints on it." She squirmed against the hard seat. "And the flower, as I mentioned to you while you were typing, might be poisonous if touched. At least that's what the associate producer said." She held out the transparent, bag-like hat with pinched fingers. "You can keep the hat or throw it away. I use it when I'm reporting in the rain, but I can get another one." Too much information. Why did she have the feeling she'd done something wrong? How long was this going to take?

The officer yawned loudly without covering his mouth. Was she keeping him up? He squeezed his eyes shut, then opened them wide as if he was bored out of his mind.

"Sorry," she said aloud.

He glanced up. "Sorry?"

She shook her head. This wasn't going well. "You yawned. I just meant I'm sorry I'm wasting your time when you could be sleeping or something." That came out wrong. Didn't he understand she'd like to go home to sleep as well, but she was afraid to go there since the guy was obviously following her? She huffed instead, just like her dog, Rory. "I haven't read the last note. It was dark, and the guy was following me, and he broke into my car. That's why I'm here. If he can break into my car, he can break into my house. I'm afraid to go home. And I don't believe in guns. So, he'll just have to kill me. I'll be tomorrow morning's murder victim." She couldn't help feeling a bit sorry for herself.

He put down the note and leaned forward on his forearms. "You're not having a very good day, are you?"

"To say the least." She huffed again and leaned back like a recalcitrant teenager, not entirely proud of herself.

"Would you like to know what the note says?"

She nodded, her eyes studying the paper in his hands, although it wasn't going to erase the fear. If anything, it would exacerbate it.

He sniffed, then grabbed a tissue from a box sitting on a pile of files. His face scrunched up as if it were a chore to read out loud. "'My Isolde'— What is that—French? How am I supposed to pronounce that?"

When she shrugged, he continued.

"My Isolde,

I knew the amphora would draw you like a bee to a flower. It hails from the Ulúa valley. If you like, I can get it for you. Soon we will be together. Yes, there will be purging—necessary for the cleansing of your soul.

Remember a kiss from a rose.

Absalom"

Officer Messner peered at her over his glasses. "Isn't that from a song?"

"What's from a song?"

He pulled up his computer and typed in some words. "This. It's a nineties song by Seal, the singer? 'A Kiss from a Rose.' Listen."

Stringed instruments preceded voices that sounded like a madrigal choir, then a beautiful voice—the moment she heard, she bolted to her feet. "Turn it off. Now."

"What did I do?" He fidgeted for the computer button and hit it. His bushy eyebrows furrowed together. "Why did you react like that?"

Her knuckles covered trembling lips. Why had she done that? "I don't know. It just brought up something visceral in me."

The officer pushed his glasses back on his head and leaned back, as if he were afraid to get too close. "All I can say is this guy's got the hots for you. That's for certain. And he sure does like to spout poetry. Could he be an old boyfriend?"

"No, sir, I think it's someone who's seen me on TV. Perhaps it's someone I reported about. There's an underlying threat in that poem. Three letters today and those flowers. My producer said they're the flowers of death. I'm afraid to go home. That's why I came here." How many times would she have to repeat herself? Her lip started quivering; she bit on it hard. No way would she lose it now. That's not what she did.

He looked her square in the face, the blue of his eyes disarming. If he cleaned up his face, he'd be almost striking, but she didn't have time for any of that.

Maddie shook her head to dispel such thoughts. All these letters and flowers had caused everything to go askew. It made her feel disoriented, like she wasn't in control. But Officer Messner was talking; in fact, he was staring at her with a curious look on his face. "What? I mean, pardon me?"

"I just asked you if you'd checked the security cameras at your work. I assume a television station would have cameras."

No, she hadn't, and a good reporter would have done that first, but then Gregory had called…still, it was important to tell the truth. "I was on my way to ask the security guard to check the cameras, but a phone call waylaid me, and then I had to prepare for the news. Since it's Saturday, we don't operate with a full staff." Her voice drifted off. The guy didn't need excuses.

"All right." He tapped the edge of the note on the desk. "No crime has been committed yet—" he put a hand up to stop her protest. "Yes, breaking into your car is a crime, but sending flowers or leaving notes on parked cars is not. Having said that, I agree with you. The tone of these notes is disturbing. Do you live alone? Will your husband or significant other be at your residence tonight?"

"No, I live alone." A thudding headache was making her right eye twitch. "As I said, that's why I came here instead of going home to my condo." She stood. "Would you mind if I threw away those wrappers? The smell is giving me a headache."

He raised his palm. "Have at it."

She used a tissue to throw away the coffee cup and the

rest of the remains of the hamburger and fries. He was watching her, but she couldn't help it. Squirting some hand sanitizer on another tissue, Maddie leaned over the desk and cleaned up the crumbs and greasy spots.

His head tilted to the side as if he was trying to figure her out. She'd seen that look before—the juxtaposition of frown lines and lips that held back a laugh.

"I'm off tomorrow, but before I leave—with your permission—I'll turn these notes over to forensics to check for fingerprints. I don't know if the flowers would have fingerprints on them, but I'll bag them anyway."

When she nodded, he continued. "On Monday, I'll pay a visit to the art museum to see if their cameras picked up the guy. What kind of a car do you drive?"

"An Audi. 2019. A4. Dark blue. It was my mother's." He didn't need to know that.

"All right. I'll know what I'm looking for in the parking lot. Perhaps tomorrow or Monday, you can check with your security people at work to see if the cameras picked up your...guy."

She frowned. "He's not my guy! It's probably some twisted viewer who thinks I should suffer for some reason." Her hands were rubbing the flesh off of each other. "Should I just go home?"

"I could lock you up." The corners of his lips turned up slightly.

Her head bobbed up. "For what?"

The officer held his palm up. "The holding cell's not pretty, but it's safe. . . . Just kidding." He pulled open the middle drawer and took out a card. "Take this with you. Call me anytime if you think something's wrong. Or you can call 911. Hopefully, it's just some crazy fan of yours that means no harm." He wrote something on the back and handed it to her. "I put my home phone number on the back. Use that number."

Oh, if it were only a viewer's prank. She took the card

expecting an official-looking police card, but instead there was a small picture of him sans uniform with a pleasant grin on his face. Two hockey sticks crisscrossed each other in the corner. The only information was his name, Brody Messner, and an email address.

Maddie was tempted to ask him about the hockey sticks, but she held back. It didn't seem right under the circumstances. "Thank you. Hopefully, you won't hear a peep." She offered the best smile she could, but it probably came out as more of a crooked line, like Charlie Brown's smile.

He stood, signaling the meeting was over. She followed suit and was just about to thank him for taking her seriously when his phone rang, so she offered a wave and left. Returning to the waiting room through which she'd entered, Maddie lowered her head, not wanting anyone to recognize her. In the thirty minutes she'd been in the detective's office, the number and volume of those waiting had risen exponentially.

The bars must have let out because the smell had changed from antiseptic to vomit and sweat. Through the hum of conversation and snores, a few voices dominated as they argued about something that had happened earlier. Why did people think being louder made them righter? At least it was safer in this room than it was outside the door where darkness could shroud a stalker.

Her car was just a few feet from the door. No stalker would be foolish enough to leave a note by a police department, would they? Unless it became more of a cat-and-mouse game that way.

Nothing new awaited her at the car, so she slipped in and immediately locked the doors. She backed out of the space and headed home as fast as she dared this close to the police station. Her eyes cut frequent glances in the rear-view mirror. Since it was close to midnight, the traffic was lighter than normal, but it was hard to tell if someone was tailing her. All headlights looked alike—menacing. It wouldn't hurt to take a quick right to see if anyone did the same.

Without turning on her signal, she veered onto a small street with mid-century houses, many in need of loving care. When she'd driven a block, headlights turned onto the street. Her breath hitched. It could be nothing. Was this her new world—eerie and threatening? She veered left, hoping she wasn't turning onto a dead-end street. Instead, she found herself in an apartment-complex parking lot. Pulling into a space between a truck and an SUV, she turned off her car, praying that this time her headlights wouldn't stay on as they sometimes did. She appreciated the headlights when she carried groceries into the house, but not so much when she was hiding from an assailant.

From her vantage point, she had an incomplete view of the street, but headlights bounced off the roofs of parked cars in the row ahead. He knew her car, so there was no point in hiding. Instead of staying on a busy street, she'd veered into a parking lot with no witnesses, like some femme fatale running into a dark alley in a horror movie. Her dead body would be found in her car weeks from now.

No, it wouldn't. With a quick prayer, she started the engine, backed up so fast the tires squealed when she raced out of the parking lot back to the safety of the main street. She risked a glance in her rear-view mirror to see if the guy was following her, then slammed on her brakes when the light turned red. This was not good for her heart. Taking a few calming breaths, she chanced one more glance in the mirror, but no moving cars were anywhere near.

Maddie headed straight home, pushing the garage-door opener numerous times before entering her driveway. New rules for this new world: Wait for the garage door to close completely before hightailing it into your condo, and always be aware of your surroundings. Pulling in, she waited for the garage door to meet the ground before racing inside, slamming the kitchen door behind her.

Barking came from the living room. Oh, no. Poor baby. She hurried into the living room and picked up the shih tzu and kissed her head multiple times. This was what she got for not planning better.

Grabbing the leash, Maddie had no choice but to take her out. "Rory, I'm sorry, but we have to make this quick because we may be taking our lives into our hands." She attached the leash, peeked out the front door, and when she didn't see anything out of the ordinary in the dark, she hurried down the steps to the grassy area. Of course, Rory was in the mood for sniffing—Maddie's punishment for not coming home earlier. Now she was a sitting duck with a dog.

Once back in the house, her breath returned to a normal tempo, and she scooted to the windows to make sure they were locked. A quick glance at the clock showed it was just past midnight. Nothing good happened after that time. The morning news always attested to that fact. She wouldn't make it easy for Absalom or whatever his name was.

She pulled the broom out of the laundry room, twisted it until the handle was free, then hurried up the stairs to her bedroom. Without turning on the light, she opened the vertical blinds of her balcony and peered out at the street below. It was as quiet as it always was, except for the meow of Mrs. Eldridge's tabby cat, which was loud enough to be heard through the glass. She stuck the broom handle in the sliding door's track. Although she prayed for God's protection, she wanted to do her part.

Sleep evaded Maddie for hours as she reviewed the biggest local news stories she'd covered. Perhaps it was someone she'd reported on who had been arrested for something, or maybe she'd inadvertently maligned someone's character. She always tried to report the news without her personal opinion showing itself, but when there were victims, it was hard.

The writer of the note had to be someone who lived locally—which meant anyone from as far east as Daytona to

Metro Orlando to Winter Haven in the southwest. The tone of the notes was accusatory. Someone wanted her to pay for some secret she kept. What could she have done to deserve such rancor?

Her social life had been nonexistent until Gregory had asked her out, so it couldn't have been a spurned boyfriend. Even in high school, she'd not dated, and hardly anyone asked. Maybe it was because she was so driven to become an investigative news reporter, already digging out any newsworthy story in their microcosmic high-school world. In fact, her best friend, Tessa, had to set her up with a blind date for the prom since no one came asking. It wasn't that she was unattractive or couldn't laugh at a joke; it was just she didn't have time, between youth work at church, community service projects, and writing college entrance essays.

One weekend, Tessa had invited her to spend the weekend at her house, so they could have a 'makeover party.' Not one that involved curling irons or mascara, but one that taught her how to 'lighten up,' as Tessa called it.

Tessa's advice was the best Maddie had ever received, beyond what she had learned in debate club about public speaking. That night, Tessa taught her to search for and appreciate the good qualities in others, including teachers and her fellow students. She gave Maddie hypothetical situations to help her practice being nicer.

"Of course, I'm not saying you're not a kind person, because you are kinder than anyone I know. You'd give not only your shirt but your jeans to anyone who needed them. It's just sometimes you're a bit—shall I say—off-putting? You like to argue, and you're always in a hurry, and sometimes it seems that you get antsy when people don't talk fast enough, and—"

"Enough. You're making me feel really bad about myself." Her lip had started quivering at that point.

Tessa wrapped her in a hug and patted her back until

Maddie regained control of her emotions. "You're a great person. So, for the whole weekend, we're making you over, so people will see the real Madeleine Caldecott."

By 'people,' Tessa meant everyone in the school, which itself was off-putting. It wasn't hard for Maddie to sympathize with the underdog. That came easily, as Maddie was always pleading people's causes to the administration. But what Tessa was trying to show her was more subtle and personal. Tessa said kindness was something as simple as a smile or a nod or making eye contact and listening—really listening.

After Tessa's makeover class, Maddie had to admit high school and college became more enjoyable.

Maybe if she'd seen appreciation modeled in her home as she was growing up, she wouldn't have had to learn it at a makeover party. Her parents were always busy—her dad with his law practice, her mother with her Junior League. It was her grandmother and Beverly, the babysitter who moved into the basement suite when Maddie was ten years old, who actually parented her. Her grandmother had prayed with Maddie to make Jesus her savior, and Beverly had taken her to church.

That relationship with the Lord had carried her through her parents' divorce, and her grandmother's move to Switzerland. How she wished Gran were closer now. She was the only one besides Tessa and Beverly who would understand how scared she felt right now. But Beverly had moved away before Maddie's parents divorced, and Tessa was living in Vancouver. What time was it in Zürich? Using her fingers, she figured it was eight in the morning.

Maybe Gran hadn't left for work yet. At seventy-five, her grandmother didn't tarry in bed too long. She'd be walking around that park on the hill near her house, every so often stopping to do strength exercises. Whenever Maddie visited her, Gran pulled her out of bed way before she was ready to get up, saying God didn't create lungs to be ignored.

Maddie didn't argue, knowing there'd be a stop afterwards at the café down the street for delicious pastries.

"Guten Morgen." Gran's words always sounded like a song.

"Hi, Gran. It's Maddie." Although her name would appear on her grandmother's phone, Gran would be hard-pressed to read it unless she was wearing her glasses.

"What a surprise. It must be the middle of the night there. How are you, my lovely?"

Gran's words felt like a warm blanket around her. "Do you have a few minutes?"

"I have a rehearsal later this morning and a child coming for a violin lesson, but that's in an hour, so I'm totally at your disposal. What is it, sweetie?"

How much to tell her? And what did she expect Gran to do about it from way over in Zürich? "Nothing really. Just an obsessed guy—maybe a viewer—who sent me three notes today and these weird flowers called spider lilies. One was left in my car. He calls himself Absalom. It's a bit disconcerting, but I'll be okay. I just wanted to hear your voice. It makes me feel safe."

Her grandmother tsked, and Maddie could almost see her shaking her head. "Ah, lycoris radiata. I am so sorry you have to go through that alone. Why don't you come over here? Take a leave of absence. It's that job of yours—being in the public eye. Everyone sees you, but you can't see them."

Maddie couldn't help herself. She started laughing. "Gran, you're priceless. No matter why I call, you always tell me to come to Switzerland. I miss you like crazy, but there are bills to pay and a mortgage. And I've worked too hard to reach a seventeen to give it all up."

"What in the world does that mean?"

How to explain? "If New York is a one, and Los Angeles is a two, and Roanoke is a thirty-three, Orlando is a seventeen. It's the size of the viewer audience."

"Ah, I understand. But with seventeen comes a whole lot of traffic and crazy people."

She chuckled. "Gran, you've got that right. But doesn't Zürich have its crazies? It's a big city."

"It does, but it just feels safe. I sure would love to have you and that sassy little Rory here." Gran paused. "You aren't going to tell your parents, are you?"

"It's funny. I didn't even think of calling them. They're so busy with their kids and jobs. I don't want to burden them with my problems." An unintended sigh emitted. "So now I've burdened you."

"You're never a burden, child. No matter what time of the day it is, you call me. I'll pray for God's warrior angels to cover you with their swords. Your crazy viewer with the spider lilies won't have a chance. Love you, Maddie Lou. Stay safe and pray."

"Yes, ma'am." That's what she'd forgotten to do—pray. Instead, she'd let that stalker drum up fear in her. Opening her Bible, she leafed to the psalms, her finger stopping at Psalm 56. There was her answer in verses 3 and 4. "When I am afraid, I put my trust in you. What can mere mortals do to me?"

Indeed, what could mere mortals do to her? Fear would not keep her from living her life. No more cowering. No more looking in the rear-view mirror. No more dragging Rory inside when she wanted to sniff at bushes.

The next morning came way too quickly. She must have fallen asleep with the lamp turned on and the Bible still sitting on her stomach. Today she'd go to work early, so she could meet with the security officer. The fear was gone, replaced with a determination to expose the guy. If he was doing this to her, he could be doing it to others. If that were the case, she needed to be a crusader rather than a victim.

Despite her new burst of determination, she took the long way to work, circling the block with her eyes on the rear-view mirror. Warriors still needed to be aware of their surroundings. This time she parked in the fenced-in employee parking lot, which required a longer walk into the building and a stop at the security desk. Maddie tarried at the desk for a few minutes, waiting for one of the cameramen to disappear. She didn't want the world to know about her stalker. In fact, the fewer people who knew, the better.

Chip Henry's freckled face broke into a broad smile when he saw her. "Hey, stranger. Long time no see."

She rolled her eyes. "Yeah, I know. It's so much easier to park in the guest lot."

He leaned forward on his elbows. "To what do we owe your presence…Princess?"

"Very funny." She peered around and, seeing no one, she moved close. "The princess has an ogre."

He backed up in his seat, his eyes now more engaged than flirtatious. "Ah, so that political bozo finally showed his true colors."

"No, it's a different ogre this time." She took out her phone and showed him pictures of the three notes and the flowers she'd taken, on the advice of the police officer. "These arrived yesterday. Would you take a look at yesterday's security footage to see who was hanging around my car in the guest parking lot?" She gave him time to read the small screen on the phone.

Once finished, he studied the pictures. "Those flowers are very colorful. It's probably that boyfriend of yours. He sounds like the kind of guy who would recite bad poetry. Now if you dated me, you wouldn't have to put up with any of that."

She rolled her eyes again. "Gregory doesn't write me poetry, and he calls me, 'Babe.' Not a chance he'd call me 'Isolde.'" She crossed her arms and tapped her fingers on her goosebumps. "Could you check the cameras? Not only did he leave notes here, but he also broke into my car last night at the art museum. He left one of the notes on the front seat."

His eyes widened. "Whoa, breaking and entering is a

different issue. Do you have any idea about the time frame yesterday? That's a lot of hours of feed to watch."

Maddie leaned a hip against the table and fought to keep impatience out of her voice. It wasn't as if the studio had a lot of crime to keep Chip busy. "I arrived about two and left about seven-ten. The note was waiting when I got in my car. Oh, and the first note was left on Dana's desk while she was in the restroom, so that should be easy to determine the time frame. You just have to go ask her." She checked her watch. "I have to fact check and talk to Morgan. Do you think I should tell him? I don't want anyone to know, so would you keep it on the down low?"

He stood to his full height, towering over her, and lifted her chin with his forefinger. "As you wish, Princess. You don't need to tell Morgan. I'll handle it. Now you take care."

"Great. I owe you one. By the way, I did tell the police last night, so they know." Waving, she hurried to her office to concentrate on bigger news stories than her own.

All afternoon, as she prepped for Sunday evening's broadcast, her mind kept straying to old local news items she'd worked on. Which ones involved a person of high intelligence accused of a crime? Anyone who used words like 'cerulean' and 'Isolde' had to be book smart. Maybe he was wrongly accused or maybe not, but for some reason he blamed her. The first note said, "past secrets, dark secrets." What secrets? She couldn't think of one. Who even knew her well enough to know if she had secrets? Maddie made sure even her coworkers didn't know her personal business. It was more professional that way. The less they knew, the more orderly her life was.

The third letter said she needed to be purged. She looked up the word in the Merriam dictionary on her phone. "Purge. Transitive verb. a: to clear of guilt; b: to free from moral or ceremonial defilement." Further down she read, "In some cultures, a ritual bath or prayer is performed to purge guilt or evil spirits. The Minoans of ancient Crete may have used human sacrifice as a way of purging the entire community."

A shiver ricocheted through her. Absalom wanted her with him, but first she had to be purged of some secret from the past. After she returned home, she'd call Tessa. Maybe her best friend from high school could shed light on something from her past—some secret she'd forgotten about. If there weren't any, she could rule out any secrets from her life before moving to Orlando. Fortunately, no flowers or notes had shown up at work that day, and her car was safe in the fenced-in parking lot. Hopefully.

Hours later, as she was stuffing files into her computer bag, preparing to go home, Chip rapped at her office door. "Knock, knock."

Maddie looked up. "You don't have to say it if you do it." When his lower lip protruded, she waved a dismissive hand. "I'm kidding. C'mon in." Circling her desk, she said, "Did you find anything on the camera?" Maybe she'd recognize the perpetrator.

Chip set the laptop on her desk, tapped on a few keys, and brought up a grainy video of a stooped-over, older woman entering the reception area carrying the flowers. The woman looked around, then placed them on the counter, spun around, and limped out the door.

"It's a woman? I don't get it. The note said we would be together. Does that woman look like a person who'd send me flowers?" She backed up, forgetting the credenza was there, and knocked over a lamp. "Oh, this is a metaphor of my life." She bent down, but he stopped her, placed hands on her arms, and shifted her around.

"You go sit down where you won't hurt yourself." He gestured toward the desk chair. "Go." Then he righted the lamp and readjusted the skewed shade.

"You're a kind fellow. So, that was the earlier picture. Were you able to get a feed from later in the day when he…she put the note on my windshield?"

He shook his head. "Sorry. When I was fast-forwarding,

something must have happened because the video went black from five o'clock on. The camera is old, so I put in a work order to get it repaired or replaced."

That wasn't the answer she wanted. "You mean there's no security right now? Doesn't that seem a bit convenient?"

His head tilted, and his shoulders lifted. "You know how tight the budget's been lately. Instead of being proactive, we wait until something like this happens." He sat on the edge of the desk. "I promise you this. I'll be watching your car and your back until we catch the person. We'll get to the bottom of this. Don't you worry, Princess. 'You got a friend in me; you got a friend in me,'" Chip warbled. "'When the road is rough ahead, and you're miles and miles from your nice, warm bed—'"

"Woody's song from Toy Story? Aww." She offered him a hug. "Thank you," she said and backed up, releasing him when it went from friendly to uncomfortable. Chip was a nice-looking man, his blondish curls and impish smile giving him a youthful, mischievous look, but he was too touchy-feely for her taste. "So, any advice, Woody?"

"About that woman. Notice how she's wearing an overcoat, and it was a nice, warm day yesterday. Maybe she's in disguise."

She rubbed against the goosebumps on her arms. "It makes sense. The limp could be a red herring. Either way, it's discomfiting."

"Whatever that means. I'll be watching you, so don't be discomfited. Trust me, okay?" He winked, brushed against her as he picked up his laptop, and breezed out the door.

Maddie felt better already. Grabbing her laptop bag, she took one glance around her office. The vase with the red flowers still sat there on her desk. She placed it next to the lamp on the credenza, almost out of sight. Tomorrow she'd be working out of the truck with her camera operator. If she could just make it, undead and unpurged, until then.

Chapter Four

"Secrets, silent, stony sit in the dark palaces of both our
hearts; secrets weary of their tyranny;
tyrants willing to be dethroned."

~ James Joyce, Ulysses

Barking met her as Maddie unlocked the garage door
and climbed the steps to the kitchen. Rory's furry little body
wagged as she opened the door. "Hey, you. It's still light out,
so how about we go for a short walk while it's still light."
Her eyes took in the whole room as she clipped the leash
onto the dog's collar. Nothing looked out of place.

Grabbing a doggy bag, she set off for the park two
blocks from her condo. The falling sun created new shadows
which lurked nearby as she and Rory walked past oak trees
and bushes. When they reached the small-dog park, she
unfastened the leash to let Rory scamper in the fenced-in
area. Only one other person stood in the corner, a man
smoking a cigarette. His cocker came over to sniff at Rory.

Maddie nodded to the man, who didn't seem to be
watching her. She'd give Rory ten minutes, and then they'd
go back. One thing she'd learned about Florida—when night
fell in this state, it fell fast, unlike New Jersey where dusk
seemed to last for hours. It was eight-thirty; she estimated
fifteen minutes of light remained.

Maddie cut a cursory glance at the man, whose hands

now were stuffed in his pockets, his head bobbing. Was he sleeping? Remarkable how every male looked sinister—like someone out of a dime detective paperback. Enough of this, she called for the shih tzu and clipped the leash to her collar. Of course, the dog pulled on the leash every few seconds as they headed home.

Finally, they reached the condo. Note to self—When outrunning a stalker, don't bring the dog. Once inside, she filled Rory's bowl with rotisserie chicken from Publix—a peace offering for leaving her home alone all day and evening.

She checked her phone after starting the bath water and dropping a lavender bath bomb in the tub. No messages from Gregory. It didn't surprise her. Sometimes days lapsed before she heard from him. Her thoughts went to Officer Brody. He'd said he was going to check with the museum tomorrow to view their security tapes. Maybe she'd have answers then. After undressing, she donned her favorite robe, and turned on the television, pressing the volume button until she could hear the television over the bath faucet.

Since Maddie worked on Sundays at the studio, she attended church on YouTube in her living room or bedroom depending on the time of day she returned from the studio. Tonight, she listened to the choir that preceded Pastor Hibbs' sermon on YouTube. The music seemed to calm her.

Settling into the soothing, hot water, she turned down the tap to listen to Jack. Fear was the topic of the sermon— how it kept King Saul from obeying God. When fear took over one's heart, irrational thoughts moved in, crowding God's Word out. Saul was so fearful he donned a disguise and visited a medium—the only one left in Israel, since they had been driven out.

It was as if Jack was talking straight to her. It seemed her best efforts to reject fear last night didn't last long. Had she allowed irrational thoughts to enter instead of finding strength in the Lord? She slipped further into the water until only her head was above it. Now the pastor on television was comparing David to Saul; in particular, the time David's men were threatening to kill him because their wives and children were kidnapped by the Amalekites. "But David strengthened himself in the Lord."

"Get to the point, Jack," she called to the TV in the bedroom. "How do I strengthen myself in the Lord?" She already knew the answer. Since David wrote most of the psalms, that seemed to be a good place to park. David had used the Urim and Thummim—sacred stones used by Israel's priests to know God's will—to determine if he should go to battle. She didn't have any sacred stones, but she had the psalms.

After putting on her pajamas, she grabbed her Bible and flipped to the center landing on the forty-sixth psalm—a familiar one she loved. "God is our refuge and strength, a very present help in trouble; therefore, we will not fear." Her finger slid down to verse 5. "God is in the midst of her; she shall not be moved: God shall help her, and that right early." Female pronouns. Was this directed at her? She wouldn't put it past Him. That's how this worked. She wondered what "that right early" meant.

Just then her phone rang. She thundered down the stairs to the kitchen to grab her phone before the caller hung up. Tessa's name played on the screen. "Hi, you. I was going to call you tonight. Is Alexa reading my mind now?"

Giggles spewed from the other side of the continent. "Hi, Mad. You've been on my mind all day. What's going on?"

Where to begin? At the beginning. Maddie filled her best friend in on the flowers and the notes as best as she could remember since Officer Messner had kept them.

"Ew. That's just weird. No wonder you've been on my mind. What are you going to do?"

She moved to the couch in the living room and tucked

her bare feet underneath her, then opened a new bottle of pearl nail polish. "Live my life and pray for protection along the way. What do you think the guy meant by a dark secret? It's almost as if the guy knew me from way back. Can you think of any tawdry thing I was involved in during high school or college? I've been racking my brain, but no secrets come to mind."

"Hmm, no, you were always the good girl. Too busy to get into trouble. Unlike me."

Maddie giggled. "You mean that time when you were about thirteen, and you stole your dad's cigarette and tried to light it while looking at yourself in the bathroom mirror?"

"Yup. I inhaled, and it tasted so bad I threw it in the bathroom wastebasket—"

"And it landed on an aerosol can and exploded."

Tessa laughed. "You remembered. Somehow, my parents didn't notice the wastebasket was missing, so I got away with it that time."

Maddie dipped the brush into the bottle, then started on her left hand. "My life wasn't half as exciting as yours, and I always got caught."

Tessa tsked. "What did you ever do to get caught? You were an angel."

"I was a skipping angel. I cut class one day to do a project for student council and passed my French teacher in the hall. My parents got a call later that night, and I was grounded for two weeks."

Tessa blew out a breath. "Skipping class to do something at school isn't skipping!"

"Well, the adults didn't agree. So, you don't remember anything else in my teens that could be considered a dark secret? I can't think of anything." She heaved a sigh, as if it were a burden not to have a secret.

"No...wait. There was one day when you left school early—twelfth grade, I think. Something happened in the restroom, but you wouldn't tell me what it was. I caught up with you as you were leaving, and you said you were never coming back to school."

Maddie stopped blowing on her fingernails. "What? You must have me mixed up with someone else. I never said that, and I don't remember ever leaving school early except for a dentist appointment."

"You did, but when I asked you about it the next day, you acted like you didn't remember. I thought that was odd, but I let it go because you seemed back to your cheery self."

Maddie leaned back against the couch. "That's weird. Why would I say that and not remember? Maybe that's the dark secret Absalom was referring to. Do you have any idea why the guy would call himself Absalom?"

"I don't know anyone by that name. We were teenagers, and teenagers do weird things. I should go. It's seven o'clock, and the dinner dishes in the sink are not going to wash themselves. I'll try to remember if there was any other secret you might have told me when we were in high school or college, but you were about as normal as a person could be."

After they hung up, Maddie sat there, her arms tightened around her chest. This wasn't normal. Nobody, male or female, should have to live, looking over their shoulder. If she'd inadvertently done something to the person writing those letters, she'd want a chance to say she was sorry and make it right, but it seemed as if he was enjoying keeping her in the dark with threats and innuendo.

The next day floated by as most Mondays did. As was always the case, she met with the producer, and he handed her an assignment to research—an old case involving a high school basketball coach who had been fired five years ago for molesting a student. Normally she loved digging into cases like this, keeping tabs on someone who'd been a danger to society, but this was too close to what she was going through. Still, she was happy to have a substantial story to work on.

"The perp, Grady Newland, got off on a technicality, then disappeared. You worked on the original story, so I thought you'd like to do the follow-up." Morgan's head tilted to the side. "You don't look too thrilled to take this on. It's unlike you. Is something wrong? Whenever I find an old case that needs looking into, you're the one I think of. What's up?" He took off his reading glasses and pointed at the chair across from him.

Surprised that Morgan hadn't mentioned anything about her stalker, she asked, "Didn't Chip tell you about what happened over the weekend?"

His bushy salt-and-pepper eyebrows furrowed. "No. I haven't talked to him today. What happened?" He leaned forward, crossing his arms.

"It seems I have a crazy fan." The words poured out without a single breath. She'd repeated it so many times it felt as if it wasn't her story anymore. "Nothing happened yesterday, but I'm still a bit undone. Officer Messner is going to check the video feed of the parking lot at the museum sometime today, so maybe I'll have more information." She leaned forward. "Tell me, is the station having financial problems?" Immediately she wished she could take back the words, for Morgan backed up in his seat as if she'd slapped him. "I'm sorry I asked. It's just that the security cameras didn't work, and I thought—"

He looked puzzled more than offended. "No, our financial picture is healthy. The security cameras were checked a month or two ago, and they were fine. I don't understand why they didn't work, but I'll notify the security team to call in a work order. I'm glad you went to the police. We wouldn't want anything to happen to our hotshot anchor and rabble-rouser."

She waved a dismissive hand at him, loving this man who always fed her hunger for righting the wrongs of society. "I am not a rabble-rouser."

"Of course not." He laughed and twisted his class ring.

"You just like to kick up the rug and see what's under it."

"Nothing wrong with that. Will Theo Andrews be going out with me today as cameraman?"

"Only the best for you." He waved, a not-so-subtle invitation to get lost.

"On my way." After she returned to her desk, put on fresh lipstick, and sprayed her curls into submission, she dug through her laptop for the original file on the abusive coach. A married twenty-eight-year-old teacher with a toddler, he'd vehemently denied the charges, saying that the student was seeking revenge for being benched for two games. Maddie had had her doubts about his guilt, but, as always, she kept an impersonal tone when reporting in front of the school, and months later, in front of the courthouse. Was he Absalom? Not likely, since her reporting didn't constitute a deep, dark secret. Had she told anyone at work that she thought the guy was wrongly accused? It was too long ago to remember, and who would she tell? She rarely confided in anyone.

Maddie spent the next few hours searching for any online clues as to his whereabouts. His wife, Gretchen, had divorced him and remarried. Summoning her courage, Maddie found the ex-wife's last known phone number and called her. It was always hard making a cold call like this, and usually the response was less than receptive. Five rings, and she was about to leave a message when a female answered.

"Hello, is this Gretchen Ashley?" She identified herself and told her why she was calling. A long pause had her wondering if the woman had hung up.

The woman's answer came in terse spouts. "I don't know where he is. He hasn't seen our daughter since then. His actions destroyed our family. Why would you want to dig all this up after all these years?"

Maddie leaned back and closed her eyes, wishing she could put the phone down and rub away the pain in her temples. The woman had a point, but Maddie needed some answers. "The court exonerated him. It's possible he was falsely accused. I just want to know if he's coaching. If he's moved on with his life."

"Grady always said he didn't do it. All I know is he left the area. No school system would hire him. I doubt he could get a coaching job anywhere. The only thing I know is every Christmas and birthday, Amazon delivers a wrapped gift for my daughter, Abby. There's no name or return address on the package, but I know it's from him."

Maddie sat up straight. "What were the gifts? Did you keep the wrapping paper?" Of course, she didn't. Why would she if she was starting a new life?

"No." The tone of the woman had descended to frosty. "My daughter was only two when he left. She has no memories of her father. Someday, I will tell her, but at this point, I don't want to confuse her. Can't you just leave this alone?"

Sometimes, she hated her job. If he was innocent and had taken on a new identity, her reporting would expose him again, and he'd lose not only his job but everything. But if he was guilty, he'd probably strike again. Pedophiles were opportunists. When Maddie was a younger reporter, uprooting evil had outstripped any bit of compassion for the suspect and the possibility he was wrongly accused. Now she was a bit more circumspect.

The woman coughed, bringing Maddie back to the present. "I understand your need to protect your daughter. How about I do a quiet search to find out where he is, and I'll let you know what I discover."

The woman's sigh expressed her reluctance before she said a word. "All right. I would like to know how he's doing. It just seemed so out of character for him to do that to a student. Grady always told me that whenever a female showed up at his office, he made sure the door was left open, or there was another person present."

"That's the school system's policy. I learned that when

I interviewed the principal. Do you have any idea where he might have gone to start over?" Morgan wouldn't be happy if she didn't file a report. She was getting soft. Maybe it would be better to check out the female student.

"Oh, I don't know. He loved sports. Soccer and basketball were his favorites. Find a town with both and check the venues."

After a few hours' work at the station, she discovered there were dozens of Floridian towns that offered community soccer and basketball seasons. It would take her forever to check out each one. If she were Grady Newland, she would have taken on a new identity. For a price, there were ways to obtain a new social security number, birth certificate, and driver's license. Nevertheless, she checked all of his old identification numbers, but the trail had died five years ago.

Because the student was a minor, her name wasn't published, but Maddie had found the name of the girl from interviewing the girl's friends. Melissa Russo had been a senior at the time, so she could be married with a new name by now. A check of social media sites showed she was already divorced and 'in a relationship.' Hm. Had the trauma she'd endured during high school led to relation problems in her adult years, or was she the kind of person who caused the problems?

Enough for today. Maddie stuffed her notes in her laptop bag and headed home. With thoughts of the assignment swirling in her head, she forgot to check her surroundings until she was almost home, but a glance in the rear-view mirror showed nobody following her. Maybe Absalom had moved on. Still, she stayed in her car until the garage door was completely down, and then she unlocked the door to her condo.

Quiet greeted her. Where was the dog? Rory always met her at the door.

"Rory?" Maddie's eyes swept through the kitchen. She

ran to the living room calling the dog's name. No barks. No little wagging body. Where was she? She ran into her bedroom and said her name; she even looked under the bed and in the closet. No dog. How could Absalom take his anger out on her helpless little dog? Tears streamed down her cheeks by the time she ran into the adjoining bathroom. "Rory?"

A note with scrawled letters hung on the mirror. Check the shed.

Chapter Five

"If you reveal your secrets to the wind, you should not blame the
wind for revealing them to the trees."

~ Khalil Gibran

"No!" Her trembling hand went to grab the note,
but reason stopped her just in time. She didn't own a shed,
so she raced to the garage, grabbing the keys on the way. Her
mind landed somewhere between agony and suspension in
another world. If her furry puppy was in any way injured or
frightened, she'd— Just then the sound of a distant
scratching reached her ears. Such a blessed sound. Rory was
alive. Where was it coming from? Maybe he'd left her
outside, but first she'd check the room in the garage, which
was the closest thing to a shed she had. What kind of a person
subjects a helpless animal to hours of Florida heat?

It took her three times to turn the knob and force the
door open. It had always been hard to open but never like
this. She steeled her eyes for what awaited her and turned on
the light. The dog wasn't there. Thank you, Lord, she
repeated in quick succession. Just in case, she checked the
containers—the red and green one in which she stored
Christmas decorations, the pink dog carrier, and the one
holding clothes she planned to take to Goodwill.

Where was Rory? Had she forgotten to close the sliding-
glass door to her patio? No, there was that note on the mirror.

As she did a slow turn, her eyes landed on a picture taped to the wall above the light switch. She almost grabbed it but stopped herself again. Reason told her this was a crime scene, but first she had something more important to do. Find her dog.

Back in the kitchen, she rushed to the sliding-glass door. At least the temperature hadn't reached the eighties today. Still there were all kinds of animals out there that would love to feast on a shih tzu. One of her neighbors had opened her front door to find an alligator on her patio. Another neighbor down the street had snapped a picture of a bobcat traipsing across his lawn at seven in the morning.

Rory wasn't on the patio. For the first time, Maddie remembered to pray. She leaned over the little table next to the patio chair where she liked to sit and have her quiet time. "Lord, you know where Rory is. Please keep her in the palm of your hand. Make this person who's invaded my home stop. I don't know why he's doing this, but make him stop."

Back in the living room, she locked the door behind her, stood, and listened. Nothing. Her eyes darted from one end of the room to the other. Nothing was out of place. Oh, she hoped Rory wasn't out running in the streets. The little shih tzu had bolted out of the door more than a few times when Maddie had opened it before attaching her leash. Maddie hadn't been able to catch her until she stopped to sniff something blocks away. Once she'd even trotted into someone's house when the door was open. Rory wasn't street-smart. She'd face down a truck coming at her, not realizing the difference in their sizes.

The balcony. She'd forgotten about it. Maddie raced up the stairs, hoping she was there. It was the least of many bad possibilities. There she was, panting from the heat, staring at her with puzzled eyes through the glass.

She flung the door open and pulled the dog into her arms. "I'm so sorry, baby. Let's get you some water. Thank you, Lord." Maddie carried her into the bathroom, then filled water to the top of the plastic measuring cup that sat next to the tub. For some reason, Rory preferred tap water in the bathroom to water from the kitchen faucet.

With another apology to the dog, she sat on the edge of the tub and blew out the longest breath. "Rory, I think it's time to call the police. I wish you could talk. You're the only one who knows what he looks like."

She grabbed her phone, but before she called, she hurried down the stairs but stopped. The perp might still be in the house. How had he gotten in? She assumed he was a male despite the old woman in the video feed. No, he wasn't in the house. She'd looked everywhere for the dog, and the place wasn't that big. There was one more thing to do before she called in the authorities.

He'd wanted her to see the picture attached to the wall in the garage, so she'd take a picture of it. It was definitely a clue, and it would provide some proof that she wasn't imagining things. Swiping at the sweat on her brow with the hem of her shirt, she headed back to the so-called shed. Flicking on the light, she turned to face the photograph.

Absalom had taped it in the one spot she'd be sure to see. It was a familiar picture, a photo taken of her parents, the babysitter, Beverly, and herself in the backyard. Her parents sat in lawn chairs in the shade of the large maple tree. Between them sat two tall glasses of lemonade on a small white table. Beverly and she stood behind them.

From her long bangs and thin legs, Maddie guessed she was probably twelve years old in the picture. Her father was scowling, or maybe it was the sun shining in his face. Her mother was wearing her public smile, which probably meant her parents had been arguing about something. Beverly, who was about five years older than Maddie, wasn't looking at the camera. Her ambivalent expression evoked more questions than answers. Who was taking the picture? And why was this picture, out of all the oodles of pictures that were stuffed in albums and manila envelopes, hanging in the shed?

After snapping a picture of the photo with her phone, Maddie headed into the house to retrieve Officer Brody's card. That's what she called him in her mind, but she didn't know why. A glance at her watch made her gasp. How could it already be eight o'clock? Was it too late to call him? He'd told her to call anytime, so she'd take him at his word. At least, the clock hadn't struck nine yet, her cut-off time for making calls.

Maddie found the card on her nightstand and summoned her courage because she really didn't like making cold calls, although it was a huge part of her job. If it went to voicemail, should she tell him to call her or blurt out everything in her message? With her luck, she'd be cut off and have to call back.

A husky voice answered on the sixth ring—she'd been counting. "Hello, Brody Messner here, may I help you?" A cacophony of screams and knocks played in the background. She'd probably caught him in the middle of a crime scene.

"Hi, my name is Madeleine Caldecott. We talked two days ago in your office? I just wanted to report something that happened earlier today." She heard him talking to somebody. "Should I call back at a more convenient time?"

"Hi, I'm in the middle of hockey practice for the team I coach. Are you in any danger at the moment? Because if you are, you should call 911."

Was she? Absalom had broken into her home. He had walked through her bedroom, past her bed, and into her bathroom. A thought occurred. What if he installed secret cameras to watch her?

"Hello, are you still there?"

"Yes, I'm here. And to answer your question, I don't know. The guy that wrote those notes broke into my house today while I was at work. He left a note in my bathroom. I'm not sure what I should do."

He breathed out a whistle. "I'm glad you called. Is there

any possibility he's still in the house?"

As she began to answer, she heard him call somebody over. "No, I'm fine. I can put chairs in front of my doors, and I'll check all my windows just to be sure."

Just then, his loud voice had her holding the phone away from her ear. "Hey, what do you think you're doing? Stop with the boarding. Go take five on the bench." Brody said something else she didn't understand. "Sorry about that. I assume from what you said you don't have an alarm system, so give me ninety minutes to finish up here, and I'll come right over. Lock up and stay safe."

The phone went dead before she had a chance to respond. Had she given him her address? At least if he was coming over in ninety minutes, she'd find out what the museum security video revealed. While she went from room to room, checking the windows, looking in every closet, and making sure the doors and sliding glass doors were locked, she thought about the picture. Officer Brody would want to know what it meant, and she had no idea.

Chapter Six

"If we could read the secret history of our enemies,
we should find in each man's life, sorrow and suffering
enough to disarm all hostility."

~ Henry Wadsworth Longfellow, Driftwood

After Brody dismissed his teenage players with a warning to spend more time passing the puck and less time in the penalty box, he thanked the assistant coach and equipment manager for hanging out in the locker room to make sure the little roosters didn't take their roughhousing outside the rink. He waved goodbye to the Zamboni driver and the two gals working at the desk and headed out to his car.

With a vocal yawn, he climbed in the car, and pulled the scrap of paper on which he'd scribbled Madeleine Caldecott's name and address. What kind of name was that? Was she a Rockefeller or something? She'd not given off any pompous airs when she'd sat across from him. Yes, she'd taken it upon herself to throw away the remains of his food on the desk, which was a first. He could tell the pungent onions slithering out the sides of his cheeseburger bothered her. She hadn't said so in so many words, but he could read her expression. He'd learned over his years on the force to read faces. They didn't lie. What he'd read on Ms.

Caldecott's face was more than disdain for onions—he'd read fear and confusion.

Brody was used to reporters. Any detective worth their salt had learned the hard way how to ward off microphones thrust in their faces while they were trying to preserve a crime scene. He turned onto the redheaded woman's street and kept alert for anyone who didn't seem to belong there. Ms. Caldecott definitely had a stalker.

His first impression of her had been cancelled by his second, and that by his third. Her elegant earrings and fancy dress, which probably cost more than a hockey helmet, had him writing her off as a spoiled socialite. But when she'd opened those heart-shaped lips to speak, she'd exhibited a self-effacing intelligence, which made him realize he'd been way off in his assessment.

As Brody pulled up in front of a block of condos, he surveyed the whole area lit only by streetlights. A woman walked her dog on the sidewalk across the street, and music sounded from somebody's open window or balcony, but the area looked devoid of trouble.

It was probably a good idea he wasn't driving a squad car tonight. He wouldn't want to draw undue attention to the young woman. She'd encountered enough attention of late. Brody knocked on the teal-colored door with an oversized fall wreath. It reminded him of his mother's front door. He knocked again, eliciting a fury of barks, or more like yips. They wouldn't scare off a thief.

The door inched open, and the voice from the other side said, "Rory, move back. I don't want to chase you down the street." The door opened wider to reveal the woman he'd seen on the news countless times, usually breaking into whatever sports program he was watching on his days off. The worry lines had vanished, and she smiled when she saw him. "Come in, Officer Br…Messner. I didn't recognize you with your clothes on." Her hand covered her mouth. "I mean, without your uniform…Come in, please." She winced and averted his eyes, ushering him in with a sweep of her hand.

He spewed out a laugh and grabbed his stomach. "Well, that's a first." She wasn't laughing, so he fought to hold back a retort that would be wrong on so many levels, even though he was off duty. Brody followed her into a charming kitchen with off-white appliances. "Is that a café oven? I saw one at Home Depot and practically salivated over it." He didn't add that it was above his pay grade.

"Would you like a drink? Water or coffee or tea?" The air was thick with awkwardness.

Her eyes still failed to meet his, and he searched for words that would reassure her it was all right. "I'm sorry. I didn't mean to laugh, but it was so like something I would say. Just the opposite of what I meant." He pointed at his lips. "Sometimes, they don't obey my better judgment. And I'd appreciate a cup of ice water. I pretty much lost my voice hollering at teenagers tonight."

Madeleine met his eyes for the first time as she glanced over her shoulder while she opened a cupboard for a glass. "Oh, you have teenaged children?"

"Do I look that old? The hairline is betraying me now. And no, I'm not married." Now he winced. Too much information. "I coach a travel hockey team. We had a practice at the Ice Den in Maitland tonight." Enough said. Normally, he didn't babble like this. He rubbed the scruff on his cheeks. Why hadn't he thought to clean up a bit before coming here? Taking a subtle sniff in the direction of his armpit, he hoped he didn't smell like a locker room.

She placed a glass of water in front of him as he stood at the island, then she took a seat on the other side, her arms folded in front of her.

Brody took a long gulp of the water, finishing off half of it, then wiped his lips with a knuckle. "Shall we begin? You rang?"

She rolled her eyes but grinned as if to say, funny guy. "Yes, I rang. But first, were you able to see the video feed of the museum from Saturday night?"

Pulling a small manila envelope from his jacket pocket, he unfastened the clip and took out the black and white photo and placed it in front of her. "It's pretty blurry and dark, but there's your perp."

Her eyes squinted as she shifted the picture. "It's a guy. He looks really tall. It's hard to tell, but it looks like he's wearing a hoody. The video feed at work showed a hunched-over old woman delivering the flowers."

"That's confusing. Too bad it was dark in this picture. It was about nine-thirty when he headed straight to your car. It wasn't like he was looking for an unlocked vehicle. He knew where he was going, and he knew what he was doing. He broke in and wasn't in your car more than a few seconds. Does he look familiar?"

She shook her head. "No. Why me?" She heaved a weighty sigh. "Wish I knew who he was. I probably won't get much sleep tonight."

He longed to comfort her, wrap his arms around her thin shoulders and draw her close to his chest. Enough of that. Although he wasn't on the company's dime, he wasn't here for social reasons. "Why don't you tell me what's happened, and we'll figure out our next steps." He took out his phone in case he had to snap a picture or take notes.

Maddie nodded, her lips taut. "I returned from work about seven-thirty tonight and didn't hear the dog bark. Follow me." She led him upstairs to her ensuite bathroom and showed him the note on the mirror. "You can imagine how I felt when I read the note, Check the shed. I was sure he'd killed my dog." She bit on her lower lip. "By the way, the dog turned out to be on the balcony." From the bathroom, she pointed toward the far wall of the attached bedroom. "I have no idea how long Rory was out there. To think he'd break in and lock my dog out there in the hot sun—" She shook her head slowly. "What if it had rained? You know what our afternoon rainstorms are like."

Luckily, he'd made a habit of keeping a spare pair of gloves in his pocket. He donned one and pulled the note from the mirror. "We can check it out for fingerprints, but most likely your perp wore gloves." He regarded the wide green eyes that peered back at him through the bathroom mirror. "Did you check out the shed?"

She visibly swallowed and nodded. "Why don't you follow me if you're finished in here?"

"I am, but I'll send someone by at your convenience to check the balcony door for fingerprints. Don't get your hopes up. The guy knows what he's doing." He winced at how that came out. "Sorry."

She blew out a breath. "It's okay, but I'd appreciate it if you'd check out the place before you leave."

"Of course." He waited for her to precede him down the stairs and followed her out to a single-car garage with a rectangular room that took up most of the back wall.

Maddie peered behind her, then opened the door, and turned on the light. The first thing he noted was the neatness of her 'junk room' in contrast to his own. Shelves lined all three walls, filled with various-colored plastic boxes, each labeled in neat letters. Nothing appeared to be out of place until he turned to face her.

She beckoned him in and pointed at the wall next to the door. "This is what was waiting for me."

Brody peered at the picture then at her. This was it? A snapshot of a family sitting under a tree? He swallowed, then started sneezing. "Sorry." His eyes watered. With a quick flick of his phone, he snapped a picture of it, then grabbed a tissue from his pocket and pulled the picture off the wall. "Do you have a plastic baggie I can put the note in?"

"Sure, let's get you out of here," she said, putting a supportive hand on his arm. "Sorry. I never thought to vacuum out here."

When his voice returned, he waved her off as they returned to the kitchen. "It's not dust in there. You should see my junk room. No, it was the picture that caught me off guard. What can you tell me about it, Madeleine? I mean—Ms. Caldecott."

"Maddie, please." She lifted a shoulder. "I have no idea what that picture means. It was taken in my backyard in New Jersey, although I don't remember who took it. That's my father and mother, probably a year before they divorced. I can tell by the looks on their faces they weren't happy. Maybe they'd just been arguing."

"Who's the other girl in the picture, your older sister?"

"No, I was an only child then. My mom and dad both married other people and had children with their new spouses. I have five half-sisters and a half-brother, all still in middle school or high school." She shook her head, then fastened chagrined eyes on him. "Went down a rabbit trail there for a moment. That girl was our maid and my babysitter, Beverly Jordan. She lived in our basement back then. Beverly had dropped out of school the year before, and my mom took her in. At twelve, I didn't need a babysitter, although we got along great, and I confided in her more than I did in my own parents."

Brody took a seat she offered at the kitchen table and studied the picture. "What happened to her?"

She shrugged, then sat across from him. "Not long after that picture was taken, she left. The last I heard, she moved to another state."

Brody rubbed his palm against his cheek. Sandpaper sounded in his ears. "Do you have any idea why she dropped out of school, and why she didn't live with her family?"

She sat back, rotating her shoulder. "Her family was poor but tight-knit. Beverly didn't talk about them much. I remember she had an older sister and brother—twins, I think, and she had a younger brother. I went to her house once, and I remember bedsheets hanging where doors should be. Beverly loved her church. She took me there quite often. It was a lot livelier than the church I grew up in." Her eyebrows knit together. "She doesn't look happy in that picture; nor does anyone else. My dad had a temper. I recall why we were posing for a picture in our backyard. The local newspaper was doing a feature on my dad for Father's Day—a young lawyer and his family. Little did they know—"

He folded his arms across his chest and stared out the window. A cardinal alighted on a nearby branch and looked at him. A chill traveled down his back. Someone had told him cardinals appeared when a loved one had recently departed. He fought the urge to cover her hand with his. "Let's go over what we know so far. Out of the blue a few days ago, you received bright red and pink flowers from someone named Absalom, who seemed to indicate through very flowery language that you held some secret."

She leaned forward. "And I've racked my brain trying to think of any secret I might have hidden. I even called my best friend, Tessa, and asked her. The only thing that came to her mind was a time I left school early and told her I was never coming back to school. I don't even remember saying that."

That was unusual. Not remembering. Maybe there was a secret she was holding onto. Perhaps the psychologist with the department could help bring it back to her mind, but that was for a later date. "And the second note was a poem by whom?"

"Omar Khayyam. I'd read his poem, 'The Rubaiyat,' in my eleventh grade English class. We'd put it to music and recorded ourselves reading it, but I don't remember reading the violent verses the stalker sent me."

She twisted her hands and seemed so lost, so vulnerable. He wished he could comfort her, but she needed to stay vigilant. "Then he left the next note in your car. That's when he called you that French name. I looked it up, and it came from Tristan and Isolde, a poem about unrequited love like Romeo and Juliet. Did you read Tristan and Isolde in that literature class?"

"I don't remember reading it, but it's possible. That was a long…time…ago." She placed another sugar cube on the tower she was building, careful not to cause it to topple over.

"What are you doing?"

"What?" She glanced up at him then down at the pincers in her right hand. "Wow." Nine sugar cubes towered on the place mat in front of her. Her eyes met his. "I did a similar thing at the dinner that night at the museum. Don't even remember doing it. This is making me a little crazy."

Brody watched as she carefully removed each sugar cube from the tower until only a dusting remained on the napkin in front of her. Interesting. "Okay, let's go over what we have so far." Her eyes locked with his, disarming him for a moment. After swallowing, he started again. "Would it be fair to say, based on the picture and the notes, that this person is someone you knew during your childhood, specifically during your teen years? Did you date anyone in high school who might be holding a grudge against you?"

She rested her nose on her knuckle and shook her head slowly. "I didn't date in high school. It wasn't until college that I went out with anyone. I think I scared everyone off."

"Why would you say that? How could you scare anyone off? I mean, look at you—" His lips tightened when he realized what he'd said, but she didn't seem to notice.

"I can be a bit compelling—is that the right word? That's what my friend Tessa always said. She told me I needed to relax. But that's not important." Her eyes squinted as if she were trying to pull information out of her head. "Doesn't it seem odd to you that of all the pictures in the garage, he'd pick one with my parents and the babysitter and me in it? If it was someone from high school, they would have picked something from the yearbook."

Brody coughed, trying to clear the grog from his throat. Maybe he was allergic to Maddie's perfume. "So, someone who is here in Orlando was in your English class back in

New Jersey, and he somehow knows a secret about your family. You said your father's an attorney. Is it possible this person was a client of your father's? Perhaps a case that didn't go in his favor?"

"He's definitely targeting me for something that happened in the past. None of the people my parents socialized with had a son in my class. There was a girl, but I don't think it's—" Her voice dropped off, but the puzzled frown remained.

He took out the picture and studied it. "Your father has quite the scowl on his face. Seems an odd choice for a Father's Day picture."

"The one they used in the newspaper was a close-up of Dad on the front lawn. I was sitting in the background on the porch with my dog, and Beverly was serving him a glass of lemonade. Only her arms showed." She shook her head. "It wasn't long after the picture shoot that my parents divorced, and my life changed forever."

Brody worried the thread of a cuticle from his thumbnail. His cuticles would get a workout on this case. The photograph was certainly concerning. The nerve of the dude to break into her car and her house. The perp wasn't fooling around. Maddie Caldecott was not safe in this house, in this city.

Her eyes locked on his. Scared eyes. "What do you think this all means?"

He leaned forward and placed his hand over hers, then removed it just as quickly. She had him rattled. "You need to install a good security system ASAP. The guy's actions are accelerating. Within a few days, he went from sending you flowers to breaking in your house. He was very intentional in everything he did, so I'd bet he wore gloves so we can't trace him." Brody didn't want to say that the guy was probably watching the place right now.

Her arms crossed across her chest, her fingers pressed tight against her arms to the point that red marks appeared.

"Do you have a friend or a relative you and Rory could stay with until the security system is in place?"

She sat back, her eyes pools of troubled water. With a shake of her head, she straightened and placed her hands in front of her. "None that I can think of. I'll be fine. I'll lock my bedroom door and stick a chair under the knob. My phone and my pepper spray will stay close at all times. I'll be fine." Her chin lifted, the quiver of her lips belying the display of false bravado.

He took a clean tissue from his pocket and gave it to her. Where was that boyfriend of hers that was running for some office? He'd never get Brody's vote, that was for sure. Brody was tempted to invite her to stay with him, but with hockey and work, he hadn't had time to clean all the fast-food bags off the tables and the counters. And the guest bedroom had become the receptacle for his laundry. When all this was over, he'd clean up the place and invite her over, but now was not the time. His job was to keep her alive, but she wasn't making it easy. "Will you at least promise to call about a security system first thing tomorrow? If you want, I can stay here until they install it. I'll park in the driveway and sleep in the car. It might provide a deterrent."

She waved him off with the flip of her hand. "The more I think of it, the more I'm convinced that Absalom chose that picture because of something my father did. Do you think I should call my dad and ask him? We don't talk often."

"Why is that?"

"I just don't want to intrude. He's a busy man with his law practice and his wife and kids." She looked away. A heavy burden seemed to weigh her lips down, but then she brushed at her temple as if to ward off a mosquito. "Sorry." A smile forced its way across her face. "I'm such a bad hostess. Would you like something stronger than water? I made lemonade this morning."

"That would be great. After hollering at goofballs at the rink, my throat is a bit parched."

She took out two tall glasses, added a few ice cubes, and filled them to the brim from a frosty pitcher. He could get used to this. Hold your horses, lover boy. But she was talking, and he'd missed it. "Sorry, what did you say?"

She spun around, her red hair doing a wide sweep to catch up. "I was just wondering how you got interested in being a hockey coach. Did you play as a kid?" She removed the water glass and placed the lemonade in front of him and took her seat across from him.

He took a sip and then another. "Oh, this is good. Long story short, I grew up in Montreal. Everyone plays hockey there. In grade nine—ninth grade to you—my father's company moved our family to Sanford. That's when I put away my skates, but I never miss a Canadians game unless I'm working or coaching. Have you ever been to a hockey game?"

She nodded. "Twice. Once in college, my roommates and I went to a Devils game against the Philadelphia Flyers. I enjoyed it, especially the fights. What does that say about me?"

He waved her off. "They're wearing padding. I've been in a few fights myself. Sometimes it's what I needed to kickstart myself. Get the adrenaline moving. What other game did you see?"

"Earlier this year, I went to a Lightning game in Tampa. Gregory had to speak at a caucus luncheon and invited me to come along. One of the men at our table gave him two tickets for that night's game. There I was in a dress and heels, but Gregory wanted to go, so I shivered my way through three periods and overtime."

He took another sip. "You don't want to go to a hockey game without layers of clothing on, but it's completely different if you're playing. Talk about sweat." Did he dare? "Maybe you could grab a coat or three and come watch my boys play." He didn't know exactly how serious she was with that Gregory fellow. Who calls a guy Gregory anyway?

She nodded. "I'd like that," was all she said. A polite answer, but her eyes sparkled. Eyes didn't lie.

Finishing off the lemonade, he stood. "I really wish you'd consider staying with a friend or a family member. You could even stay at my place, although it's a bit of a mess." He hazarded a glance at her already knowing the answer.

"I'm going to be fine. I'll call if I need help. How far do you live from here?"

"I live in Maitland, not far from the rink. Probably about eight miles? I can be here in no time, but please consider installing a security system ASAP, the kind that monitors your entryways, okay?"

She walked him to the door. "I'll be careful, and I have my guard dog here." She pointed at the furball that pranced near her feet.

He didn't like her chances. "Would you be okay with me parking in the driveway? I'd sleep better knowing I'm close."

"What will Mrs. Eldridge next door think? She'll probably call the cops. Go home, Officer Brody. I'll be fine."

She brushed against him as she opened the doors, causing his breath to hitch. Had she felt it too? A charge, kind of like static electricity but more exciting. He'd do his best to keep her alive, and maybe she'd live to see another day.

Chapter Seven

"Some secrets are meant to be taken to the grave, and that's what I plan on doing with all mine. They're not necessarily my secrets to tell. I'm the gatekeeper of other people's secrets."

~ Quentin Tarantino

A night of comforting activities would make the evening pass more quickly. Maddie would keep her mind focused on painting her nails, brushing the snarls out of Rory's fur, and reading a few chapters of the book of a civil-rights author she would be featuring in a few weeks. With relaxing music playing from a YouTube video in the background, her mind would overcome the matter of the guy stalking her.

It was working, she thought, as she yawned for the second time. Now if she could just fall asleep without thinking too much about the picture. Nope. I shouldn't even invite the picture into my thoughts or there'll be no sleep, and the dark and the sounds will be too much. At ten o'clock, after reading the next chapter in her Bible, she turned off the light and snuggled into her pillow. Some people counted sheep; vacuuming worked for Maddie. She pictured herself vacuuming the living room—back and forth, back and forth, then the dining room, then the kitchen. Each stair with the small attachment. And by the time she reached the fifth step—

The cell phone sitting on her bedside table jolted her awake. Her heart was beating at a fast clip as she glanced at the alarm clock. Eleven-thirty. Who would call this late? She donned her glasses and read Gregory's name on the screen. Why was he calling her at this time? This was not like him at all.

"Hello, Gregory? Are you okay?" She could hear voices and glasses clinking in the background, the kind she often heard at galas and banquets and restaurants.

"I'm more than okay. We just received two big donations. I'll have enough to buy a few television ads."

"That's great. Good for you." She struggled to sit up without moving the dog who leaned against her feet.

"You sound like you have a cold. Are you okay?"

Didn't he have a clue what she was going through? "No, I just went to bed early."

"Oh, I'm sorry. I'll get to the point. Are you free on Wednesday night to go with me to a fall fair in Kissimmee? I have to judge pies or jams or something, and they're giving me five minutes with the mic. It could be fun. You won't have to dress up this time. What do you say?"

At any other time, this would have sounded so exciting, even liberating, and it would give her a chance to escape these walls that were beginning to close in on her, but these walls were also protecting her. This was the first time Gregory had asked her to do something fun instead of all those dreary dress-up affairs. Still, he hadn't even asked about her stalker. Shouldn't that have been his first question?

Climbing out of bed, she padded over to the window. As suspected, Brody's car sat in the driveway. How sweet. "All right," she said. "As long as you agree to go on the Ferris wheel with me and eat something totally unhealthy."

"Do you know how unsafe those rides are? Who knows if those traveling carnivals follow safety codes."

"They're fine, and it'll be a good photo op for you." She hoped he didn't hear the snark in her voice.

"Deal," he said with less conviction. "Corn dogs, it is. A far cry from the foie gras I just ate."

After Maddie ended the call, she waved at Brody, although she couldn't see him. His headlights flashed twice in response. She giggled despite herself at her big protector with the scratchy facial hair and the mustard stain on his shirt. At some point in her mind, he'd morphed from Officer Brody to Brody. What would he say about her date with Gregory on Wednesday? She hoped he'd be a little jealous. Where did that thought come from? With another glance at the car below, she called his number.

Brody picked up on the first ring. "Is there a problem?"

"Not at all. And that's why you should go home."

He yawned aloud. "I'll stay right here until that alarm system is installed."

"You are such a nag, although I'm grateful. I was thinking about what you said about that picture on the wall. Maybe you're right. Absalom must have had something against my father. After all, Dad was the focal point of that picture. Maybe my dad was Absalom's lawyer. Tomorrow morning, I'll give my father a call to see if any of his clients have been released from prison lately."

"It was probably Absalom's father, since your stalker was too young to be part of a lawsuit. He knew about your English class, so he's most likely your age. Do you remember anything about the boys in your class?"

He was right. "I don't. Could be my dad lost the case, and his father spent time in prison. Absalom's bitter that he lost precious years with his father, and he blames my dad—" She returned to the bed and plopped down. "And he's taking it out on me. But that doesn't explain the 'secret' I supposedly have."

"You make a good point." He gasped. "Don't know why it didn't occur to me before. I must be getting spiritually unsavvy. What do you know about Absalom in the Bible?"

She racked her brain for Old Testament history. "I know he was King David's son, but he rebelled against his father so that he could become the king. He tried to turn everyone against King David, but he ended up dead when his hair got caught up in a tree. Am I right?"

"Yeah, so it's no accident he chose that name. It has something to do with his father…or your father. Maybe Absalom viewed your dad as a father figure."

"To my knowledge, I don't have any brothers around my age, although I have a half-brother, but he's only seven years old and lives in Clifton, New Jersey. He's certainly not old enough to break into my condo or send me flowers."

"The name's important; that's all I'm saying. It's a good idea to call your father. Ask him about the picture. Who took the photo? Ask him if he can remember anyone about your age who might have regarded him as a father figure. Maybe he can shed some light on why Absalom chose that particular picture."

"Thank you. By the way, I agreed to go out with Gregory on Wednesday. To a county fair in Kissimmee. Do you think that's a good idea?"

When Brody finally answered, a sigh preceded his words. "As long as you've engaged the alarm system, you should be safe. But don't tell anyone your password, okay?"

"What about you? I can trust you, can't I?"

His voice became husky. "Yes, you can trust me, but don't tell anyone else your password."

"Deal. Here's how I choose my passwords. I use a spoonerism based on the company's name, then the first letter's alphabetic number, then an exclamation point. So, what security company should I choose?"

"I use Frontpoint Security. It's reliable and not too expensive. Now, refresh my memory on what a spoonerism is. I haven't thought about them since ninth grade."

"Just exchange the first letter or diphthong of the first

syllable with the second. So pontfroint16!"

"Ingenious, but that won't work because all you need are numbers."

"Oh. Then I'd use my favorite verse from the Bible. The first numbers would be the book's number, then the chapter, then the verse. So, Psalm 71:16,17 would be 19711617."

"Wow, that takes a lot of thinking, but nobody could crack that code. Psalm 71. I don't think I know that one."

"Well, I'll sing it for you. That's how I memorize things, by putting the words to a tune and singing it every day. 'I will go in the strength of the Lord God. I will make mention of His righteousness, of Yours only. O, God, you have taught me from my youth, and to this day I declare Your wondrous works.'"

Applause emanated from the phone. "You are a woman of many talents. I like the way you think. Good night, Madeleine Caldecott. Sweet dreams."

She climbed in between the covers, feeling a lot safer than she had when the phone rang. Brody was out there getting a stiff neck, so she'd call the security company first thing the next day. As much as she appreciated his presence in her driveway, he had better things to do with his work and his hockey team. She closed her eyes. His presence made her feel warm and comfy just like these blankets.

Chapter Eight

"It is wise not to seek a secret, and honest not to reveal one."

~ William Penn, Some Fruits of Solitude

In the morning, after she'd made an appointment with the security company for the next day, she sat on the edge of her bed, already dressed, hands folded on her lap, waiting for nine o'clock to appear on the clock. That rule she'd learned from her parents about not calling before nine still guided her practice.

It wasn't easy calling her father. There was never a good time, whether he was home or at work, but she'd already practiced her words. He'd appreciate her getting to the point.

His cell phone rang four times—she had counted. At five she planned to hang up instead of leaving a message, but he answered.

"Madeleine. How nice to hear your voice. It's been a while."

Yes, it has. "I hope I'm not interrupting your work."

"I have a few minutes. What is it?" In other words, get to the point.

"I...um—" The words weren't coming as she'd practiced. "I seem to have a stalker, who broke into my car and into my condo." She heard an uptake of breath.

"Have you called the police?"

"Yes. And a security system will be put in tomorrow. This guy calls himself Absalom and has left letters about some secret in my past. And he posted a picture of our family—the one that was taken in the backyard for your Father's Day feature in the newspaper. I'll send you a copy of it. Just a minute." She pulled up the picture and sent it to his phone. "Did you get it?"

"Give me a sec. Okay, there it is. Interesting. So, he posted it on Facebook or Instagram?"

"No, in my garage. He must have gone through my photo albums when he broke in. And that's the one he hung on the wall."

Muted voices sounded. Her dad was saying something to them. "I'm sorry, but I have to leave. What do you want from me?"

I want you to hug me, and tell me I matter? No consolation, no encouraging words. "I want you to think back to that time. Was there some young man about my age who might have had a grudge against you? Someone who looked up to you as a mentor, or someone whose father was one of your clients. Maybe someone who did time and was recently released?"

He blew out a breath. "No one comes to mind, but I'll give it some thought. Why don't you call your mother and see what she has to say."

And there it was. She heard the dismissal in his voice. "Okay, thank you. Sorry for bothering you." He wouldn't call her back. The minute he mentioned her mother, Maddie became the ping-pong ball they'd batted back and forth since she'd been a teenager. Never would she get married if ping-pong was the end game.

A day later, she scribbled notes down as Hal, the security guy, took her on a tour of her condo, giving her way too much information, and she had to be at work in an hour, then rush home to take Rory out and dress down for the date with Gregory. That was a first.

"Uh-hum," she said for the dozenth time as she wrote sideways in the margins of the paper. This was much more complicated than she'd thought, but if it helped her sleep better at night, the fifty-dollar monthly fee was worth it. She hadn't heard anything from Absalom since Sunday. Maybe he'd moved on. Still, she felt better knowing he wouldn't be able to enter her condo without the security people knowing it. Which evoked a question. "Hal, what if my stalker knows his way around your security system? Is there any way he could disable it?"

He linked his thumbs in his belt loops and rocked back and forth on his heels. "Good question. No system is foolproof, but it's never happened with the model we've installed in your house. Unless the interloper knows your password, he can't turn the alarm off. Make sure you pick a good password that no one knows."

"No worries there. Bible verses are my go-to pa—" She stopped mid-word. How quickly she'd forgotten her promise to Brody. This man was a stranger.

Hal took off his ball cap and scratched above his ear. "Now there's one I've never heard of. Just be sure you keep it to yourself and change it often." He scribbled something on the invoice and handed it to her. "I added my phone number if you have any problems." With a two-fingered salute, he took his leave.

The day flew by as she fact-checked her assignment by making phone calls and doing Google searches, met with the producer, and joined the anchors for their monthly lunch meeting. Usually, she enjoyed spending time with the other five anchors who handled the six o'clock and morning news. From the time she'd started at the station, they'd been her mentors and helped her through all the mistakes she'd made as a rookie.

Now a well-manicured hand patted hers, bringing Maddie back to the present. Sydney Hamrick gathered her long blond locks, then gave her a one-armed hug. "You seem awfully quiet today. What's going on?"

This presented a problem. How much should she tell her? Since it seemed to be more of a personal vendetta than a work-related one, she decided to forego spreading the bad news. It would only make them feel sorry for her, and that would make matters even worse. Sydney was waiting for an answer. "Just some personal issues." She pasted on a smile that wouldn't fool anyone, especially her perceptive seatmate, and it didn't.

Sydney tsked. "Yeah, well, that's not what I heard. We've all had stalkers at times. Don't try to handle this yourself. We're all here for you."

So, word had leaked. "Thank you." Enough said. She wasn't used to relying on others. There was only room in her small circle for her grandmother and Tessa, and both lived in other countries. But she'd taken care of herself for a long time, and Officer Brody was mere miles away if she needed immediate help.

For the first time in a long time, Gregory actually picked her up at her condo. The moment she opened the door, Maddie couldn't keep from smiling at this new version of Gregory. His mouth curved up on one side, clearly uncomfortable in his new duds—jeans with a crease, a denim shirt with a red neckerchief, and pointy-toed cowboy boots that looked a bit stiff. "Looks like you're ready to do-si-do."

"Not even close." He ran a finger under his kerchief. "But if you want to dance, I'll give you a whirl. We should be going."

"Just a minute." She entered the code on her security panel before smiling back at Rory then shooing Gregory out the door.

"I don't remember you having a security system before. Not a bad idea with the hours you keep."

A sigh preceded her words. He hadn't even asked. "It was installed just this morning." She wouldn't tell him why. Gregory wouldn't remember anyway.

He opened the Tesla door for her, and she slid in, the scent of new leather wafting toward her nose.

"Do you still use spoonerisms?" he said before he closed the door.

"What? How did you know?" So much for discretion.

He climbed in and pushed the button to start the car. "You told me once. I thought it was a unique idea and even tried it a few times." He backed out of the driveway and headed out of her neighborhood.

Mixed feelings filled her as they sped toward Kissimmee. Why had she'd been so loose-lipped with Gregory about her password method? Had she told anyone else? Calling to mind all her coworkers, she couldn't think of a single person she'd told. She didn't tell secrets of any kind. Outside of her colleagues at work, no one else came to mind.

Clearly, Gregory didn't like to linger behind slower-moving cars—that is, cars that were going over the speed limit. He swerved in and out of several lanes, and they arrived at the county fair in no time.

Loud country music and the aroma of french fries wafted her way as they headed toward the entrance from the grassy parking lot. Gregory was still grumbling about the cars being parked so tightly that there were sure to be dents on their return.

She took his hand. "Cowboys don't care about car dents. C'mon, let's have some fun."

The county fair didn't disappoint. Screams rose and fell in unison from a tilt-a-whirl, and more sporadic shrieks came from the haunted house. As they passed food stands, her stomach gurgled. "What time do you have to do the judging?" Hopefully the scent of fried onions would work up his appetite.

"Hm? Oh, at seven near the stage. My assistant did some research for me, so I know how to evaluate jams. They must be translucent in color with no debris or layers, and the jam should spread easily." He pulled her over to the side away from the crowds. "Would you mind if I hung around the stage? It's a good opportunity for me to make some connections. If you want to get something to eat, go ahead."

She nodded and offered her professional smile. How foolish of her to think this was a date; it was just another photo-op. Her appetite ebbed as she strolled among laughing couples holding hands and a gaggle of teenagers huddled together over cotton candy. A child with a petulant frown pointed at a larger-than-life stuffed bear at a water-gun game. Next to the whirly-bird was the entrance to a maze.

Fall wasn't fall without a corn maze in New Jersey. She bought a ticket and passed through the pumpkin-festooned entry. Always go left was her habit in grocery stores, flea markets, and malls. She turned left, and the blinking lights and the din of voices lowered to dimness and a haunting wooo. Maybe this wasn't the best place to be a solo walker in the dark. She increased her pace and applied logic and habit past haystacks, jack o' lanterns, and hanging spiders interspersed with costumed ghouls with water pistols.

After returning to the same place after thirty minutes, she realized her method wasn't working. Gregory would be so mad if she wasn't at his side. Should she call him? Yes. She stopped at a lantern and called, then left a message when he didn't answer. Since going left wasn't working for her, she'd follow the next group of people who passed her. Eventually, they'd lead her to the exit, but no one came by, although she heard a rustling sound on the other side of the cornstalks. "Hello?" she ventured.

No answer. More rustling. Maddie hurried on, hoping the two rows would intersect at the end of the row. They didn't, so she turned left not wanting to lose complete control of her orientation. Again, the rustling sounded when she walked, and it stopped when she stopped. Her breaths came in spurts. Absalom was on the other side. He wouldn't give up just because she'd installed a security system. She'd provided him with the perfect opportunity to 'purge' her.

Using the flashlight on her phone, she aimed it through the cornstalk. "Hello, Absalom?"

A dark figure moved on the other side close enough to reach out and touch. Why didn't he answer?

Turning off the light, she turned and tiptoed in the opposite direction, hoping to reach another group or find the entrance. When she reached a safe distance, Maddie began to run, and she kept running until the lights and crowds and the entrance brought her heart rate back to normal.

Within minutes, she was back at the stage, smoothing her hair which had picked up a few hitchhiking straws. Maddie took a seat at the end of the second row. Gregory was onstage telling one of his favorite anecdotes, which brought a titter from the small crowd that gathered in the seats around her. He glanced her way and lifted his chin, but he didn't smile. Somehow, she knew the small crowd would be her fault.

Finally, he thanked the people in the audience, made another joke that brought a bigger laugh, and jumped off the stage. An ample woman in a straw hat took the microphone and directed him to a seat behind a table of jam jars. For the next ten minutes, he applied the knowledge he'd garnered to make comments as he scrutinized texture, color, and taste. By the end of the judging, he held the crowd in his sticky hands.

After chatting with those who lingered, he joined her, any irritation now dissipated. "Wished you'd been here for the pies. Now I'm stuffed. Did you get something to eat?"

They left the stage area, turning right, which meant they were heading to the exit. "No, I didn't have the chance." She told him about the maze, omitting the part about the rustling on the other side of the cornstalks.

He stopped at a mini-doughnut stand, which he must have seen her gawk at on their way to the stage. "Does this look good? I wouldn't want my date to die of hunger."

When she nodded, he took his place at the back of the line. "Did you say there were guys on skates dressed up in costumes?"

"Yeah, when they jumped out at me, I almost wet my pants." Her hand covered her mouth, which brought a laugh.

They'd reached the front of the line, and he ordered her a cider and a small bag of powdered, cinnamon doughnuts that fit perfectly with the ambiance. "Is this okay, or do you want caramel corn or one of those bags of hot almonds?"

"This is fine." She blew on one of the little rings of goodness before taking a bite. Then she savored a few more, licking her sticky fingers. They were now heading for the exit, and she was quite sure Gregory wouldn't want her to eat in his car. It wouldn't surprise her if he stopped someplace to hose her down.

It was dark in the parking lot, and the breeze had changed from pleasant to chilly. He was chatting about one of the pies he'd sampled that had been so dry he almost started choking, but he stopped mere feet from his car. "Oh no, no, no, no."

She peered up at him. "What's wrong?"

"I just bought the car three weeks ago, and already—" He hurried to the car and removed the note attached to the windshield. "Just as I thought—someone hit the side of the car. There wasn't enough space to park." Gregory circled the car, using his phone's flashlight to show any points of impact.

Maddie already knew he'd find his car just the way he'd left it. She hung back wrapping her arms across her chest to give herself the comfort he should be giving her. This was not about him.

"I can't see anything in the dark. Tomorrow, I'll take it back to the dealer." Gregory rejoined her, opening the note for the first time. He skimmed its contents, reading the words under his breath. "What is this? I don't understand. It's probably from one of those religious cults. Should have known right away. They're drawn to Teslas. Probably want the money that comes with them." He threw the note on the ground, "C'mon. It's chilly out here," noticing her shivering for the first time.

"Was it from Absalom?"

"Yeah, didn't you get one of those messages at your work? I can see that happening. They probably love the publicity." He opened the door for her, waiting.

Before she got in, she took a tissue from her small backpack and picked up the note, then put it in her backpack without a second glance.

"Oh, right. Littering is bad for the environment. It's okay at one of these venues. Can you imagine what the place looks like at the end of the night?" He climbed in the other side and started the car.

Curiosity and dread threaded together, preventing her from talking on the way back to her place. Gregory didn't seem to notice. Even the Tesla was silent as he wove through traffic. He filled her in on the other candidates and told her about a televised debate at one of the local colleges. "

"Madeleine?"

The sound of her given name brought her back to the present. "Sorry?"

He glanced at her for a long moment. "Where are you tonight? I said Sydney Hamrick will be the moderator. What do you think? Does she lean to the left or the right?"

"I don't know. At the station, we try to keep our personal preferences to ourselves. If it ever got back to the station manager that we were talking politics, we'd probably lose our jobs. That's one of the things I like about working there."

With a nod, he covered her hand. "Then I'm amazed that you still have your job. I mean, look at you. You're out with me at fundraisers and party gatherings."

"Right after you asked me to accompany you to the first benefit, I talked to the station manager. He said he couldn't tell me what to do in my private life, but he strongly advised me to keep a low profile, which I've tried to do. Except for one guy at work who's a big tease, nobody's ever said anything about me attending events with you."

He patted her hand then chuckled. "If I had any say about it, I'd want you to be the moderator at the debate instead of Ms. Hamrick. Would you be able to sit in the audience? I'd really like your support."

"Sure. Just let me know when." They'd turned onto her street, which made her feel relieved and apprehensive at the same time. Hank, the security guy, had said there was no foolproof system.

When they entered the condo, she reached for her key in her purse to open the door when the note fell out. Gregory must have noticed because he bent down to retrieve it. "I thought you were going to throw this away." She tried to grab it from him, but he pulled it out of her reach and read it aloud. "'Vengeance is Mine, and recompense; Her foot shall slip in due time; for the day of her calamity is at hand, and the things to come hasten upon her. Remember a kiss from a rose. Absalom.' What is this, some type of joke? Does the guy have something against Teslas?" He handed it back to her. "You can throw it away."

Maddie took it and stuffed it into her pocket then unlocked the door to Rory's bark. Good. She didn't really want to invite him in, but he lingered in the doorway, so she quickly turned off the alarm, then turned to him. "Thanks for a fun evening. Let me know when you have more details about the debate. I'll try to be there."

His eyes settled on her face, then he took her hands in his, pulled her close, and kissed her. "Thank you. Sorry I wasn't with you in the maze. Maybe some other time. Good night."

She touched her lips after he left. He almost seemed contrite. This was a new side of him—a gentler, humbler side. Maddie liked this version better than the political one.

Rory's tapping claws and wiggly body brought her back to the present. She grabbed the leash and clipped it to the dog's collar. "Just a short minute, Rory. Do your business, and let's get in the house. I have to call Brody." Hopefully, she wouldn't catch him during another hockey practice.

Rory quickly did her business, then raced for the door. Odd, usually Maddie had to coerce her to come in the house. As soon as they entered the house, Rory emitted a strange little sound and stared up at the stairs.

"What's wrong, baby? Do you want to go to bed? I'm ready. Just give me a moment." She turned and set the alarm, then she turned off the lights, and headed up to her bedroom with Rory on her heels. Something was off with Rory. She wasn't used to Maddie leaving her all day when she went to work and then going out at night, although it happened from time to time.

Once in her room, she thought about changing into her nightgown, but it was getting late, and she didn't think it proper to call Brody after nine. Her watch said 9:45. No, she should call him. She ambled onto the balcony and pressed his number. After eight rings, it went to voicemail. She cleared her throat. "Hi, this is Maddie Caldecott—in case there was another Maddie in his life—I received another note. It was on Gregory's windshield. We were at the county fair in Kissimmee. The car was in the parking lot. What should I do? Thank you, Goodbye." That was lame.

A glance at her day planner which she kept by her bed showed that she had to drive to Sarasota to interview Gretchen Ashley, the ex-wife of Grady Newland, the coach who'd disappeared after he was arrested for molesting a student, then got off on a technicality. Grady and Gretchen. It was as if they were meant to be together, yet Gretchen had remarried, unable to believe he didn't do it despite his denials. A family broken apart by a false report. She'd promised to keep her research quiet, and she'd tried to be fair. Reviewing the facts of the case, Maddie still felt Grady had been wrongly accused. But if she was wrong, there was probably some other girl out there who had become a victim.

Walking into the bathroom, she put on her nightgown, brushed her teeth, washed her face, and decided to try a new facial masque Sydney had recommended at lunch. Pulling her hair up into a ponytail, she rubbed a paste that smelled of cucumbers on her cheeks, chin, forehead, and nose. The instructions said to keep it on for twenty minutes, then wash it off with a gentle washcloth.

Just then, Rory started growling. What was going on? The only time she ever growled was when Maddie ignored her when she was eating chicken. "Rory, why are you—" The dog's eyes were focused on the hall outside her door. "What is it?"

Rory barked again, her eyes not leaving the hall. Maddie searched for her phone, which was sitting on the bedside table next to Rory. If someone was out there, they'd see her if she went for the phone. She opened the top drawer of the bathroom's cabinet and grabbed a pair of scissors.

What was she barking at? Her alarm was on, so nobody could get in. But Absalom had broken in somehow even when the door was locked. Could it be Absalom? Her breath was coming in tremulous spurts. She recited a verse she'd memorized for such a time as this, then returned to the bathroom door, glancing at her masque-covered face. Two courses of action presented themselves. She could try to reach the door without him seeing her, shut the door and lock it, then call 911. Or Rory was just barking at a light or a shadow, and she and her scissors could go check out the house just to be sure. Or she could do both.

Maddie slid against the wall, hoping her reflection didn't show from the balcony's sliding glass door. She inched to the door, flung it shut, turned the button to the right, and hurried to her bed to grab her phone. Then she stopped. Should she call 911 based on a dog's growling? Life presented such hard choices.

She said a quick prayer for God's protection, then went to the door. Planting her ear next to it, she stood listening for any sound on the other side. Nothing. Maybe her own skittishness was rubbing off on the dog.

With a glance back at Rory, she grabbed her phone, inched the door open, and peered into the hall. Nothing out of the ordinary. Opening the door wider, she crept out, feeling vulnerable and wishing she carried a better weapon than a pair of scissors. If she aimed at the right place with the right amount of thrust, she could do some damage.

Something wasn't right, although she couldn't explain why. Maddie hurried toward the door of the guest bedroom, flicked on the light, then entered. Could a human hide under the bed? First, she hoisted the scissors in one hand and opened the folding closet door with the other. Luckily, it was so small no human could hide in it. Which left the other side of the bed and under it. Releasing a stream of short breaths, she checked out the other side, then knelt to look under the queen bed. What met her eyes were piles of shoes and clothing and bedspreads she'd hidden under there for the winter season.

Maddie walked out of the bedroom, rolling her eyes at her overwrought imagination. Absalom didn't know it, but he was exacting revenge without doing a thing. Did she even have to waste her time checking the guest bathroom and downstairs? That's what the alarm system was for. With that in mind, she flicked on and off the bathroom light and was about to turn to leave when she heard a creak, then felt a breath on her neck.

An arm circled her neck and pulled her back. The stale odor of beer melded with cinnamon, reminding her of her mother's gum which she always carried in her clutch with a hanky and her lipstick. Maddie's thoughts jumbled and stumbled over each other, and the faces of Tessa and her grandmother played in front of her eyes.

A spray of saliva to the top of her ear preceded a gruff

whisper. "We finally meet."

The scissors almost dropped from her clenched fist. Scissors. One chance for life. With a quick backward thrust of her fist, she stabbed with all her might behind her.

A grunt escaped from her assailant. The arm around her neck loosened. She used the momentary surprise element to stomp her bare foot into his instep. No power in it at all.

Maddie didn't wait. She started for the bedroom, then changed her mind. It was safer to leave the house where the darkness could hide her. As she scrambled down the stairs, heavier footsteps gained on her. She had to reach the door before he did. Her feet thudded down the stairs. If she could just make it to the door, but then he'd get her when she took the time to unlock it. At least the alarm would g—Her foot missed a step and she plunged to the bottom, landing face-first on the hardwood.

Her breath evacuated her at the moment of contact with the floor. She wasn't ready to die. Not here. Not like this. Get to your feet. Run to the door.

Then he flattened her, his body on top of hers. Air whooshed out. She grasped for a breath. Coughing against the acidic taste in her mouth, Maddie tried to pull her body forward to gain a modicum of space. Anything to get away, to breathe. Lord, save me. Rescue me.

Rough hands tore at her thighs, pulling up her nightgown. No.

"Don't do this. God, help." Tears streamed down her cheeks, running into her mouth, pooling by her nostril. "Don't...do...this." Suddenly, she was hovering above her body, somewhere near the ceiling. Detached. Nothing mattered. She observed from afar, as if she were watching a television crime show. Since the room was dark, she could only make out shades of dark and semi-dark. The scissors lay on the area rug, mere inches from her hand. Grab the scissors. Grab the scissors.

The man wore a balaclava. She couldn't see his face. He

looked rough, unkempt, tall, lanky. Jeans, a khaki jacket. His body covered hers, so she could barely see herself. He grunted like an animal. He was an animal. She could hear her own hysteric sobs, but it was as if she was watching and listening to someone else. And then he stopped moving and the grunts and sobs stopped.

Then she was back on the floor, his head nauseatingly close to her ear. She jerked away and focused on the area rug. Think about the rug. Maddie had loved its warm shades of burgundy, teal, and beige. The moment she'd seen it, she knew she had to buy it. She'd throw it away if she ever made it out of here.

The only light came from a nightlight under the table where she left her mail and keys.

The scissors, gleaming, sat in the middle of the larger circular pattern. Her hand inched toward the scissors. His breath came in short spurts, actually causing the hairs near her neck to move. Vomit burned her throat, bubbling up in her mouth. Her hands landed on the scissors. How was she going to strike a blow when she was on her stomach with his weight holding her down? Any backward thrust would lack power, and he could see it coming.

She had to try. Clenching the scissors tight, she stabbed backward with what strength remained. Her fist made contact with what felt like jeans—she couldn't tell if it had penetrated skin.

He snorted like a donkey, and he grabbed the scissors. Then his voice whispered so close to her ear it made her gag. "Now why'd you go and do that? We were even—eye for an eye. You for my sister. Now you have to pay up again. Don't move, you hear?"

A waft of mint met her nose. She'd never chew gum again. The weight of him moved and lifted. The front door opened and closed, cold air coming in. The alarm didn't go off. Her eyes closed. He needn't worry. What reason was there to move? She'd just as soon die.

Chapter Nine

"Every man has his secret sorrows,
which the world knows not;
and often times we call a man cold when he is only sad."

~ Henry Wadsworth Longfellow, Hyperion

Maddie had been driving for hours from one highway to another, her dog sleeping next to her, snoring in a regular pattern. Patterns. There was something comforting about patterns. They were trustworthy and normal and safe. Her chin throbbed from where it had hit the ground. She was sure an ugly bruise covered that part of her face and the other parts where she'd made contact with the floor. Contact with…

She caught a glance of her face in the rear-view mirror and almost scared herself. The low light and whitish masque she still wore made her resemble the Joker. Her fingers touched her face. It felt tight and dry. She started peeling off bits not caring that they fell willy-nilly in her car.

Dawn was shedding light on what had been cloaked in darkness. Her gas gauge showed less than a quarter tank. Time to go home. Time to get ready for work like any other normal day. Patterns. Rory needed a walk and some food. The shih tzu had been at the top of the stairs, shaking like a leaf in the wind. Now the dog slept on the passenger seat, probably traumatized. Maddie hadn't known where to go when she climbed into the car and pulled away from her condo, only that she couldn't stay there.

She'd forgotten to turn off the alarm that she'd engaged after she'd picked herself off the floor. It scared her to death when it went off as she went into the garage, sending jolts of fear through her all over again. Great job it did in protecting her.

Once she and the dog were back in the kitchen, Maddie opened the pantry door, took out a can of dog food as she did every day, and spooned it into Rory's bowl. Then she poured fresh water into her other dish, gave the dog a little pat, and went upstairs to take a shower. It was the one and only thing she desperately craved. Not daring to glance at the mirror, she took off her nightgown and threw it on the floor. It would kill her to leave it there, but for some unknown reason she didn't feel like following her normal pattern.

Now she encountered her second deviation from her daily routine. On any other day, she'd feel the temperature of the water before stepping in, but this time Maddie turned the knob as far as it would go to the left. Steaming hot water prickled her skin. Good. The hotter the better. Absalom's need for her purging was satisfied now. Hot tears tumbled down her face, joining with the flood at her feet, then disappeared in a circular motion down the drain.

Using the stiffest brush she could find, she swiped it against her skin back and forth, harder and harder, to make it go away. A verse from Psalm 51 came to mind. "Purge me with hyssop and I shall be clean. Wash me and I shall be whiter than snow." If only the shower could wash away everything.

The water had already turned cold as she stepped out of the shower, noting the red slashes on her legs and arms in the mirror. They'd leave in time. As she wrapped a towel around her hair and went to her closet to pick out an outfit to wear to work, she broke out in giggles of all things. How many times had she, in her investigations for a news report, shook her head at girls who'd been raped and kept it to themselves, washing any evidence down the drain. Now she knew why they did it. Sometimes reason had to yield to silence. Maybe someday she'd tell the authorities…someone, but it would be her choice when and to whom. In the end, it was all about control. What else did she have control over?

As she drove to work, she turned the radio up loud. Anything to keep from revisiting the events of the night before, but her memories intruded unbidden over the noise. Remembering how it felt to watch what was happening from the ceiling made it impersonal, as if it were happening to someone else. It was dark enough that she couldn't see much from her post above. Thank you, Lord, for taking me out of there for the worst of it. I'd asked You to help, and You delivered me from evil. Just like the Lord's prayer said. How many times had she recited the prayer not really knowing what it meant? Now she knew. Now she knew.

Then her mind traveled back to what she did know. She never got a look at him because his full weight held her down. He wore a dark hood, so she couldn't see his features, although she had the impression he was tall. What else? He'd said something in a gruff whisper. Had he said his name? She couldn't remember. Something from the Bible. What was it? Nothing came to her. Enough. She turned into the studio parking lot.

Before Maddie stepped out of the car to go into work, she pulled down her visor mirror to check her face. After her shower, she'd come up with one new rule: Don't let anyone know. As a result, she'd applied three layers of concealer to hide the bruise on her lower right cheek and the inverted rainbow of an abrasion under her left eye. Long sleeves covered her upper arm that sported a huge bruise from where she'd hit the floor. The lower bruises hid behind long pants. As long as she didn't get too close to anyone, she'd make it through the day.

Maddie opened the side door to the studio and wished she'd parked in the guest parking lot instead. The last person she wanted to see was the security guard, Chip Henry. He wasn't the kind of guy who'd let her pass by with just a hello. She turned to scoot out the door when he noticed her.

"Where you going, Princess?"

Turning around slowly, she offered a crooked smile. "Just back to my car." Now she was stuck. If she parked her car in the guest parking lot, he'd be sure to notice. Pulling her nametag out of her suit jacket pocket, she slipped it on, and waved to him as she passed. "How's it going, Chip?"

"Not too bad." He leaned forward on his elbows. "Can't say the same for you. You look…What happened?"

She huffed and waved him off. "Nothing really, I just didn't get much sleep last night. I'll make up for it tonight. See you later." If she kept walking, she wouldn't be pulled into an awkward conversation. Cloying, he was, and she had no use for flirts. Not before last night. Not now.

Somehow, she survived the day without anyone noticing, although she'd ducked behind her desk when she saw Chip Henry enter the newsroom. He was looking for her, she could tell. Fortunately, she and Theo, the camera operator, would spend most of the day in Sarasota interviewing Gretchen Ashley. Anything to leave Orlando, but at some point, maybe later tonight, she'd have to make some decisions.

Would Absalom come back?

The thought caused her to grab at her desk to keep from swaying. Never would she ever go through that again—the R word, even if it meant moving to a different city. It wasn't as if there were anyone to keep her in Orlando.

Chapter Ten

"The face is the mirror of the mind, and eyes without
speaking confess the secrets of the heart."

~ Saint Jerome

For the fifth time, Brody checked his phone to see if she'd responded to his message. He'd left his phone in the kitchen and hadn't checked his messages until today. That's when he saw her voicemail. Why wasn't she answering? He listened to it again. She'd been at a fair with that political guy. If she saw the message on Gregory's windshield, then the guy named Absalom must have left it there while they were in the fairgrounds. She didn't say what the note said. What time did she call him? The voicemail read 9:48 last night. Would she have called him from his car, or would she have waited until she was back home? Logic told him she'd call from home.

Now it was the next day twelve hours later, and she still hadn't called him back. Had that guy, Gregory—he'd have to look up his last name—done something to her? The alarm system wouldn't be worth a cent if she invited him into her home. Was he Absalom? No, it couldn't be. It had to be somebody from her past. At this time of the day, Maddie should be at work. Since she wasn't picking up her phone, he'd call the station and see if she'd shown up. He dialed the number and a woman answered.

"Hello, this is Officer Brody Messner." He winced, wishing he hadn't said his name. Damage already done. "I've been trying to get in touch with Maddie Caldecott, and she hasn't returned my calls. Did she come into work today?"

An uncomfortable pause ensued, then she said, "I haven't seen her, but I'll patch you through to her assistant."

After five rings, an out-of-breath female answered, "Page Grisham."

"Hello, this is…I've been trying to get in touch with Maddie Caldecott all morning. Is she in today?"

"No, I haven't seen her, but she had scheduled an interview in Sarasota, so that's probably why she hasn't returned your call. Is there something I can help you with?"

Now he was the one who paused. If this Page was her assistant, she'd know about Absalom's notes. "This is Brody Messner. I was calling about the notes." That should draw her out.

"Notes? Is this related to a story she's working on?"

This wasn't going well. "Um, no, it's related to a note she received—"

"Oh, you're referring to the note she received a week or so ago from some screwball?"

He expelled a silent breath. "Yes, that would be the one. I'm with the police department."

Another pause. "So, you called her cell phone, and she hasn't returned your calls, is that right?" Her voice had taken on a strident tone.

"I'm just concerned about her. You're suspicious, and that's a good thing. Call the department, if you must, and ask for Brody Messner. Better yet, would you try to call her or the cameraman, then call me back. I just want to know that she's okay."

"I will." Click. Will what?

There had to be a reason Maddie wasn't returning his

calls. Nobody at the studio had seen her today, but there might not be anything to worry about. After all, the alarm system would keep her safe. Still, something didn't seem right. Brody always liked to have a plan for the next few steps. He'd go over to her condo and see if she was there, and if not, he'd call Gregory. Hopefully, it wouldn't come to that.

Maddie's street couldn't have looked safer. Manicured lawns, flower gardens, and sabal palms adorned the front of craftsman-style condos attached in pairs. Because of the curve of the road, residents couldn't see their neighbors because their porches and driveways were separated. Perfect for a person's privacy. Perfect for felons.

Maddie's garage was closed, so he couldn't tell if her car was in there. He pulled into her driveway, went to the front porch, and rang the bell. No answer. With a glance at the house across the street, he went to the garage and tried to figure out the code to open its door, but nothing worked. Back on the front porch, he checked under the mat for a spare key, since most people hid a spare somewhere near the front door. He felt above the door lintel and in the hanging plant. Nothing. Where to look? His eyes dropped to the statue of a puppy. Picking it up and turning it over, a key jangled inside.

Now he had to get past the alarm system, but he wouldn't enter until he knew her password. Thinking back to what she'd said, the password had something to do with her favorite Bible verse. He remembered her singing the words, something in psalms. A few of the words came to mind, O God, you have taught from my youth. He typed them into his phone, and up popped the verses. Counting the books from Genesis on his fingers, he came up with 19 then added the chapter and the verse numbers.

Putting the dog sculpture back on the step, he looked around, then opened the door with the key. He'd only have seconds to get the code right. Holding his breath, he plugged in the numbers and pressed enter, preparing himself for the blast of the alarm. It worked. Even if the alarm had gone off, he would have shown his ID and explained the situation to the security company. He was more worried about Maddie's reaction when she discovered he'd broken into her house, but he had a good reason to. And they'd have a chat about the key in the dog statue.

Rory walked up and sniffed at his shoes, her tail wagging at the sight of him. Very cute but not very intimidating. He bent down and ruffled her ears, making her whole body sway to the side. "Where's your mama?" She didn't answer but maneuvered her little body around, so he'd scratch her back.

His eyes took in the foyer, then he stood. A trail of small drops of blood led from the front door toward the stairs. "Maddie? You home?" He yelled, then went to the garage to see if her car was there. It wasn't. Good, he guessed. Maybe she was in Sarasota and was so busy she hadn't had the chance to check her messages or call him back.

The absence of her car didn't explain the blood on the floor. Brody returned to the hall and turned on the entry light. A pair of scissors lay on the rug. Had she cut herself with them? Digging in his jacket pocket, he pulled out a pair of gloves, an evidence bag, and a Q-tip. He bent down and swabbed a spot and then another, now congealed and turned a brownish tone. It could be nothing, but knowing Maddie just a little, he knew she would never leave a trail of blood on the floor. Everything had its place, she said. In fact, he'd wager she wouldn't leave for work until she'd wiped up the blood and the scissors were put back in their proper place. Things weren't adding up here.

He took a slow walk around the first floor, the dog at his heels. Nothing appeared to be out of the ordinary. Then he walked upstairs, steeling himself for… he didn't know what. At the top of the stairs, he stopped as was his practice whenever he encountered what could be a crime scene. To the left was the guest bedroom and a bathroom. Straight ahead was the master bedroom, which he'd been in once before. From his place at the top of the stairs, everything appeared to be in order. "Maddie?" he called out just in case. Nothing.

He headed to the master bedroom first to make sure she wasn't there. When she wasn't, he let out the breath he'd been holding. Good. He'd be back to spend time in the room, but first he headed to the other two rooms. The guest bedroom looked untouched, the opposite of his own guest bedroom that held boxes and giftwrap and old clothes to the point the bed was completely covered. Maddie's held a quilt-covered bed, a dresser, a bedside table with a lamp and a Bible on it, and a single picture on the wall. Not a hint of dust, not a wrinkle on the bed. He needed to hire a cleaning service before he invited her over.

The bathroom looked pristine as well, except for a few drops of blood on the floor just outside the bathroom door. He bent down and took a sample. This was so unlike the Maddie he knew to leave bloodstains on the floor. Was it her blood? It had to be. Because if it wasn't, that meant her stalker had somehow found his way into the house and injured her. Or worse.

But her car was gone. So, she'd been able to drive herself perhaps to a hospital. Why hadn't he thought to call the hospitals? He'd call them after he checked her bedroom. Brody checked his phone again. No messages, so he called her again, imploring her to call him back immediately even if it was just a word or two to tell him she was okay. That would be enough to calm his heart.

His breath was coming in fits and starts now. An officer of the law was supposed to be objective. Brody knew better than to let himself fall for a crime victim, but he'd broken his own rule. Pushing to his feet, he plodded toward her bedroom, swallowing past the pit of despair that lodged in his throat.

The room was light and airy since the balcony draperies

were open. The bed was made, and the room was as neat as the rest of the house. The walk-in closet held a hint of cologne. He breathed in, savoring its scent, which caused his lips to quiver. He bit his lower lip hard to stop such nonsense. What kind of an officer of the law was he? Do the job required and do it well.

The bathroom told a different story. The shower door was open, and on the shower floor lay a scrubbing brush—the kind he used on his nails after working in the garden. Maddie must have been in a hurry because on the bathroom floor lay a nightgown, a blue jean jacket, and a bath towel.

Something was really off here. The Maddie he knew would never leave clothes lying on the floor. Brody picked up the jacket. A faint hint of cologne met his nose—a familiar hint. He had savored it when he opened the door for her and leaned over her shoulder to see the photograph in the garage.

The towel was damp to the touch, plush, mint-colored that smelled of shampoo and soap. She'd taken a shower this morning and had gone to work. Normal things. But the pile of clothes and the blood on the floor were anything but.

He picked up the nightgown and froze. Dried blood splayed near the hem in an unusual shape as if the gown had been folded—no, bunched up since the stains were random. He looked for the tag and determined the blood was on the back side, about where her knees would be. Had she cut her leg? Was this the same blood that stained the floor outside the other bathroom or at the bottom of the stairs?

He didn't have an evidence bag large enough to put the nightgown in, but he'd find a bag somewhere in this condo to secure it properly. Everyone had grocery bags or large freezer bags. Reason battled with panic. Why wouldn't she return his calls?

Brody blew out a breath to clear his head. He was a cop. The evidence was all around him. He needed to calm down and make sense of the scene as he returned to the first floor and looked for a plastic bag. He remembered a lesson his captain had taught him. Occam's Razor. Leave the zebras to the jungles. Always look for the simplest explanation first.

Okay, Maddie had come home from her date with the politician named Gregory—he couldn't help the scrunch of his nose when he said the name in his head—and she had called Brody afterwards about finding another note on his car. She'd been home when she called him. But he hadn't called her back, so she went to bed, or did she? The simplest explanation was the one that felt the best. No, that was wrong as well. He was letting his heart lead instead of his logic.

It was last night because Maddie was wearing a nightgown, or it could be early in the morning, but the blood was in the hall in front of the other bathroom. Brody returned to the area to see if there was any sign of an accident. Had she cut herself while shaving? Nicked an artery and had to go to the hospital? But if that were the case, there would have been a trail of blood down the stairs and through the kitchen to the garage.

Brody retraced his steps more slowly this time down the stairs. Yes, a drop on one step and then another a few steps down. The only other drops started a few feet from the stairs and led to the front door. He went outside to follow the trail where it went, then went back to attach the leash to Rory and take her for a quick walk. Whether in Sarasota or elsewhere, Maddie would appreciate her dog being taken out. He could even tell her in a message, but then she'd know he'd been in her condo.

While waiting for Rory to finish her business, he bent down to study the sidewalk leading to the driveway. There on the pathway was a single blood drop. With eyes focused on the ground, he slowly headed to the driveway, his car blocking most of the space. Since the blood trail showed up outside, it couldn't be her blood unless she was forced into the perp's car. Which would mean this was much more than nicking her leg while shaving. Common sense told him the dude named Absalom had broken into the house, but he wouldn't have parked in the driveway.

Brody headed down the short driveway and stopped where it met the road, Rory pulling him toward the sidewalk. Since the street was blacktop, any bloodstain would be difficult to distinguish from any other stain. He bent down to examine a spot on the slope of the driveway when a car braked mere feet from him.

Angry eyes glared at him from the windshield of the Audi. The door opened, and Maddie stepped out. "What's going on?"

He rose slowly, choosing his words while he reined in Rory who was yanking at the leash to reach Maddie. Rubbing a hand against the growth of whiskers on his cheek, he resisted the urge to envelop her in a relieved hug. "You didn't return my calls, so I had to come check to make sure you were okay." Alive.

Her face was devoid of color, her jawline taut. Smudges framed her eyes as if she'd been crying. "Sorry. We were filming in Sarasota. Page told me you called. I thought she was going—"

"To call me? She didn't." He knelt and picked up the dog, already knowing Maddie wouldn't take kindly to him having entered her condo without her consent. The fourth amendment came to mind. He searched for an exception to an illegal search. "You left a message that you'd received another note, and when I called you and you didn't answer multiple times, I thought something might have happened to you. That's why I—"

"Broke into my condo?" She huffed, then whipped around to her car. "Could you back up so I can put my car in the garage, and then we'll talk." The way she said 'talk' brought back memories of his mother's use of the word before he was grounded.

He nodded, handed her the dog, and moved his car onto the street, then he waited at the front door until she bade him enter. It seemed the right thing to do under the circumstances. He fidgeted like a middle-school boy, anticipating the imminent scolding.

Long minutes later, the door swung open. Her pale face was unreadable, her jawline still taut as if she was holding back her anger.

He stepped in but remained on the welcome mat—feeling anything but. "I'm sorry," he spoke to her silence. When she didn't respond, he continued. "I'm sorry I entered your condo without your permission, but when you didn't call after having left me a message, I had to make sure you were…alive." That was the unspoken motivation he'd honestly had. He pointed at the blood drops by the stairs. "Are those yours?"

Maddie didn't react right away. When she did, it almost seemed to take all her strength to turn her eyes to the floor behind her. "I don't know." She wheeled toward him, her eyes pools of pain.

"Did you cut yourself?"

Without a word she strode to the living room. He followed her but kept his distance. "What happened? Please tell me." Maddie straightened the throw pillows on the sofa and then bent to collect Rory's toys to return them to the straw basket in the corner next to the television. He'd wait as long as needed to get to the truth.

After minutes went by, Maddie finally turned to face him, took a seat on the sofa, and pointed toward the wingback chair. "After I called you, I got ready for bed. As I came out of the bathroom, I noticed Rory was focused on something out in the hall, the way she gets when someone's at the door. I grabbed a pair of scissors from the bathroom and went to see what had caught her attention. The alarm was set, so I wasn't worried about an intruder." Maddie frowned and blinked as if she were reliving what had happened.

Brody moved from the chair to the sofa, but she

stiffened and backed up in the seat, as if his proximity was distasteful to her.

"I checked the guest bedroom, then went to the bathroom and turned on the light. Everything looked normal. I berated myself for letting my imagination run in all kinds of directions, and that's when I discovered my imagined fears were reality."

Her lips were trembling now. Brody tried to offer some comfort, but she lifted her hand to stop him. "The guy put his arm around my neck from behind so I couldn't see his face. He said something to me—that's how I knew it was a man. I don't remember what he said because I was busy summoning enough courage to stab him with the scissors."

"The bloodstains in the hall upstairs were his. It wasn't your blood."

She shook her head. "I broke free and ran as best I could in bare feet to the stairs and raced down, but he was right behind me. At one point, I missed a step and fell to the bottom of the stairs, landing facedown." Her head lowered.

Brody let out a pained groan. He knew what was coming and didn't wait for her approval to pull her into a hug.

She jerked back, but then acquiesced with a shaky sigh. Maddie didn't talk for the longest time as he made awkward circles on her back with the palm of his hand, then fingered her curls. "I wish I'd been here," he whispered. How did the guy get past the alarm system? If he'd left a note on her date's windshield, he'd used the time they were in the park to break into her place.

When Maddie's breathing seemed to settle, Brody separated himself from her by sitting back. They needed to talk, and he had to tread lightly, or she'd sprint away like a deer.

Maddie sat up, swiping strands of hair away from her face. "Sorry, I lost it."

"No need to be sorry. Honest emotions are the best." He put up his hands to show he wasn't going to touch her. "Let yourself mourn. Just sit with the sadness."

She nodded, her lip twitching. They sat for a long minute, the clock's tick the only sound.

Finally, he whispered, not wanting to break the silence. "Please don't hide from me. I want to catch the guy and put him away, so he doesn't hurt you anymore." He kept his voice low and calm. "If we knew what he said upstairs, we could figure out what he's after."

With eyes closed, she shook her head from side to side. "I've tried. It's like I blocked what he said. Again."

He moved a strand of hair away from her eyes, which were now swollen and red. "You said you fell down the stairs face-forward. How far did you fall? Did you hurt yourself?" He still hadn't told her about taking her nightgown. She wouldn't appreciate him nosing in her private business without her consent, so he'd have to tread even more lightly than before.

"I fell about four steps from the bottom. It took my breath away, but I didn't even notice because all I could think about was getting out of the house before he caught up with me." Maddie looked everywhere but at him. She wasn't telling him the whole truth.

"Did you?"

"Did I what?"

"Did you get out before he caught up with you?"

She bolted to her feet. "I don't want to talk about it." Grabbing the afghan that lay over a recliner, she unfolded and refolded it.

Brody got up and gently put his hands on her arms to turn her around, but she whipped around and pushed him so hard he almost lost his balance. Backing up a few steps, he lifted a palm to waylay her fears. "I'm a police detective, but I also care about you. If that guy hurt you in any way, let me find him and put him away so you don't have to live in fear."

She remained with her back turned to him.

He swallowed deep. "I must confess something to you.

You're not going to like it. Could you turn around please, so I can tell you?" Something had happened so horrendous that Maddie couldn't face him. When she finally did, the look on her face let him know this would not end well. "When you didn't return my call, I found your key in the puppy vase then used the information you gave me regarding your method for coming up with your password—"

"And you broke into my home without my permission." Her jaw twitched with anger.

"Remember, you said you could trust me, but yes, I disabled the security system, but I only did so to make sure you're weren't…you were okay." He paused to let her react. When she didn't, he continued. "When I saw the stains on the floor by the stairs, I called your name, then checked the whole downstairs, then went upstairs. That's when I saw the blood on the floor by the bathroom. So I went in your bedroom, checked your closet, then went in your bathroom."

Tears traveled down her cheeks. She swiped at them with the back of her hand.

"There I saw the pile of clothes on the floor. I don't know you that well, but what I do know is you're, well, very tidy, so the pile heightened my concern that something had happened. When I saw the bloodstains on the back of your nightgown, I took it—"

A gasp spewed from her lips, and her lips started quivering. He was making things worse, but she needed to know.

"I did this to preserve the evidence." He took a few steps toward her but froze when her hand went up.

"Don't come any closer."

His own eyes secres watering. "Don't you see my heart is breaking? This has never happened to me before, but I had to sublimate my feelings…and do my job." His own voice was cracking like a juvenile. "I didn't know if it was your blood or someone else's. But whoever's blood it is, we…I can find your assailant—your stalker—through his DNA.

Please, work with me on this. Tell me everything that happened. Nothing you say will change my feelings for you." Enough said.

Her arms hugging her chest, she kept her eyes glued to the floor.

When it was clear her response was not forthcoming, he headed to the kitchen where he'd left the grocery plastic bag he'd found in her pantry—the bag containing her nightgown. He fought the urge to hide it behind his back like a naughty boy. "I'll be on my way then. Don't worry, I'll return your…garment." He hadn't felt this empty and heavy at the same time since—he couldn't remember. Despair made his chest hurt. It was just as his hand touched the doorknob that her voice, monotone and so low it was hard to hear her, stopped him in his tracks.

"The fall took the breath out of me for a moment. As I tried to get to my feet, he jumped from behind, keeping me down, making it hard to breathe."

Brody pivoted on his heel to find Maddie on her knees in the living room, her body sunken, her head down. He dropped the bag and went to her, holding her in his arms, pressing her head gently into the crook of his neck. "It's going to be okay," he whispered and kissed her head.

"I tried to grab my scissors, which lay on the rug. Must have dropped them in the fall. I couldn't move. Maybe I should have tried harder. I didn't see him, but I heard his voice and smelled him. And no, I don't remember what I heard or smelled. I just know that I did."

"Did he?" Brody couldn't say it without making it become real, even erecting a wall between them. Although she didn't answer, her sobs told the story. "Well, I'll send the blood I found to get it tested, but I may not have results for weeks."

She was talking again, low and monotone. "He wore a balaclava, and he was tall. Wonder how I knew he was wearing a hood when he attacked me from behind? Oh, yeah.

When he was on top of me, I… or rather my spirit…floated to the ceiling and watched from above."

She pulled away and squeezed her eyes shut as she rubbed her temples. "It was dark, so I couldn't discern color, but I could see his dark shape completely enveloping mine. He was wearing a black hood. And jeans. Everything was dark. The only light I saw was the gleam of the scissors lying on the rug. I think God took me out of the situation for a few moments…minutes? I had no concept of time. Then I was back under him, revulsion undulating over me in waves.

"His breath smelled like my mom's gum. Dentyne. I don't even know if they make it anymore. And he said something to me, but I can't remember what he said. Then he stood and left through the front door as if he was finished with me. As if he hadn't just—" Maddie chuckled, something Brody hadn't expected. "Since I was getting ready to go to bed, I'd covered my face with a masque—the kind to make your skin healthy and shiny. Doesn't every girl want healthy, youthful skin?" A bitter laugh erupted. "My face would have been a better weapon than the scissors."

Brody could tell she was spent by the weight of her head against his chest. She'd told him enough. When her breathing became more regular, he gently tipped her chin up, her eyes still closed. "I promise you I'll do everything in my power to put the guy away forever. Please, take some time off from work. Mourn. Go visit Tessa or your parents."

A shrill laugh spewed out. "No, my parents would probably blame me." Swollen eyes peered up at him. "I don't understand how he got in. The alarm was on when I left, and it was on when I returned from the county fair." She swiped at a smear under her eye. "What is the point of having a security system if he could so easily break in?"

Brody couldn't tell if it was a rhetorical question, so he didn't say anything, but he'd been wondering the same thing. Cameras. They might tell the story. Had Absalom thought about the cameras when he entered her place? Until now, he'd covered his tracks very well. Still, he'd call the security company to see if they'd caught anything. It was something he could do, and he needed to do something for Maddie. "Will you take some time off?"

Her dismissive wave and smirk answered his question before her words did. "I can't afford to take time off right now. There's a case I need to finish. Work will help me…heal. It's just I can't understand why God would let this happen to me. I feel so foolish, as if somehow this was all my fault. I couldn't even protect myself. What was I going to do with a pair of scissors? They're not even a good pair." Her lower lip started quivering again.

What could he say that would make any difference? Everything sounded trite. Using the bottom of his shirt to dab at the tears on her face, he brushed her hair back with his other hand. "I'm going to make a report about this, okay?"

Her eyes shot up. "Absolutely not. Reporters will be knocking at my door and waiting for me after work. Everyone will see me as an assault victim, and I don't want that. I just want it to go away." She buried her head in her hands, then bolted to her feet. "Enough of this." She peered at him through eyes that had no hope. "Don't tell anyone. Promise me you won't file a report. It must be kept secret. Please."

He stood. "As you wish, but I am going to call the security company. See if there's anything on the camera in the foyer—"

"But no checking the blood for DNA. It will lead to too many questions. No DNA." She strode to the front door and opened it.

Brody got the message. "All right, please keep me informed of any more notes or anything that seems out of place." He stopped at the threshold. "You wouldn't consider staying at my place at least until I'm sure—"

"No, I have my dog, and I'll be careful. Thank you…for all you've done." She waved him off and closed the door behind him.

He waited for the sound of the deadbolt and the ping of the alarm system before he left. That little mop of a dog? Lord, please protect them from the predator. Unfamiliar tears formed. What was going on with his heart? Falling for a reluctant, obstinate, OCD-driven woman who obviously didn't return his feelings.

Chapter Eleven

"Nothing makes us so lonely as our secrets."

~ Paul Tournier

Autumn had given way to the crisp evening air of December, and Maddie had almost missed the change. She brushed the dead brown remains of the leaves off her windshield, the chilly air causing a shiver to travel down her neck. Gregory asked her to arrive early to the debate at Rollins College. He said she was his lucky charm and buoyed up his confidence. It was the least she could do.

Pulling out of the parking lot, Maddie did a quick check in the rear-view mirror, although no one had followed her in over two months. Still, habits were slow to break, and she couldn't be sure that Absalom wouldn't strike again, but there'd been no more notes or break-ins. Thoughts of the notes brought Brody to mind, and she couldn't help but smile.

A few times a week, he called her just to check up on her, he said, but he wasn't fooling her. His warm eyes locked on hers and remained there when he returned her nightgown, apologizing that he'd taken samples of the stains in case she ever wanted to pursue a DNA test.

"I checked with the security cameras, but your guy had dismantled them without being seen. Sorry."

She offered a poor excuse for a smile. "That's okay. I haven't heard from him. Maybe he's moved on."

"You need a distraction. How would you like to come watch a hockey game at the rink? Then I can keep my eyes on you while I'm watching the youngsters play."

"I'd love to, but as I said, Absalom's moved on." She waved a hand. "You don't need to watch me. There have been no notes or flowers."

He reached up and brushed her cheek with the palm of his hand. A shiver traveled through her at its intimacy. "Come anyway, but dress warm. Rinks can be cold."

Brody was right about the chilly arena, but it also reminded her of a high-school gym locker room mixed with a hint of popcorn. It surprised her that she enjoyed hockey much more than the elegant events Gregory took her to. The mothers screaming in the stands were much more interesting than the women who fawned over Gregory. Brody, pacing back and forth in front of the bench flapping his arms, was much more fun to watch than Gregory telling the same old stories at every banquet. Even the teens on the ice, pushing each other out of the way to get to the puck, were more real than the political players schmoozing for more votes.

After the game, Brody suggested a late breakfast at Denny's. They drank hot chocolate, trying to outdo each other's marshmallow mustaches. That was the first time she'd allowed herself to laugh since that day.

When she pulled into the parking lot at Rollins College, she drove up and down the aisles until she found an empty parking space a long way from Annie Russell Theatre. Since it was already dark, she used Siri to guide her to the college auditorium.

Gregory was waiting for her, pacing in front of the entrance. She could tell he was rehearsing his responses because his lips were moving.

"I'm here," she said quietly, sensing his rigid posture bespoke his nerves.

Gregory stopped midstride, as if in a bit of a daze, then pulled her into a hug. "I'm so glad you're here. I need my muse close at hand." He grabbed her elbow and led her into the building. "Let's go find a place in the back. I'd appreciate it if you'd run some lines with me."

"What does that mean? Run some lines?" Maddie had never seen him so lacking in confidence.

Gregory pulled her down next to him. "I have twenty minutes before I have to go backstage. Work your magic."

"Okay?" She blew out a subtle breath, not sure what a muse did. "Gregory, you know the answers to every question thrown at you. This isn't your first debate, so you know your opponents are going to try to rile you up, but you're not going to allow it, are you?"

He patted her hand. "You're right. I can do this. I just need to keep my cool and refuse to fall for their barbs and innuendos. All right, thank—"

"Sorry. I just—" Bolting to her feet, Maddie covered her mouth and dashed as fast as her Louboutins would let her to the exit. Where is the restroom? As her eyes searched for the sign, she huffed loud enough for anyone to hear. I can't believe this is happening when Gregory needs me the most. A passing teenager gave her a quizzical look—the crazy-lady-who-talks-to-herself look. Surely there was a restroom for a venue this big.

Past the popcorn stand, which evoked an extra rush of nausea, she finally saw the sign. She threw open the door. Three college-aged girls were chatting near the sinks, one of whom was applying a fresh brush of mascara. A glance at all the stalls showed feet facing forward except for the last one—which was the handicap stall. Was the flu enough of a handicap to use the only available stall? Too much to think about. The moment she entered, breakfast, lunch, and that Snickers bar flowed out of her into the toilet, spattering onto her sleeve. Just great. Now she smelled bad, and she didn't have any mouthwash.

When the undulating waves seemed to abate, she dabbed at her lips and chin, washed off her sleeve, and hurried out, although a slight wave of vertigo made her slow her pace. Something she had eaten didn't agree with her, which surprised her since she had an iron-clad stomach.

The lights were dim now. Good, although the squeak of the door into the auditorium made a few heads in the back row turn, Maddie made it to her seat while Sydney Hamrick was introducing each of three debaters—a candidate from the progressive party named Holly Winter, and Gregory's biggest nemesis, incumbent Rick Welker, and Gregory. He must have regained his confidence because he didn't look a bit nervous. Neither did the other two for that matter.

Sydney went over the rules, then asked the first question—something about the growing cost of insurance after the last hurricane. From the first question on, all three candidates were already throwing barbs at one another, interrupting each other, touting their own records, and going over the time allotted for their responses.

Debates were hard to watch—not unlike wrestling matches. Maddie admired Sydney for keeping her cool when the arguments became too heated. Her head was pounding, whether from the flu or the tension in the room, she didn't know. She glanced back at the exit. What if she left? It wasn't like Gregory could see her since the room was dark, and she'd done her duty by encouraging him when he needed it. He was doing fine on his own.

Maddie waited through the next question, which involved what the candidate would do about the teacher shortage in Florida. Holly, having been a school superintendent, answered with the most eloquence. The other two agreed it was a huge problem and said it would be a top priority. With that, Maddie slipped out of the room.

The smell of popcorn again made her cover her mouth as she hurried out of the building. Breathing in the chilly evening air, her clouded head cleared a bit as she walked as fast as she could to the car. Gregory would not be happy when he discovered her absence. She didn't really care. If truth be known, she was tired of being his 'muse' as he called her. It was time to tell him so when he called her to find out why she'd left.

Habit made her check the windshield as she dropped into the driver's seat, although there hadn't been any notes in the two months since the night of the attack in her house. Attack is what she called it, although she knew differently. Her eyes glanced behind her seat just to make sure no one was crouching there.

Satisfied her car was safe, she swallowed past the acidic gulp that burned and drove away. Could it be? She counted the days since that night—seventy-five days. That was more than ten weeks. No, no, no! More than two months had passed with no period, and she hadn't even noticed. It explained the fatigue and cloudiness she felt as she went to work and trudged home, the sense of darkness following her around. She felt her chest—tender to the touch. Her head slammed back against the headrest. Lord, how could it be? *I don't know how I'm going to survive a pregnancy, especially one borne out of violence. Alone, in the public eye, unmarried? How do I handle this?*

She stopped at a red light, noting a CVS on the opposite corner. Something Brody said came to mind. Take the next step. The next step would be to buy a pregnancy test. Before she lost it. Before she fell apart.

Christmas music met her when she entered through the sliding doors of the pharmacy. "God Rest Ye Merry Gentlemen." It wasn't a gentleman that had put her in this position. Gentlemen didn't have to worry about pregnancy tests.

Plastic red and white candy canes lined the aisle. Maddie pulled her ball cap further down on her head. She didn't need anyone to recognize her.

Where in the world were they? She headed toward the

pharmacy in the back right corner, away from the hair dye, deodorant, and face cream aisle. Her watch read eight-forty-five, which meant the store would be closing in fifteen minutes. She passed vitamins, cold medication, and veered left, checking each side until she found them. Them. How to choose? So many options. She needed clear results, so she chose Clearblue Rapid Detection, and headed to the counter. Along the way she picked up a bag of red licorice—something to hide the smaller box from any curious eyes.

The teenager behind the checkout counter probably didn't watch the news, and there was no one behind her. Still, Maddie kept her eyes averted just in case. After paying, she drove over the speed limit to reach her home. Now that the possibility existed, she wanted to know right away. Christmas lights twinkled from several of her neighbors' houses, and Mrs. Eldridge next door had propped up a fake snowman on the lawn.

In any other year, decorations and Christmas carols brought joy to her heart but not tonight. Closing the garage door behind her, she hurried into her condo, the lights on in almost every room, a residual necessity since the attack. Shadows and closets held too many secrets, and Rory didn't need to sit in the dark, which settled in late in the afternoon.

Maddie made quick work of taking the dog out, her eyes darting around her while Rory took her sweet time. Once inside, she turned on the security system and raced upstairs with her new purchase. In the bathroom, she put on reading glasses and followed the instructions. Summoning every bit of strength she could muster, she read the results. A dark pink line next to a fainter line told her what she already knew. She was with child, pregnant—an expectant mother, a single one at that, with no idea who the father was. The colored line left little doubt, but she took a second test just to be sure.

Next step, make an appointment with her doctor as soon as her office opened in the morning. The step before that was to make it through the night. She studied her stomach, still flat, unchanged, but the bile in her throat confirmed the result. Who should she call? What about her job? What would her boss say? What would the viewers think about a single news anchor with a baby growing inside her stomach?

Seek ye first the kingdom of God whispered in her mind. Take the next step. She needed wise advice on what to do. The easy answer was elimination—wipe out the results of the attack in a single procedure. That was the advice she'd receive from her parents, from her friends, and from her coworkers. How much detail should she go into? If she revealed to any of them she'd been raped, they'd definitely tell her to have the procedure. Would God tell her the same thing? After all, what child born out of a violent act would want to face life that way?

Her grandmother's face came to mind. It was early morning in Zürich. Maddie sat on her bed, picked up her phone, and dialed her number.

"Good morning, Maddie. What a surprise. Is everything all right? I just woke up."

"Hi, Gran. I'm sorry to wake you, but I need wise counsel, and you came to mind."

"Good grief, child, what is it? Did that boyfriend of yours break up with you? Please don't keep me in the dark."

Maddie bit her lower lip which was twitching. "No, he didn't break up with me. I can assure you, Gran, he is clearly not my boyfriend. I'm a mere prop on his arm." She summoned a breath—just say it. "I just discovered I'm pregnant, and I don't know what to do."

The expected silence for a few moments ensued. "Oh. Are you sure?"

"Yes, I'm sure. I just took a test, and the results didn't lie. I am with child."

"My goodness. Are you excited about it? Who's the father? Is it that politician?"

Maddie could almost hear the hesitancy in her

grandmother's voice. "No, to being excited about it, and no, Gregory is not the father." She blew out a breath. "Truth is— I was raped."

Her grandmother gasped.

"All I know about the father is his pen name, Absalom. At least that's what he called himself in the notes he left. Three months ago, he broke into my condo and was hiding upstairs when I returned from the county fair." She let out a mournful sigh, then she told her grandmother everything that had happened that night. "So, I need your advice. Tell me what to do because I'm at a loss." She barely got the words out before her lips started quivering again.

"You'll come here, of course. But first, did you tell the police?"

She grabbed a tissue and blew her nose. "Kind of. Brody Messner, a detective with the Orlando police department, knows that someone broke into my place and that I was attacked, but I didn't tell him I was raped; nor have I told him I'm pregnant. You're the first person I've told. Brody's a really good guy, but I don't want his pity, and I don't want anyone to know—except you and maybe Tessa. I don't even want to tell Mom and Dad."

"Why not, honey? You did nothing wrong. Whoever this Absalom is, he needs to be put behind bars, so he doesn't hurt anyone else. You didn't see his face?"

She couldn't stand going over it again and again. "All I saw was the black hood on his head. It was as if I was outside my body looking down from the ceiling of the entryway, but it was dark, so I couldn't see much. Just that he was tall, and his head was covered."

"Did he say anything to you?"

All these questions didn't help. "Yeah, he did, but I don't remember what. I don't like to think about it. Can you just tell me what to do?" The pause was too long. "Gran, are you still there?"

"I am. You have options, as you already know. First

though, you need to contact that detective and tell him the truth."

Uncomfortable, she flopped over onto her stomach, placed her phone on the pillow, and pressed speaker phone. "No. I don't want everyone in the city to know. Word will get out. Then people won't see me. They'll see a poor rape victim and pity me. That's the last thing I want. Why did this have to happen to me?" Maddie sounded whiny even to herself.

"I know you don't want to hear this, but you've asked twice for my advice, so I'll give it to you in the form of a question. What about the baby? Is any of this the baby's fault?"

Hmm. Good question. "No, none of it is. It is Absalom's fault, and maybe my fault for not being…able to properly protect myself. If I'd just been more careful going down the stairs, or maybe if I'd put up a bigger fight." She shook her head to erase the plague of thoughts of that night. How could she bear this even for another day?

"This is not your fault, Maddie. Don't take that guilt on yourself. You need all the strength of character you can muster to decide what you're going to do. Have you prayed? Have you sought God's advice?"

She flopped over, sat up, and wrapped her arms around her knees, resting her head against them. "Not enough. I don't want to do the wrong thing, Gran. You know what Mom and Dad will tell me to do, so I don't even know if I'm going to tell them. It will just add more pressure to their lives. So—" she managed a chuckle, "I'm adding more pressure to your life."

Gran's chuckle came all the way from Switzerland. "Don't even think that way. You need support right now, and don't let anyone tell you you've done anything wrong. This is what I think you should do. Buy yourself a journal. Start with Psalm 139, then just keep reading. Write everything down God tells you to do, no matter what it is. Second, call that young man of yours—and I'm not talking about that political guy; I'm talking about Officer Messner—is that his name? A serious felony has been perpetrated on you, and justice must be served—"

Tears pooled, and she swiped them away with the back of her hand. "I don't want anyone to know. You don't know what it's like to be in the public eye. Everywhere I go, people cast a second glance at me. Even at church, I can see people whispering about me."

"That's something you're going to have to deal with. You can either choose to hide from everyone, or you can face it head-on. Think of others who have gone through the same thing—they're hurt, bewildered, unsure. You don't have to make any decisions right away—"

"Oh, but I do. Sorry to interrupt you, but I can't go on with this hanging over my head. I have to make a decision right away!" Her voice was getting louder. This was making her crazy.

Gran's voice remained calm. "I will be praying for you, love. Please keep me in the loop, and tell that officer what happened. Don't let the attacker get away with it. You, Maddie, are a strong woman in every way."

Her grandmother's words buoyed her confidence. "Thanks, Gran. Just for the record, what do you think I should do about the baby?"

"Honey, that's between you and God. No one else. Don't make any decision until you've given it lots of time and prayer. Right now, it's too new, too raw. Remember, you're not just deciding for yourself."

Once Maddie hung up, she leaned against the wooden headboard, barely noticing its hardness. The amount of thinking she had to do would prevent any sleep in the next couple hours. She already knew what awaited her in the psalm her Gran had recommended. That verse about being fearfully and wonderfully made always came to mind when that little voice inside made cutting remarks about the way she looked on camera.

Maddie picked up her Bible, opened to the middle of book, and found the psalm. She'd read it so many times. In essence, everyone had worth. God didn't make junk. But what if the child inside her wasn't part of God's plan? Her finger trailed down the psalm, and there it was in verse 13 her lucky number:

For You formed my inward parts.
You covered me in my mother's womb.
I will praise You, for I am fearfully and wonderfully made.
Marvelous are Your works,
And that my soul knows very well.
My frame was not hidden from You,
When I was made in secret,
And skillfully wrought in the lowest parts of the earth.
Your eyes saw my substance, being yet unformed.
And in Your book they all were written,
The days fashioned for me,
When as yet there were none of them.

There was no doubt what the verses were saying to her. This would be so easy if she was married and this child was planned, but how was she going to keep her growing belly a secret from the viewers? She'd worked with other female newscasters who hid behind a plant or carried a book to cover their baby bumps, but they weren't fooling anyone. How was she going to go through this alone with no one to help her? And the child—how could she ever tell her daughter—somehow, she felt it was a girl—that she was the product of a violent rape by an unknown criminal?

Take the next step. The next day she donned a wig, drove to a nearby urgent care and, using her grandmother's name, she obtained confirmation she was indeed pregnant. After work, where she'd made a beeline to the restroom twice to empty what remained of her lunch from the previous day, she drove home, put on her pajamas, and scrubbed the foyer floor clean with ammonia. The strong smell ensured it was really clean. If only she could be. Then she wiped down the refrigerator and the cupboards. By keeping busy, she held onto a modicum of control over the life Absalom had ripped away from her.

Christmas music played from YouTube on television. It did little to buoy up the heaviness that weighed on her shoulders like a big gray anvil. She finally flopped onto the armchair, her phone on her lap. Whenever unwelcome tasks lay ahead, Maddie made a list and checked them off, feeling some amount of satisfaction with each checkmark. Next on the list of people to call was Brody Messner, followed by her parents and Gregory. She was quite sure she knew how Brody would react, as well as what her parents would say.

Do the next thing. She dialed Brody's number, hoping she could just leave a voicemail if he didn't answer. Was her news something to put in a voicemail? Four rings, five…good, she'd hang up on the sixth. Lo and behold, he answered.

"Hi, stranger. How are you?"

His voice sounded as warm and smooth as cocoa. Even in her depleted state, it brought a smile to think that once again she compared him to food. "Hello, I hope I'm not interrupting hockey practice. Is hockey still going on?"

"No, you aren't, and yes, it is, but with Christmas coming in a week, we're taking a break. What are you doing for Christmas?"

Christmas. "Nothing much, just attending a party at work next Friday and going to church on Christmas Eve. How about you?" It wasn't exactly the right season to break the news to him.

"Work. Since I don't have a family, I always volunteer to let the other guys have the day off. Crooks usually take off Christmas, which makes it easy." He paused. "If you don't have anything going on, maybe the two of us can celebrate together—"

"Brody, I'm pregnant." Her head hit the back of the chair, her eyes squeezing shut as she waited for his response, which didn't come right away. "I'm sorry to throw this at you, but I've never done this before."

"Are you at home? I'll be right there." Click.

Maddie stared at the phone, then crossed his name off the list. Gran was right. She needed to tell Brody. He'd done so much for her. After he left, she'd make quick work of the other people on the list, and that would be the end of it. While she waited, she made coffee then threw it out in favor of decaf.

The doorbell rang, and she ran to turn off the alarm, then opened the door. Brody stood there, his shoulders slumped, his eyes on her. Sad eyes. Disappointed eyes.

"C'mon in." She stood back. I have to get used to people looking at me like this when they find out.

He stayed in the threshold until the wind whipped snowflakes into the foyer. Closing the door behind him, Brody turned to her. "I don't know what to say." The tremulous sigh that followed made her regret following her gran's advice.

She stared at the ground, anywhere but at him. How she wished she hadn't told him. If this was the way everyone reacted, it would be better to go someplace and hide for the next few months. Somehow, she'd figure this all out by herself, but he was talking—

"So, how are you feeling? I bet your boyfriend is happy—there I go rambling again." He straightened and bobbed his head. "Congratulations." His eyes said the opposite.

"Gregory? I haven't even told him yet. I haven't told anyone except my grandmother and you." She could feel her head squeeze in and out like an accordion. All she wanted to do was go to bed and sleep off the headache.

Brody took a step toward her; she backed up. He blew

out a breath. "I don't know what to say." He inclined his head, so she had to look at him. "Are you happy? I mean, a baby—"

Her arms wrapped tight across her chest. "I don't know what I feel. My whole life has changed, and I don't know how to handle it." Her lip started quivering to the point she just gave up talking, pivoted, and shuffled into the living room.

"Have you gone to see your doctor?"

"This morning. I just found out last night by taking one of those tests." She felt Brody's touch on her arm, and he turned her around.

"What can I do to help? I want to be here for you. Whatever you need." He drew her to his chest and kissed her temple, and for the first time, she let go and allowed herself to lean into another human being, her throbbing temple feeling good against his cold jacket. His hand smoothed her hair as if she were a cat, and it felt comforting.

"To tell you the truth, I just want it to go away." Her voice muffled into his shirt.

"Okay, so it's not a good time for Gregory with the election and all? Is that the issue?"

She pushed him away. "You think I—? Gregory is not my boyfriend. Never has been. Ew." Maddie watched as the light went on, his eyes transitioning from befuddled to aware to agonized.

"Oh. Oh." He pulled her to his chest again. "I understand. Now I know why you don't know what to do. What you must be going through, and to do this alone." He lifted her chin. "Maddie Caldecott, will you marry me?"

What? "What? Are you nuts?"

He blinked a few times. "Nuts? Maybe, but I don't think so. Ever since you cleaned up my desk, I've wanted to be part of your life. It would be my honor and great delight to be your husband and this baby's father. I know it's not the way you planned it, but sometimes life hits us in the gut." He peered down, then up. "No pun intended."

Maddie burst out laughing, then covered her lips at his crestfallen face. She'd hurt his feelings, and he was trying so hard. Pulling him into a hug, she whispered in his ear, "You are such a dear man, and I am honored that you would even ask me, but we can't make a life decision like this just to solve a problem."

He straightened, and his eyes didn't share her mirth. "Why not? Who needs all that fluffy stuff that comes with planning a wedding? I don't take marriage lightly; it's a holy covenant between a man and a woman. You're having a baby, and I want to help you raise the child as if it were my own. Do you have any better offers?"

She pushed away, averting her eyes. "No…" How to say it without hurting his feelings? "What about love? We don't know each other well enough to rush into marriage. I grew up with parents who barely tolerated each other, and I promised myself I would rather remain an old maid than be in a marriage like that."

He pulled her to the sofa and plopped her down, then sat next to her. "I'm sorry you grew up with a poor image of marriage, but I grew up with parents who loved one another. Did they hug and kiss all the time? No, but they were kind to each other, took care of each other, and laughed a whole lot. They honestly enjoyed each other's company." A smile pulled his lips up as he finished speaking. He turned to her. "That's what I want. I want to laugh with you. I want to enjoy life with you. I want to share this child with you, take care of you—" He stopped when his eyes filled with tears, and his lips pressed together.

Maddie gently framed his face with the palms of her hands, then kissed him gently. "You paint such a lovely picture. That sounds exactly like what I hope love looks like. But I don't want to make a huge decision like this before I've had time to pray about it. I'm sure my parents and friends will advise me to get an abortion. They'll think it's wise because of the way… it happened. Even if we were to get married quickly, people could do the math and figure out we'd had to get married."

Brody bolted to his feet and paced. "Who cares what they think? What matters is you and the child. Nothing else."

"Sit, Brody, please. My head is pounding like crazy, and you moving around like that is making it worse." She patted the seat next to her. He plopped down, crossed his arms, and frowned.

She took his hand and held it in both of hers. "I've thought about abortion—" When she saw his eyes cloud over, she continued. "But I know this little packet of genes inside me needs a chance to make her own mistakes. I'm not sure what I'm going to do yet, although it is a tempting way to uncomplicate things at work." She raised her hand when he started to say something. "But I've interviewed enough women to know they don't get over the procedure easily. What I need is time and a place where I feel safe to make that decision, and I don't have that here in Orlando."

His face looked so woebegone she squeezed his hand. "After I call my parents and Gregory, I'm going to take a leave of absence from work, and then I'm going to go spend the next few months with my gran in Zürich. When I return, we can pick up where we left off. We'll know by then." She ran her knuckles gently against the stubble on his face. He looked every inch the epitome of a lost boy. She could easily fall in love with that bump on his nose—he'd said it came from hockey—and the crooked smile. Maybe love wasn't about Cinderella and a prince named Charming; maybe it was about caring and protecting and laughing, as he'd described his parents' love.

Now crestfallen joined woebegone, and she could tell he was disappointed.

"You can only stay for six months legally, isn't that right?"

"Yes, and then I'll be back." She didn't want to think

about coming back alone.

He stared at her. "You've already made up your mind, haven't you?"

She shrugged. "I've worked hard to keep my private life private. I don't want to be one of those anchors who holds a laptop or a book over her baby bump. It's better if I just go away."

"But what about when you return with a newborn? Won't people be talking then?"

"If I return with a newborn. I don't want anyone to know I'm pregnant, and I certainly don't want anyone to know I was raped. It will just be better if I go away for a while."

He kissed her on the forehead, stood, and headed to the front door, then he turned around. "Don't be surprised if I show up in Zürich. I've got tons of vacation time coming, and I'd like to be there with you…when the baby's born. Please let me."

What a man Officer Brody Messner turned out to be. Appearances were certainly deceiving. "Yes, of course. I would love to show you around Zürich and introduce you to my grandmother. She's quite a character—I want to be just like her someday." She gave him a kiss on the cheek and closed the door behind him.

Somehow Brody had rid her of the doldrums. Now it was time to complete the last three unwelcome tasks, then she'd say goodbye to Orlando and be in Zürich in time for Christmas.

Pouring herself a cup of coffee with extra caramel cream, she called Gregory. Normally she would prefer to tell him in person, but now it didn't matter. She was nothing more than arm candy anyway.

He answered on the fourth ring. "Hi, Babe. Long time no hear. What's up?"

She could hear voices in the background, so he'd be distracted. "I'll get to the point, Gregory. I never told you this, but the night of the county fair after you dropped me off, a man broke into my house and attacked me."

The pause was way too uncomfortable. "Oh…Oh…I am so sorry. Why didn't you tell me?"

She sighed. "You're in the middle of your campaign, and I didn't want to bother you with my problems. I don't feel safe here, so I'm going to stay with Gran in Switzerland. That's about it. It sounds like you're in a busy place, so I'll let you go."

An unsufferable silence ate up her patience, but it was a lot to drop on a person, so she waited for his response.

It finally came, and his voice was subdued. "You know you can call me anytime."

No, she couldn't call him anytime. Gregory wouldn't be there for her, not when every decision had to be sifted through his political life. "Thanks, but I won't be calling you. You should find someone else to be your 'companion' from this point forward. Good luck with the election." Goodbye, Gregory. Check.

Next, she called her mother, who might be more compassionate than her dad. Her mom answered right away.

"Hi, dear, I was just telling Jerry I needed to call you. How's the job in Orlando going?"

"Fine." She could hear the voices of her stepbrother, his voice cracking as he tried to out-argue his sister, who was in middle school. Since it was close to Christmas, they were on break. "Mom, could you give me a few minutes, so I can talk to you about something? It's important."

"Of course, dear." She heard her mother shoo the kids into another room, and quiet ensued. "Sorry about that. Those two have been arguing since they were toddlers. Now what is it, honey?"

Where to begin? "In September, I started receiving notes from someone who basically said we belonged together, but I needed to be purged of some secret I was holding onto. He called himself Absalom."

"It sounds like you have an obsessed fan. There are a lot

of crazies out there. Did you call the police?" Maddie could hear cupboards opening and closing. Her mother was in the kitchen putting away dishes.

"Yes, especially after he broke into my house, and he hung a picture from one of my photo albums up on the wall. Remember when Dad's picture was in the paper for Father's Day?"

"Do I ever. We'd just had the biggest fight because he'd forgotten to pick you up from swimming lessons. Father's Day indeed! Why would your fan put up that picture? He broke into your condo?"

"Yes, can you think of any guy about my age who would have something against Dad? If I could just figure out the answer to that question, then I'd know who he was and could protect myself."

A long sigh emitted from the other end. "Your father has a lot of enemies, but I can't think of anyone that young. Why do you think it's someone your age?"

"Because in the three or four notes he sent me, he quoted poetry that I studied in World Lit in eleventh grade. Another thing he alluded to in the notes was a secret I was keeping. Mom, do you have any idea what he might mean by a secret? I've racked my brain, even talked to Tessa, but the only thing she remembers is a certain day when I left school early. I told her I never wanted to go back to school again. The next day, I was back and didn't remember even saying that."

"Hm," was all her mother said. Just as Maddie was about to talk, her mother spoke up. "I do remember a time when you came home. Your eyes were swollen, and you said the same thing—that you never wanted to go back to school. Someone had said something to you in the restroom about your father. When I asked you about it, you clammed up. Said you didn't want to talk about it. You said you wanted to lie down. Whatever it was seemed to vanish because you were back to your old self the next morning, as if nothing had happened."

Maddie blew out a frustrated breath. "It's weird that I don't remember. It must have been something so bad I blocked it. Maybe that event is related to the notes I've received. But there's something else I have to tell you—" She summoned her courage. "Here goes. One night in September, that guy who wrote the notes broke into my place and attacked me."

"Oh, Maddie!"

She took a deep breath and quietly said, "I'm pregnant."

That same silence followed as it had with Brody and Gran. "Oh, sweetie. I don't know what to say. Of course, you saw him. Did you recognize him?"

"I didn't see his face. He grabbed me from behind. As I tried to get away from him, I tripped down the stairs and fell face first. That's when he assaulted me. It was dark, so I didn't see his face."

"Well, you simply must make it go away. No one would blame you. It's the wise thing to do."

The last thing Maddie wanted was to get in a fight with her mother. "I just wanted you to know, Mom. Could you tell Dad for me? I just can't right now. I'll be going to Zürich to spend time with Gran. Give my best to the kids and Jerry, and if you think of anyone who might have had a grudge against Dad, call me. It's the not knowing that's killing me."

"Of course, I'll tell him. Love you, Maddie. Take care of yourself. Do the right thing, then everything will be back to normal." Click.

Normal. There would never be normal again. She stared at the phone for the longest time. Three down; one to go. Maddie wasn't surprised that her mother would want her to snuff out the life growing within her. There would be no baby shower for this little one. Maddie had to admit life would be a lot easier if she followed their advice. After all, her mother wanted what was best for her, and maybe for themselves as well. How would her mother and Gregory explain away the child?

It didn't surprise her that her mother hadn't asked her to come stay with them, but it hurt. Why did she keep on letting them disappoint her? What was the saying—insanity is doing the same thing over and over and expecting different results? The sigh that emanated held a lot of angst. No, it was time to stop feeling sorry for herself. She'd always made her own way. Keeping her private life separate from her public life kept everything orderly and free of drama. Until now. The only thing she could do to keep everything in its place and maintain control was to take a leave of absence.

The last person to contact would be best to tell in person. She grabbed her coat and purse and drove to the studio, rehearsing what she would tell Morgan and what she wouldn't. By the time she parked in front of the building, she'd decided to tell him the truth and hope he'd let her keep her job.

His office door was partially open, and she could hear him talking on the phone. She wanted to get this over with as quickly as she could. When she tapped on his door, he waved her to the chair across from him. Morgan finished the call then leaned forward, crossing his arms. "To what do I owe the pleasure of your visit? How's the Grady Newland piece coming? I know you asked for an extension."

Maddie shifted in her seat. "Mr. Newland has left the area and taken on a new identity. His ex-wife said their daughter receives an anonymous gift every Christmas, which she assumes comes from Grady. She told me she'd save the packaging this year so I can follow the crumbs to his location." She winced at how soft she was getting. "But I don't think he did it; I think the high-school girl made up the whole thing. The guy's life is already ruined, and I don't want to expose him to public scrutiny again just to get a follow-up."

Morgan's eyebrows formed a V. He stood, circled the desk, and sat on the edge of his desk. "What's wrong,

Maddie? It's not like you to give up on a story."

Her chin lifted. "I didn't give up on the story. A week ago, I followed Michelle Russo, the 'victim' to a nightclub where she was sitting with a bunch of girls drinking martinis. I'd read on Instagram she'd invited friends to celebrate her divorce."

Morgan's head tilted to the side.

"Yup, and she was a few sheets to the wind by the time I sat down at the next table." Maddie could feel the satisfied smile on her face, relieved she'd finished the case before her life took a different turn.

"Don't keep me in suspense. What did you find out?"

"Melissa recognized me as the reporter who covered the story involving the coach years ago, so she invited me to join her and introduced me to the three other gals at the table. One of them asked her what the coach had done. Melissa shrugged and said, 'I did what anyone would do when he sat me on the bench when I was his best player. Tit for tat.'"

Morgan frowned. "Too bad it's just inuendo. We can't do much with that."

Maddie nodded, then straightened the three pens that sat on his desk. "So, I asked her if the coach had…you know…come onto her."

Morgan leaned forward. "What did she say?"

"She shrugged and said, 'I'm sure he wanted to.' Then one of the girls at the table said, 'So what happened? What did he do to you?'"

"Melissa said, 'He got fired is what happened, and I got to play every game after that.' I've never seen such a self-satisfied smile in my whole life." Maddie held up her phone. "It's all on here. I put together the shoot, and it's ready to go to the producers."

Morgan leaned back and clapped. "That's my girl. Bravo. Do you have any ideas what story you want to tackle next?"

Tears fought to brim. Not now. Blinking them back, she

stood, closed the door, then returned to her chair. "I have something to tell you, but promise me you won't tell anyone…here or anywhere."

His eyes held concern as he drew an X on his chest with his pointer finger. "What's happened? I noticed you seemed a little…strained of late."

No time for reticence. She spewed out the same words she'd repeated all morning. "I'm pregnant." When his eyebrows lifted, she held up her palm. "It's not what you think. Remember the guy who left notes on my car?"

He returned to his seat. "Yes, was it him? Did you finally meet him?"

She straightened then leaned back. "No, he broke into my house and assaulted me. That's why I'm here. I need to take a leave of absence. To sort things out. I have big decisions to make—decisions with eternal consequences. I can't make those decisions here, so I'm going to Zürich to stay with my grandmother." Maddie leaned forward, her arms crossed on his desk. "I don't want anyone to know. That means no one here at work. You're the only one I'm telling. Please respect my privacy. I've worked hard to separate my personal life from my public one." She paused until he nodded his acceptance. "I won't return to work for several months—maybe even into the month of July. That is, if you allow me to retain my position."

The silence was uncomfortable. She was asking a lot, but surely, he understood she hadn't asked to be attacked.

Finally, he came around and wrapped her in a hug. "I'm so sorry, sweet girl. I can't imagine what you're going through. Have you told the police?"

No words were forthcoming, so she nodded, her tears soaking his suit jacket.

Handing her a tissue, he leaned against his desk. "You did the right thing telling them, although I bet it was hard."

She blew her nose. "I'm no hero. I didn't tell Officer Brody Messner I was raped until yesterday, but when I didn't return his calls right after it happened, Brody entered my house and found blood on the floor where I'd stabbed the guy with a pair of scissors. I was—and still am—so worried about this getting out to the press, so I told him not to check for DNA. Maybe someday, but not now." She shrugged. "I've become the typical victim who wants everything to go away." She shook her head. "It always flabbergasted me that the victims I've interviewed didn't go to the police to stop the guy from attacking other women. Now I get it. How naïve I was."

"Do you still think it's one of our viewers?"

"No, I'm fairly sure the attacker was someone from my high school in New Jersey, but only because he hung a photograph of my family on the wall, and the poetry he wrote in the notes was from a specific class I took in high school. It could be he moved here to exact revenge for something either I or my father did. Whatever it is, I've blocked a lot."

Morgan blew out a breath. "My dear girl, I'm so sorry, and yes, you can take a leave of absence. We'll just say it's for personal reasons. Of course, I'll have to find a replacement for you, and I can't hold your position open for that long, so you'll have to take whatever's available when you return. Don't worry about that right now. You take care of yourself and that baby of yours."

He stood, signaling the end of their meeting, so she stood. "Thank you." Fresh tears brimmed. She hated being such a needy girl. "I've loved working here."

"We love you too. You'll receive a portion of your income for three months. Long-term disability will kick in after that. I'll take care of it, and I'll be praying for you." He pointed at her midsection. "Whatever you decide." As she opened the door, he said, "Your condo. Would you be up to subletting it?"

Maddie hadn't even thought about the condo. How was she going to make the payments and pay the utilities without a full paycheck? "I haven't even thought that far ahead. Do you know of someone who's interested?"

"Yes, I have two interns who will be working here for six months. They're young men just out of college. Do you have two bedrooms?"

"Yes, I do."

He joined her at the door. "Don't worry, I'll read them the riot act about taking care of the place. You just take care of yourself." He gave her another hug, and she left feeling better than she had all day.

The next week was a whirlwind that left her falling into bed at night fast asleep as soon as her head hit the pillow. Even with lots of sleep, Maddie felt so listless. The pressure of tying up business at work, meeting with her two new tenants, updating Rory's papers for the trip overseas, and packing for six months made her long for a nap. There was still so much to do, and her flight left the next afternoon. Once she was at Gran's house, she'd have time to slow down and reflect. Then she'd make her decision, but like everything else, she'd do it after carefully considering all the information she could collect.

When her phone buzzed, she dropped onto the bed and picked it up. Brody. A mixture of confusion, contentment, and something akin to remorse filled her. She pressed the button. "Hi, Brody."

"Hey, how are you, Maddie?"

The way he said her name made her heart calm. "I'm good. Busy. I'm leaving tomorrow." Brody always made her feel warm and cozy like a comfortable blanket, but she didn't deserve him, and he wanted a deeper commitment than she could give him. In a different time, in a different situation, Maddie could easily fall for him, but she needed to guard her heart. It was unwise to make a commitment when everything in her life was in upheaval.

"I know." A sigh preceded his words. "I'd like to take you to the airport if that's okay."

"I was just going to call a cab, but okay, that would be

helpful. You should know my two suitcases are so heavy they're liable to break your back. I also have the dog."

He chuckled. "Duly noted." When they agreed upon a time, he seemed unwilling to say goodbye. "What did your boss say?"

"Morgan was very nice about it. He told me not to worry about my job, although he couldn't promise to keep it for me. Two interns will be moving in next weekend, so my mortgage will be taken care of. I made Morgan promise not to tell anyone why I was leaving."

"That's great. I know it's important to you to keep your private life out of the public eye."

Something about his tone bothered her. "Is that so wrong?"

"No, of course not, but someday it might help someone else who's going through the same thing to heal. They'll listen to you because you've gone through it."

Maddie's lips tightened. How could he possibly know what she was going through? "I'll be ready at ten o'clock," her words spat out.

"I'm sorry. My timing is awful. I'm going to miss you so much. I just wish—"

"It's okay. I'll be ready. See you tomorrow." She hung up before words of anger ruined their relationship—what there was of it.

Chapter Twelve

"The man who can keep a secret may be wise,
but he is not half as wise as the man with no secrets to
keep."

~ Edgar Watson Howe, Country Town Sayings

The drive to the airport was prickly, although Brody tried to lighten the mood with an anecdote about a car chase he'd been involved in. She responded with a forced laugh. He'd offended her with his advice. How quickly he'd forgotten the value of just listening. Hadn't he just read about Job's friends who'd given him unsolicited counsel? What did Brody know about being attacked and pregnant? Instead of apologizing, he should zip up his lips, which he did, but his mind was running as fast as his car.

He headed up to the airport hotel's parking lot, which would allow him to accompany her into the airport instead of just dropping her off outside the terminal. Maddie was quiet, as they headed to check in her two very heavy suitcases.

"Books?" he said as they stood in line for the next airline rep.

"A few. Sorry," she said as knelt to look into Rory's dog carrier and touched the dog's curious nose with her finger.

"No need to apologize. If I was leaving for six months, my hockey equipment would weigh more than these two suitcases." At least she was talking to him. After dropping off her bags, they headed to TSA, which would be his last chance to let her know how he felt. What he wanted to say she wouldn't want to hear—that he'd fallen hard for her, despite the fact they'd hadn't been on a real date. Despite the fact she regarded him as a mere friend. He wanted so much more, but he'd keep his feelings to himself until she was ready. One call from this lady with the red hair and green eyes, and he'd be on the next plane to Zürich.

It seemed Maddie knew a lot of the TSA staff, who hugged her when she told them she was heading to Zürich to visit her grandmother. He noticed she didn't tell them how long she'd be there. Brody trailed behind her, feeling out of place, but still wishing she'd give him a few moments so he could apologize. He didn't want her to leave with things the way they were.

When she'd reached the place where he had to leave, Maddie turned to face him, and before he could say any of the words he'd recited in his head, she wrapped her arms around him, her cheek next to his. "I'm going to miss you so much," she said. "You've been the one constant in my life for the last few months." She kissed his cheek, the scent of her cologne or hairspray—he didn't know which—lingering after she broke contact.

Brody tipped up her chin, gently forcing her to look at him. "Will you call me, please?" His voice was husky as he swallowed past the lump in his throat. "Whatever you want, whatever you need—" He stepped back, wishing for just a little more time. His mother had taught him many lessons, but one had stayed with him when he'd tried to keep a wounded bird in a shoebox. She'd said, "You can't own the bird, so let it go. If it comes back to you, good, but if it doesn't, you never owned it to begin with."

This bird touched him just under his eye, where a tear betrayed his attempt at a stolid expression. "I will." She ran her fingers gently down the side of his unshaven face. He hadn't had time to control the stubbly mess. "I'll miss you."

She and Rory disappeared into the crowd behind the TSA agent.

His father's face came to mind. "Do the next reasonable thing." Apt advice. The next reasonable thing was to find Maddie's attacker. Brody remembered the time she'd walked into his office, her nose scrunched at the scent of stale coffee and onions. The first thing that had come to mind when he saw Madeleine Caldecott was—what a snob. How wrong he had been. From that first time she'd wiped up a ketchup stain on his desk with a disinfectant wipe, he'd fallen for her, and he'd tried to honor her request, even though she'd hamstrung him by not letting him pursue a DNA search. But not anymore.

As soon as he left the airport, he drove to the station and headed to his office where he'd bagged and tagged samples of the perp's blood from Maddie's nightdress and her carpeting. With those same samples now hidden in a gym bag, he headed to the crime lab where Sonny Jeffers worked as a tech. If anyone could come up with definitive answers based on the attacker's DNA, it was Sonny.

His eyes were glued to a microscope when Brody knocked on the open door. Sonny's head bobbed up like an ostrich who'd just realized it wasn't alone. "Hey, Brod. What brings you to the bowels of the building?"

He used his ace in hand. "Remember those tickets I scored for the Lightning playoffs in Tampa last year?"

The bespectacled lab tech blew out a slow breath and nodded. "Ah, it's pay-up time." His ponytail hung to the side of his tilted head. "For what relative do you want me to analyze their DNA?"

Brody chuckled. "Why would you think I'd ask you to do that? It's against policy."

His arms stretched out in a yawn. "Doesn't stop anyone from calling in favors. What's yours?"

Brody unzipped the gym bag and removed the small plastic bag. "A friend of mine was raped. This blood was found on the floor, on the carpet, and on her nightgown. I want to find out who did it, but we gotta keep the results on the down low. My friend doesn't want to know, but she's not thinking straight. I have to stop the guy. He's a crazy dude." Brody dropped the bag into his friend's hands.

"Okay, so this is for your eyes only?"

Brody nodded.

"It will take a few weeks, but it should be back by the new year."

"Good. If there's no hits on CODIS, could we send the samples for a genealogy test? This guy's a rapist, and he's out there. I want to get him."

Sonny's smile widened. "Okay, but we're even."

"Understood." Brody hoped Maddie would understand.

Chapter Thirteen

"To keep your own secrets is wisdom; but to expect others
to keep them is folly."

~ William Scott Downey, Proverbs

Coming to Zürich was like coming home. Here
Maddie could be safe and anonymous. She felt the
ubiquitous knot at the back of her neck loosen. Normally she
would have taken the train from the airport and walked the
short distance to her grandmother's home, but with the dog,
two suitcases, and a backpack, she hailed a cab instead.

Although it was the middle of the night back in Florida,
here the day was just beginning, and the sun and the crisp
winter air invigorated her with their welcoming arms. Rory
was going to love staying at Gran's. She lived a mere block
away from Lindenhof park, which sat as a crown on the regal
head of the city overlooking Old Town, with its beautiful
view of the Grossmünster Church. Although there wasn't
any grass in the park any time of the year, there were so
many trees to sniff that it would never grow old for her dog.

Once the taxi had navigated up the narrow lanes,
Maddie directed the driver to pull in front of 16
Fortunagasse. She paid him with the Swiss francs that
remained from her last trip to Zürich two years before. Gran
didn't own a car since public transportation was so
accessible in this city, so whenever Maddie visited, she

found her own way to Gran's house. As expected, the gray shuttered windows lined with flowering plants were wide open despite the brisk temperature, welcoming her in.

She pushed open the door, peering at the four stairs that led to the living room. "Gran?"

A squeal came from the kitchen. "Oh, my sweet Maddie, I'm coming. Just taking the muffins out of the oven." As Maddie climbed the stairs and let Rory out of her carrier, her grandmother appeared around the corner, white hair in a stylish bob framing her smiling face, her dark blue eyes twinkling. She enveloped Maddie in a warm hug. "Oh, girl, I'm so glad you're here."

"Me too," Maddie whispered, her voice muffled in her gran's sweet-smelling scarf. Tears welled up—from jetlag or from everything else, she didn't know. This whole ordeal had made her cry at everything. This was where she needed to be—her safe place with one of the few people she trusted.

"Let me take a good look at you." Gran straightened her arms, her eyes glistening then dropping to Maddie's midsection. "How are you feeling? I remember being very tired those first few months, and I was barely out of my teens." Without waiting for a response, she cupped Maddie's face in her flower-dusted hands. "I will be with you through this whole thing. You have me and you have God and you have this beautiful town. What more do you need?"

"Nothing, I guess." Her lip still quivered. "I'm just at a loss."

Gran kissed her cheek, then took her hand. "I know just what will do the trick. How about a cup of hot tea and a warm, gooey muffin? We have all the time in the world to talk about things." Rory's prancing taps on the floor caught her attention. "And look who's here." Gran knelt down and let Rory lick her nose. "I love this dog. We'll have lots of fun. You two will bring a lot of liveliness to this old house." With that she turned and hurried into the kitchen, the dog bouncing at her heels. Maddie headed down the four steps to retrieve her luggage and lugged the first one up the stairs.

Her gran walked fast. She was used to walking everywhere, as most Swiss people did, up and down the hills of Zürich. Maddie was already breathless from climbing up and down the four steps in the foyer. "I'll catch up with you, but I want to take my bags to the room, if that's okay."

Gran's voice came from the kitchen. "Oh my, what was I thinking? You shouldn't be carrying those heavy bags up by yourself. Leave them. I'll get them after we've had tea."

"I'm not dying," Maddie said, grabbing the backpack and the other suitcase. "I can manage."

"You know where your room is, but come right out. I don't want the tea to cool down."

Just being here soothed her soul. The living room's wall-to-wall bookshelves filled to the brim with books her grandmother enjoyed, the baby grand in the corner, the heavy wooden table that held Gran's Bible and study books; they all comforted her. This was certainly the best kind of therapy—to listen to her gran play the violin, to shop for Christmas presents with Gran, to stroll the many lanes of Old Town without having to look over her shoulder.

Maddie entered the bedroom to the right of the living room, across from the small bathroom that would be hers for the next few months. She looked at it with new eyes, envisioning a bassinet by the lowest slope of the ceiling. Not yet. Until she'd made up her mind once and for all, she shouldn't complicate things by imagining what might never be.

Setting her suitcases on the single bed covered by a colorful quilt Gran had made, Maddie pulled out a fresh top and put it on, noticing no tightness yet. Wiggling into slippers, she headed to the kitchen, where Gran was plating fresh muffins and covering a pot of tea that smelled of orange and cinnamon with a cozy. Maddie took a seat at the island, a place she always associated with long conversations, wise advice, and encouragement.

"May I?" Gran said without waiting for a response. She poured tea into a proper teacup from her hutch. "I hope you like this tea. I find it very comforting when the weather turns colder. We're supposed to have a cold, snowy Christmas. Isn't that wonderful? Just like He meant it to be."

Maddie smirked at her. "God lives in Florida as well, Gran."

"If you say so." She poured herself a cup, then took a sip. "We'll have to take a stroll around the shops of Neumarkt. I always find the most interesting things I don't need there."

Maddie stifled a yawn, jetlag reminding her that she hadn't slept in twenty-four hours. "I feel like I've come home when I'm here. Thank you for inviting me."

"Of course." Gran leaned forward. "I hope you don't mind, but I made a tentative appointment for you with Dr. Annette Schneller for tomorrow morning at eleven. She's the daughter of our bassoonist, Herb Schneller, and she's an OB/Gyn. Did I misstep already?"

The quickness of it startled Maddie, and she was inclined to tell her grandmother she'd find her own doctor, but she held back, knowing fatigue was making her edgy. Maddie reached for her gran's hand and took it in hers. "That's okay, but, Gran, I haven't decided for sure whether I'm going to keep it. I mean, would a child born of violence want to live in this world?"

Gran's head lowered, and she didn't speak right away. Maddie knew she'd hurt her. When Gran finally looked up, she said, "I'm sure Dr. Schneller will be able to direct you to the best place to abort the child, if that's what you choose to do."

She'd only been here minutes and she'd already hurt Gran. "I'm sorry, but don't you see? This…person who attacked me—he targeted me because of some secret from my past that I can't remember, and when he finds out I'm going to have his baby, I'll be linked to him for the rest of my life, as will this child." She'd never been one to feel sorry for herself, but she sure was wallowing in self-pity today.

Sympathetic blue eyes stared into hers, then Gran nodded. "I can't imagine what you've been through, and I pray every day that God will bring beauty out of the ashes you're in. He promised to do so in Romans 8:28, and my God does not break His promises. Whatever you choose, you'll need the advice of a good doctor, so humor me—go to your appointment. I forgot to mention that you'll also have an ultrasound tomorrow. Will you do this for me?" She handed Maddie the doctor's business card with a penciled-in appointment time.

She reluctantly took it. "It's probably the right thing to do."

Chapter Fourteen

"A secret remains a secret until you make someone promise
never to reveal it."

~ Fausto Cercignani

The next morning, after taking the dog for a quick walk around Lindenhof park and enjoying a mug of coffee and one of Gran's moist muffins, she set out on foot to the appointment which was a bit over two kilometers away. Siri gave her good directions to the office, so Maddie could enjoy the view around her, and it was postcard-perfect no matter where she looked.

Brody would love this town so much, with the sheer age and intricate beauty of the buildings' designs, some from as far back as the Middle Ages. People walking in all directions, some hurrying to work; others strolling with a leashed dog or a baby in a buggy. The aromas of spiced pastries and coffee emanating from a corner bäckerei. Brody would love this, at least she thought he would. She and Brody had never talked about art or architecture, but somehow, she sensed he'd love every bit of this town.

In no time Maddie stood before the doctor's office, and she hadn't yet rehearsed what she would say. For some reason, she regretted being alone. Gran was busy rehearsing for a Christmas concert at the opera. It was probably just as well. Two competing choices pulled at her—to have the baby regardless of anything else—this she felt was God, Brody, and her grandmother's choice. The other choice seemed the easier, more efficient, and less dangerous path for her. Maddie needed a level, dispassionate head today of all days because she would make that choice in the next few hours before Gran could make the decision for her.

The office waiting room was empty except for one woman who was tapping on her phone. Maddie approached the window and signed in, then took a seat, forcing herself to figure out how much information she'd give the doctor or the PA or whoever questioned her. If there was ever a time that required forthrightness, it was now. This doctor needed to have all the information in hand, so she could inform her of the pros and cons.

Twenty minutes later, she sat with a warm sheet around her naked body. At least it wasn't one of those crepe-paper covers that always ripped apart. Her legs dangled over the edge, her feet showing toenails that needed tender care. Maybe she'd treat her grandmother to a pedicure. A nurse had already taken her vitals and a urine sample, so at least that part was done.

Two taps and the door opened. A tall woman with a long black braid and big red horn-rimmed glasses entered, smiled, and extended her hand. "You must be Madeleine. I'm Annette Schneller. It's so nice to meet you." Her smile was warm, and her English held only a slight German accent.

She seemed awfully young to be a doctor, but maybe that was a good thing. Maddie took her hand. "Es freut mich." She hoped the Swiss version of 'pleased to meet you' was the same as the German one.

The doctor set her laptop on the counter then turned and leaned against it. "Did your grandmother tell you she taught me piano when I was a teenager? I love her, although I wasn't the best student."

"No, she didn't tell me that, Dr. Schneller. Gran also

tried to teach me piano, but I was a lost cause." They both laughed as they chattered about the scales and arpeggios their common teacher had required, and soon Maddie felt completely at ease.

The doctor poured a glass of water and passed it to her, then pulled up a chair. "Please call me Annette. Drink up. This is for the prenatal sonogram. Now, tell me everything."

And it wasn't hard to do so. Maddie told her about the attack—she still couldn't quite call it what it was—and described what she knew about the attacker. All the while, Dr. Schneller nodded and typed a few notes.

She set the laptop aside. "So, may I hazard a guess? You've still not decided what you're going to do."

All Maddie could do was nod.

"All right, let's do an ultrasound, just to see where we stand and how far along you are, and then we'll talk." She patted her hand and stood. "Don't worry. I can tell you want to do what's best."

A few minutes later, Dr. Schneller—Annette—returned with the sonographer, whom she introduced to Maddie. "We're going to do an abdominal ultrasound which will tell how the baby's doing and how you're doing as well." She dimmed the lights.

The technician asked her to lie back and relax. With jetlag and the lights dimmed, she almost fell asleep as the woman applied a warm gel and slowly spread it around her stomach with something very soft. The doctor's eyes were focused on the screen, which was slightly tilted away from Maddie, but she could see it with a move of her head.

Oh, there was the baby. A large head with closed eyes and a cute little button nose. Tiny fingers hovered near the baby's mouth. Ten little toes. Just then its eyes opened, and the fingers formed a tiny fist. How could anyone call this a fetus?

She should never have looked at the screen. Verses fifteen and sixteen from Psalm 139 assailed her, even stabbed at her:

"Your eyes saw my substance, being yet unformed.

And in Your book they all were written, the days fashioned for me,

when as yet there were none of them."

But the baby wasn't 'unformed'; she had knuckles.

Before Maddie knew it, the doctor turned on the lights, then pulled off her gloves. "Now that wasn't so bad, was it?"

"It almost put me to sleep like a very soft massage." An unintended sigh issued forth.

The doctor took a seat next to Maddie and tapped on her laptop. "From what I can see, the baby looks like it's developing nicely. I see no problems. I'd say you're twelve weeks along, as you'd said. And twenty-eight more weeks takes us to the fourth of July." She leaned forward peering into her eyes. "You have a lot to consider. Emilia Weiss, the nurse, will bring you information if you decide to terminate. I don't do that myself, but we have several facilities around Zürich that have good reputations. However, if you decide to keep the baby, I would be happy to be your attending physician. We'd do monthly appointments and schedule another ultrasound at about the twentieth week. You can decide if you want to know the gender of the baby at that time." She scooted the chair to an upright position and took her hand. "Whatever you decide, I'm so happy to have met the granddaughter of one of my favorite people, and it would be an honor to walk with you through this pregnancy."

Maddie shifted around so her legs hung over the side. "May I ask you a few questions?"

"Absolutely." She reached up and turned off the searing bright light. "What would you like to know?"

How to put it? "This man…who raped me did so out of revenge but also out of obsession. He said that once I was purged, we'd be together forever. I'm afraid that this baby will not only tie us together for the rest of my life, but he will also want to be in the baby's life. That's what scares me.

Another question. Will this child carry the rage, the insanity that her…its father has? I don't know a lot about genetics, but I know children often have a propensity to adopt their parents' behaviors—alcoholism, drug addiction, abuse."

"Those are two loaded questions." The doctor looked at her watch. "How about joining me for lunch? It's just after twelve, and I don't have another appointment for an hour and a half. We can reminisce about arpeggios and scales, and we'll sift through your questions."

Surprised that a doctor would want to fraternize with a patient, Maddie was inclined to say no, but it quickly hit her that she had no friends in this town outside of her grandmother, and what better friend to have than a female doctor? "Sure. Why not?"

The doctor stood. "Wonderful. You get dressed, and the nurse will bring you information, which we can go over if you'd like. I'll just need ten minutes to fill in my chart, and I'll meet you in the waiting room." With that she hurried out the door, her long dark braid bobbing behind her.

Grabbing her clothes from the chair before the door opened, Maddie took a moment to run her hand over her abdomen before putting on her pants. There was a decided bump that hadn't been there the week before, which made this whole situation more real. Closing her eyes to block out images of the baby with that tiny fist in her mouth, she zipped up her pants and slipped on her sweater, fingering through the snarls in her hair the wind had produced.

Emilia Weiss, the nurse, tapped twice then inched open the door. "Is it okay to come in?" When she said yes, the door opened. "I brought you a pile of papers and a folder to keep them in." The middle-aged blonde wore blue scrubs with a dalmatian-puppy motif. She motioned for Maddie to join her at the counter. "Here is a list of clinics to contact if you want to terminate the pregnancy."

Maddie cringed at the way she said it. It sounded so banal—Here's a list of places to get rid of your kid. Yet, there was nothing in the nurse's tone to imply judgment. It was simply a product of Maddie's imagination.

Emilia handed her three more slips of paper. "Here is a prescription for prenatal vitamins, reminders of your monthly appointments, and a list of things to avoid over the next months, if you choose to keep the baby." The woman's nostrils flared, something Maddie couldn't interpret, but for some reason she felt judged.

"Thank you." She managed a weak smile.

"Call the office if you need to cancel the appointment. Good day." She bustled out of the room.

Swallowing past the uncomfortable lump in her throat, Maddie grabbed her coat and the folder and headed to the waiting room. Swiss people were known to be reserved and efficient, so the nurse wasn't being judgmental. Even if she were, there would be many more Emilias in the next few months; there always were.

The waiting room was empty when Maddie entered. She couldn't sit, not when she had so much on her mind, so she stared out the window at the tram stopping to pick up people on the corner three floors below. The Bahnhofstrasse, the main street in Zürich, bustled with shoppers, bankers, and tourists hurrying to get out of the snow that was falling at a fast rate. The light jacket she wore was not going to do much to keep her warm on the walk home.

The doctor flew into the room, shouldering her handbag. She'd replaced her white lab coat with a wool coat and scarf. Her smile lit up the room. "Come. I know a great café that's only a block off the main street. We'll be able to get seats inside since it's too cold to sit outside. Do you like Thai?"

"Yes." As they rode down the elevator, Maddie asked the doctor how she'd learned to speak English so well.

She waved a hand. "Most people here speak English. We take it in school along with another language of our choice. I watched a lot of American movies, which helped more than classes, but mostly I learned English as an exchange student in Jackson, Michigan, during high school."

"Ah," she said, wishing she were more competent in German and French. She'd tackled both in high school and college, but the old saying was true—'if you don't use it, you lose it.' With six months ahead of her, she'd make an effort to regain what she'd lost by using German instead of relying on others to speak English. "Isn't Swiss German different from the German we studied in school?"

"A bit. It's more of a dialect difference. We learn the same German as you do in school, but most cantons have their own ways of pronouncing words, ordering sentences—things like that. Zürich German is different than, say, Basel German, but they're just small differences."

When they reached the ground level, Annette took the lead, turning left outside the front door. As they waited at the light to cross the street, she asked, "How is your German? Your grandmother said you've visited a few times."

Maddie rubbed her gloved hands as they waited. As a Florida girl, she wasn't used to below-zero temperatures. "I took it in school, but it seems like whenever I try to use German here, everyone responds in English. One of my goals for the next six months while I'm here is to use German whenever I can."

Once the tram had passed, they crossed the street and walked half a block to the restaurant. The bamboo-style door opened to a busy but charming restaurant. They were seated quickly in a small room away from the crowd.

"Wow, that was fast," Maddie said as she placed the cloth white napkin on her lap. "It smells wonderful. My stomach's gurgling." It was hard to believe she'd spent the day on a plane yesterday, and here she was having lunch with her new doctor. It still amazed her and felt a bit uncomfortable that this beautiful stranger sitting across from her had invited her to lunch. Was this her grandmother's doing?

The doctor asked for glasses of water as the waiter

handed them menus. Opening the menu, Maddie could only understand a few words—tofu, fisch, pad.

"Do you want me to translate?"

She peered over her menu. "That would be a relief, Doctor. I usually order pad thai, but I'm open to trying new things."

"Call me Annette; otherwise, I'll have to call you Ms. Caldecott, and that's not easy to pronounce."

"I have trouble saying my full name as well. Do you remember how you felt when you saw your teacher in a grocery store or at the gas station? That's how I feel right now. Did my grandmother put you up to this?"

Annette waved a dismissive hand. "I don't usually have lunch with my patients. Most of the time, I don't even take a lunch break, but we're closing the office early today, and we'll be closed for two weeks. My husband and I are taking our two boys skiing."

"That's sound exciting. Two boys? You look so young."

"I don't feel so young, but let's go over the menu. They only have four choices today for specialties—two vegetarian, a chicken, and a crispy fish with vegetables and rice in a curry sauce."

Maddie set down her menu. "I guess I'll have the fish." She'd had enough chicken on the plane the day before, and she wasn't a fan of tofu.

The server returned, a diminutive woman with a gentle voice, and they each ordered the same dish.

Annette took a sip of her water, then set the glass down. "I confess that I did have a reason in inviting you to join me for lunch. I wanted to tell you my story, but it wasn't appropriate to do so at the office. Your grandmother didn't ask me to tell you my story, but she did play a role in it."

Okay, that explained things and raised more questions. "I appreciate that. The more information I have, the better able I'll be to make the right decision for myself."

Annette sat back and peered at her. "I can't say I've been

in your shoes, as you Americans say, but I've had the same decisions to make as you do. When I was in college, my boyfriend then—now my husband—and I got pregnant, and it couldn't have been at a worse time. I was studying for our version of the MCAT and getting ready to spend the summer in Rwanda on a short-term mission trip. I'd been brought up in the church but had distanced myself from it when I got caught up in college life. My roommate and I went to the campus clinic, filled out an application, and had the procedure on Friday, so I wouldn't have to miss any classes." She heaved a tremulous sigh. "I didn't even tell Klaus. Figured it was my decision. What I didn't anticipate were the dreams."

Maddie rested her chin on her elbows, then straightened when she remembered that was bad manners. "What do you mean by dreams?"

Just then the server brought their meals in large steaming soup bowls, set down four skewers of crusty fish, and filled their water glasses. Annette took her hand, which surprised her, and said a blessing over the food. Then she picked up her spoon and took a sip. "Oh, I find this so soothing."

Maddie followed suit, taking a sip of the broth, her eyes watering at the spicy heat of it, yet it warmed her insides, relaxing her as any good bowl of soup would do. "Yes, it's delicious but very spicy." She took another sip.

The doctor patted her cheeks with her napkin. "It's making me sweat. About the dreams—they didn't come right away, but when they did, they bothered me so much I refused to lie down for days at a time. I'm not going to go into the details, but the dreams were related to the procedure I'd had. It took me months of counseling, fasting, and prayer to reach the point where I wasn't terrified to close my eyes at night. You're not going to read about dreams as possible side effects on any brochure, but they do happen, and there may be other psychological changes that occur."

Maddie separated a few pieces of fish from the skewer and added them to her soup. "Does this happen to everyone?"

Annette shrugged. "All I know is it happened to me, and I'd never had problems sleeping before. It almost felt demonic. A few other women have told me they had dreams, or they fell into deep depression. It could be due to hormonal changes, or it could be something else. Nobody can deny that it's a traumatic thing—to be pregnant and to abort."

They ate in silence for a few minutes. Finally, Annette put down her spoon. "That was good. How do you like yours?"

Maddie leaned back and patted her stomach. "It's delicious, but I'm getting full. You've given me a lot to think about. Being raped is reason enough to suffer depression. It changed everything. How do you think the child would react to finding out its life was the result of a violent act? I can't imagine how I'd feel if I found out my mother was raped and then found out she was pregnant with me. Why did God let this happen to me?" Now the tears brimmed, adding to her runny nose from the hot soup. "I'm sorry. Just having a Job moment." She swiped her whole face with the already-wet napkin.

Annette took her other hand. "I'm the sorry one. Here you just arrived from Florida, and I throw all this at you. Please forgive me."

"It's not you; it's me. I'm a bag of hormones right now, but I do have to decide, and I'm grateful to you for telling me about your experience. It gives me more information to help me make a wise decision. Another factor that I should tell you is the fact that I'm a news anchor in my town on the weekends and a reporter during the week, so I'm in the public eye." She heaved out a quick sigh. "I also have…compulsions, one of which is an unhealthy phobia of the public knowing anything about my private life, so you can understand how a protruding belly might lead to speculation."

Annette leaned forward. "You have a lot to consider. Your situation is so much more complicated than mine was. Mine was one of bad timing and perhaps a need to keep secrets, but yours—is there anything I can do to help you? At least you know the baby is coming along fine, and you're also doing well physically."

The server brought a pot of hot tea and two delicate cups and poured tea for each of them. Annette sniffed, then took a sip. "Chamomile with mint? It's enough to put me to sleep, but I still have two patients and a whole lot of packing to do before I close these eyes. Try some."

It was soothing and made her wish she didn't have to brave the cold weather to reach Gran's house. "It's very comforting, as is your counsel. If I hadn't seen that screen this morning, I would have probably taken the easy way out. But that image I saw on that screen had little fists with knuckles. How big would it be at twelve weeks?"

Holding up her palm sideways, Annette measured from the edge of her hand to the thumb side. "That much, about three inches. Most of the parts are there; they just have to develop. That's what I love about my job. I get to watch God at His creative best."

When the server dropped off the bill, Maddie grabbed it before Annette had a chance. "On me," she said when Annette started to object. "Nope, you don't even know me, but you were willing to tell me about a hard time in your life. This is the least I can do." She stood and put on her coat. "I hope you have a wonderful Christmas with your family on the slopes, and I'll probably see you at my next appointment. Merry Christmas."

Popping to her feet, Annette enveloped her in a hug. "The merriest of Christmases to you. Enjoy every moment. I sense we're going to be good friends, whatever you decide. Just don't get me fired for giving you unsolicited advice."

"That's not going to happen. Not that my broken

German would be understood anyway." After she paid the bill, they walked out together into the cold, hugged again, and headed in separate directions. Maddie walked to the massive train station just three blocks away to buy a month rail pass for seventy-five Swiss francs, which would allow her to get around town on tram, rail, or boat. It was expensive, but at least she wouldn't have to walk everywhere.

Before she returned to her new home, she'd also have to buy boots, warm socks, mitts, and a heavier coat. Maddie was within three blocks of the hill leading to Gran's condo when mannequins dressed for cold weather beckoned her into Lehner Versand, a clothing store similar to Burlington's in Orlando. She grabbed a jacket in a subtle shade of blue in her size off the rack, then glanced at her stomach and chose a size larger instead. The price of everything was less than a hundred Swiss francs, and the clothes would see her through the cold months ahead.

It occurred to her, as she slowly crept up the hill against the wind, that she'd already made her decision with the purchase of the coat.

Chapter Fifteen

"How can we expect another to keep our secret if we
cannot keep it ourselves."

~ François de La Rochefoucauld, Maxims

The next week whirred by, full of Christmas delights.
Maddie's new coat, scarf, and boots daily came in handy as
she reacquainted herself with this festive, old city. The daily
snowfall turned to rain when it touched the ground or her
clothes, and her outerwear was always wet when she
returned to Gran's house.

She loved walking the streets and gasse or alleys full of
people, their chatter mixing with Christmas carols ringing
from stores, hourly church chimes, and distant trams. Gone
were the outside eateries, now replaced by festive Christmas
kiosks offering mulled cider, Glühwein, and waffles filled
with bananas and chocolate.

Now that she'd decided to keep the baby, she embraced
her choice. Christmas markets sprouted up within walking
distance of her grandmother's home, and more than ever she
delighted in heading to a different outdoor market every day,
always on the lookout for trinkets to fill Gran's stocking or
hang from the imitation tree they'd put up in the living room
corner next to the hearth.

Her appetite had increased—from a new stage in

pregnancy or from the relief of having made a decision—she didn't know which, but now she woke up early and enjoyed a breakfast of coffee and toast and muesli with Gran. As soon as Gran left for the opera, Maddie pulled out her Bible, reading the next chapter with an eager eye to what little gift she'd find in it. Then she was out the door with the dog, first to Lindenhof for Rory's morning walk and sniff, then onto another neighborhood, always on the lookout for something for the baby. Sometimes she found a bib or a little onesie. At this rate, she'd be well-equipped for the baby's birth.

Maddie felt safe. Wherever she looked, there were people, all heading this way or that. She was anonymous in Zürich. No one gave her a second glance, and for that she was glad. A couple passed her, hand in hand, laughing. Brody popped into her head. He'd love this whole town, and she'd love sharing it with him. The poor guy had never known her as anyone other than a frightened, suspicious woman, but here she was more like her real self. Maybe life in the public eye wasn't for her. Maybe her compulsive need to get to the bottom of a story wasn't as important to her anymore. The difference between black and white was graying.

Today she strolled through Weinachtsdorf market where she bought a Christmas-tree ornament and a handmade wooden toy for the baby, then headed to Werdmühleplatz to watch the singing Christmas tree. It surprised her when the chime of the clock made her look at her watch. It was already 4:30. Where had the time gone? With only two days remaining before Christmas, she needed to buy wrapping paper for the gifts she'd hidden around the house from her grandmother's eye like a squirrel hiding nuts.

Stopping at a paper store two blocks down from her new home, she bought three rolls of giftwrap, then headed up the hill to drop them off and take the dog for her second walk before meeting her grandmother at the opera. The walk up the hill had been easier the last time she was in Zürich, but the interim years and possibly the baby within made it more of a challenge.

Rory was waiting at the door for her, eager for their walk to the park, which offered a view of the whole city in all its Christmas glory. The retractable leash allowed Maddie the chance to sit down on a wet bench while Rory sniffed at every tree. A group of tourists took pictures of Grossmünster Church, the Eiffel Tower of Zürich. Children chased each other around the fountain as their parents snapped pictures of them as they passed. Two teens lugged chess pieces from one square to another on the now snowy chessboard. A man lit a cigarette by the tree where Rory strained at the taut leash. His tall height and slender shape made her catch her breath. No, not here—not in her sanctuary.

She retracted the leash. There were thousands of tall, thin Swiss men. He paid her no attention. She was being silly. Still, it was time to meet Gran at the opera for the children's Christmas show she'd been rehearsing. Maddie pulled the leash taut and headed for the stairs closest to her gran's house, but she changed her mind at the last second. If this guy was the one, she didn't want him to know where she lived, so she took the stairs by the chessboard which added a few blocks to reach Gran's.

Was she being paranoid? If it was him and he was at Lindenhof, he already knew where she was staying. Was fear, her constant companion, which she'd worked so hard to overcome, coming back like an unwelcome guest? No, she wouldn't allow her mind to go there again.

In her haste down the hill, she slipped on an icy patch and fell, skinning her knee on the edge of a cobblestone. The leash slipped out of her hand as she fought to reclaim her equilibrium against the ice. "Rory, stay here." Note to self, pay attention to the cobblestones when walking up and down the hill. "Rory!"

"Careful," said a gruff voice behind her. A hand grasped her arm, causing her breath to hitch, and helped her to her feet. "Thank you." She spun around, and a gasp spewed out. The same man from Lindenhof, a stocking cap hiding his head, stood there staring down on her, his eyes unreadable black pools. Was this the end of the road for her?

In that moment, her thoughts rushed to the young life within her, her hands shielding her midsection. A glance down the hill revealed the shadow of someone slowly limping up the road. An old woman perhaps. It would have to be enough. She yelled as loud as her breathless voice would let her. "Help. Rory, come back."

The man must have seen the woman because he backed up a step. Maddie didn't have time to react; she had to find Rory who had taken off. Maddie swiped a hand over her knee, feeling the tear in her jeans and the warm wetness of blood. She headed down the wet, uneven pavement, reaching the woman who held onto the wall on the other side of the small road. "Thank you for being here," she said.

The woman's head lifted in her direction. It was too dark to see her reaction, but the tilt of her head said she didn't understand. Maddie greeted her instead, "Guten abend, Frau. Have you seen mein hund…my dog?"

The stooped-over woman smiled, although it was hard to see her features in the dark. "Ja, der hund ist da drüben. Ein klein hund." She pointed a gloved hand toward some bushes next to a business about a block below.

"Yes, she's little. Danke." At least, if Rory was busy sniffing, she wouldn't run away, and it would be easier to grab her leash. As she approached, she heard Rory's cry. What had happened to her? "Rory?" Again, Rory's squeal reached her. There she was between two bushes, her leash caught tight within their branches, not letting her move. "Oh, you poor baby." She freed the leash from its captors and picked up her shivering, wet dog. "I'm so sorry. This wasn't a good idea, was it? I should have taken the short route back to Gran's." Now they were both a dirty, wet mess, and she was supposed be at Gran's Advent performance in twenty minutes.

The walk home was uneventful, and she entered the house, realizing that she couldn't just leave Rory the way she was, so she carried her to the bathroom and put her in the clawed tub, washing her off with shampoo, then picked the twigs and burrs out of Rory's coat.

Wrapping her in a large towel, she carried her into the bedroom, closing the door so Rory would only get her bedroom wet while she changed clothes and tended to the cut on her knee. Her favorite jeans were now ruined. The waistband was getting a little tight, but even so, they'd served her well. She'd never been one to wear holey jeans, but maybe they could be salvaged. Throwing them in the wash basket, she quickly slipped on the one dress she'd brought, foregoing fashion for utility for the walk down the hill. She didn't want to disappoint Gran by being late, but if she hurried, she could slip in unnoticed.

With one last look around, she hurried into the living room, turned on a few lamps, then shrugged into her warm coat, and left the house, the cold wind slapping her in the face as she headed down the hill. Her sense of peace had evaporated, and now her eyes reverted to casing the area as she did back in Orlando. The whip of the wind made her pull her furry hood over her head. What had the tall guy said? Had he spoken in English or German? Her memory evaded her.

Not here. Not in her sanctuary. At the same time, Maddie refused to be foolhardy. The only people who knew she was here were Brody, Gregory, her parents, and her boss. Had one of them told others? She had to trust they'd honor her plea to keep her secret quiet.

Reaching the bottom of the hill, she joined the throngs of people who strolled the roads that lined Lake Zürich. Christmas lights made everything beautiful and festive, but she couldn't think about that now. Six blocks took her to the large square that fronted the stately opera house, now filled with the largest Christmas market she'd ever seen. The air was full of delicious aromas of familiar foods—curry, ginger, and garlic. Oh, she was going to gain so much weight because everything made her stomach grumble.

But there was no time to satisfy her hunger right now. Her watch told her she was already ten minutes late. Rushing up the staircase, she handed her ticket to the docent who stood by the entrance, and she slid into the lobby behind a group of well-dressed couples and followed them up the stairs to a large hall and found a seat in the back.

Many rows of heads blocked her view of the dozen or so musicians, so Maddie closed her eyes, already relaxing to the beautiful rendition of "O Little Town of Bethlehem." She tried to pick out her grandmother's violin from the other stringed instruments. Her eyes opened and took in the ornate, gilded ceiling of the large room, hundreds of years old. How many centuries of people had sat in this very room, celebrating the majesty of the birth of their Savior?

After the applause died down, a child's face peeked over the top of the podium. She recited the words from Luke about the angels' message to the shepherds. Then began "Hark the Herald Angels Sing," and everyone joined in.

As if on cue, her hand went to her stomach, which seemed to undulate like a little fish. It couldn't be. She wasn't far enough along to feel the baby move, but there it went again. Was her baby responding to the music about another baby? Wonder filled her. Maybe her baby was reacting to the music in the same way John the Baptist had moved in his mother's belly at the presence of another baby within his aunt, Mary. Yes, this baby deserved to live, no matter what anyone thought, and she would raise this little person to lift her head high.

After the second encore, Maddie waited for Gran as she greeted a few well-wishers. Gran stood straight and confident, her eyes sparkling as she thanked guests and their little ones for coming to the advent concert. This was the woman Maddie sought to emulate—wise, kind, hardworking, never complaining. Whenever Gran's sciatica acted up, she'd wave it off with a dismissive hand. "I've earned these aches and pains. At near eighty, what do you expect?"

Gran finally broke away, slung her violin case over her shoulder, and joined her, handing her a peppermint cane. "Saw you sneak in during the third song. What happened?" She guided her toward the entrance, nodding at people they passed.

The woman never missed a beat. Maddie hadn't kept anything from her, and she wouldn't start now. "I thought I saw him when I took Rory to the park to do her business, so I took the long way back to your place to prevent him from knowing where I was staying. In a hurry to get home, I wasn't paying attention to the slick pavement and tripped, hurting my knee. I also dropped the leash, and Rory took off and got caught in a bush, so I had to give her a bath."

Gran linked arms with her as they walked out of the opera. "You have to be careful, girl. I've fallen a few times on the icy incline. In fact, I usually take the stairs during the winter months. What do you mean, you saw him at the park?"

Maddie massaged the knot in her neck with her free hand. "The guy who attacked me. I thought I saw him. He seemed to be watching me. I panicked and took off, but that same man offered a hand to help me up when I fell. I didn't know what to do, then I saw a woman coming up the hill. When I called for help, he took off." She stopped in front of the first of many Christmas kiosks that lined the square in front of the opera to get out of the rain. "The last thing I want to do is bring danger to you and your home."

Gran rubbed her shoulder. "Don't worry about that. That's the least of my worries. Are you sure you didn't just imagine things?"

She lifted her shoulders. "Maybe. He was tall and thin

and watching me, but maybe I'm just being paranoid." With a shake of her head, she took Gran's hand and led her to one of the kiosks that offered Indian food. "Let's not talk about that. How about I treat you to some dinner from one of these places? We have raclette and waffles and pizza and sausage and curry at this kiosk. What's your pleasure? Then we don't have to cook tonight."

"Good idea," Gran said, pulling her lapels together. "Waffles are too messy. How about raclette? Little potatoes and gherkins with melted cheese over the top."

Maddie squeezed her hands together. "Let's get some glühwein. The scent of all those spices always puts me in the Christmas spirit."

"You shouldn't be drinking wine." Gran nodded toward Maddie's abdomen.

"Why not?" When the only reaction she received was a frown, she added, "It won't hurt me to smell it, will it? You know what?" She cast a sly smile toward Gran.

"What, child?" She rolled her eyes. "You're trying my patience."

They stopped in front of a raclette booth, and Maddie ordered two with ham. After paying, Maddie pulled Gran over to the side, both of them rubbing the cold from their arms. "You're not going to believe this, especially after hearing me talk about seeing the guy in the park, but tonight when I was listening to 'Hark the Herald Angels Sing,' I distinctly felt the baby move inside me. Is that even possible at this point?"

"Land's sake, girl, that seems pretty early, but it's been a half a century since I carried your mother, so what do I know? I wouldn't put it past the Lord to favor you with a baby gift for doing the hard thing."

"That's something I'll never forget. I'll get the food." Maddie blew out a vapored breath as she collected napkins and forks, then balanced the two cardboard containers of gruyère wonder over to where her grandmother stood under an awning. "Here you go. I'll go grab us some hot drinks. It's getting mighty chilly out here." Training her nose toward the scent of cinnamon and cloves, she hastened to a booth where the teen behind the counter poured one cup of mulled wine and another of hot caramel apple cider and handed them to her. Maddie sipped the drink to warm her insides as she hurried back to Gran and their raclette which was sure to be lukewarm by now. "Here you go."

They stood there under the awning of the kiosk, out of the falling snow that turned to rain as soon as it touched the ground.

Gran took a sip and closed her eyes. "This hits the spot. You'd better hurry and finish your food before it gets cold."

"Gran, you've been saying that to me since I was six."

"Maybe so, but we need to go home before we're both popsicles, and that hill will turn to ice before long."

They huddled together as they headed up the sidewalk that lined the Limmat River. "Aren't the lights beautiful?" Gran said pointing toward a large hotel on the other side of the river. "I love Christmas in Zürich. How about we go to my church tomorrow night for the Christmas Eve candlelight service?"

Maddie squinted past the snowflakes that fell in her eyes. "Could we also go to Fraumünster tomorrow for their Christmas service? I won't be able to understand what they're saying, but it's so serenely beautiful there."

"Sure, we can go to both churches." As they completed their climb, their breaths were coming in spurts as they turned onto Gran's road. "I can't wait to start a fire in—" Gran froze in place, holding Maddie back with her arm, then she pointed at her front door. "Is that the man who followed you?"

Chapter Sixteen

"Man is not what he thinks he is; he is what he hides."

~André Malraux

Her breath escaped. Had the man seen or heard them? Maddie pulled her grandmother behind a tree. A tall man faced the front door, shifting from foot to foot. A hood concealed his head, but he wore a different type of jacket than the one worn by the guy in the park, although he could have changed his coat. Still, the guy that helped her up was leaner and swarthier than the guy standing on the front step. She grabbed her grandmother's elbow. "It's not the same man, but I don't recognize him. Do you?"

"No, but I don't know all my neighbors."

Maddie didn't realize how tightly she was grasping Gran's arm until Gran pulled it away. The guy now turned to face them, probably having heard their footsteps on the wet pavement, but the fur on his hood shadowed his face.

"Hello?" Maddie ventured, her voice cracking and smallish.

The man hopped off the porch. "Maddie? It's me. Brody. Surprise!"

What? Brody was standing mere feet from her in Zürich? "I can't believe it. What are you doing here?" She ran toward him and threw her arms around his neck. "I'm sorry. Did I miss some message? I didn't know you were coming." Realizing where she was, she released him and spun to face her grandmother, whose hand on her upper chest conveyed her surprise.

Maddie grabbed his hand and pulled him behind her. "Gran, this is Brody Messner, the police officer I told you about—the one you said I should call and confide in. He's here in the flesh." She pointed next to her. "Who knew?"

Gran clapped her gloved hands. "The Cavalry's arrived."

He reached for Gran's hand and shook it. "Very nice to meet you. I'm sorry to show up like this. It was a split-second decision. The department gave me three days off, and I found a flight to Zürich that left early this morning. I just arrived." He took a breath, then swung around to face Maddie. "You look wonderful." His mittened hand went to her cheek, then he must have realized what he did and pulled it way. "I mean, you look so… healthy." His face scrunched in such an adorable way. There was something refreshing about a guy who wasn't the least bit suave.

She spewed out a laugh. "Healthy? If a wet dog is healthy, I guess that's me. Come on, let's get out of rain…snow… whatever this is." Then she remembered where she was and turned to Gran, not wanting to presume on her hospitality.

"Of course, any friend of yours is a friend of mine. Welcome, Officer Messner."

"Call me Brody. I'm off duty for three days, and I don't want to think of anything related to law enforcement."

Maddie unlocked the door and ushered the two in as the yapping started. When Rory entered the foyer, she made a beeline to Brody and jumped up and down to be picked up. "Rory, down. Let him take his coat off first before you assault him."

Gran sidestepped the three of them. "I'll make some hot chocolate or tea. What would you prefer, Brody?"

"Hot chocolate please, but either one is fine. It's a mite colder here than in Florida." He pulled off his hood, disheveled dark wet hair popping out in all directions, then unzipped his black jacket. "Brr. It's the rain that goes right through, but it's a beautiful city. I can already tell even though it's dark."

Oh, he looked good. She couldn't help herself; she wrapped her arms around his waist and hugged him. "Merry Christmas. I'm delighted you're here." Then she backed up, cringing at her lack of decorum, and slipped off her coat and her boots.

Questioning eyes traveled from her bedraggled hair slowly down her form and landed on her waistline, then they rose to lock with her eyes.

She merely nodded, and he blew out a breath and smiled. Taking his hand, she pulled him into the kitchen where Gran stirred a saucepan of hot chocolate. She pointed toward a seat at the island, then she helped Gran by unwrapping a plate of cookies and bringing cups, small plates, and Advent napkins to the island. "Gran, tell Brody what these cookies are called."

Gran set a teapot on a trivet, then carried them over to where he sat. "Oh, I forgot about those cookies. I bought them at a stand outside the opera house. Maybe Maddie can take you over there tomorrow. Switzerland loves its Christmas markets." Gran examined the cookies. "These rectangular ones are called Basler Lackerli. They're spice cookies, and these little chocolate stars are called Basler Brunsli." She took a bite of one. "I love the smell of them. Brody, I hope you'll join us for church tomorrow night, and afterward we'll come back and have soup and open presents."

It suddenly occurred to Maddie that Brody had nowhere to stay—no room in the inn, so to speak, and the inns were prohibitively expensive in Zürich, especially during the season.

Her gran must have read her mind because she stopped pouring hot chocolate into his cup and set the white pitcher on the table. "Brody, we have a pull-out bed in the study. Would you like to stay here? Then you won't have to brave the elements to get here tomorrow."

Bless you, Gran. Both sets of eyes were on him.

"Thank you, but I managed to get a room at the Adler. I checked in before I came here. They gave me a great map that helped me find my way here."

"The Adler? Oh, they have the best fondue there, but how did you know how to find me? I don't think we shared addresses, did we?" Maddie leaned on her fist.

He tapped the side of his head. "Always thinking. When I called you, I didn't get through, so I tracked your phone." He shrugged. "I'm a cop—what can I say?"

Checking her phone, she said, "Oh, I forgot. I turned it off during Gran's concert. Sorry."

"Concert?" Brody said, sipping his drink. "Yum, this is good."

"Yes, Gran plays violin in the chamber orchestra at the Zürich opera. Tonight was their last Advent performance, right, Gran?"

"That's right. I wish you could have attended tonight, Brody. We don't start up again until the new year." She covered a yawn. "Sorry about that. Maddie, how about you two attend the candlelight service at Fraumünster tomorrow night? I'll go to my own church and find out what's going on with my friends, and we can meet up here afterward for some midnight soup. Now if you'll both excuse me, it's been a long day, so I'm going to bed." Gran nodded toward Brody. "It's a pleasure to meet you. Thank you for looking after my granddaughter." She rounded the island and kissed Maddie on the temple. "Leave everything. I'll clean up in the morning."

Maddie cast a sideways smirk at that not-so-subtle matchmaker. "I'll clean up. See you in the morning. Love you, Gran."

Once she'd left the room, Maddie grabbed the pitcher of cocoa. "Would you like some more?"

He patted his stomach. "No thanks. Too many cookies. I'm stuffed."

"Let's go sit in the living room. I'll make a fire, something I've learned how to do since I've been here. Not a lot of need for a fire in Florida." She poured herself a cup of tea and headed into the living room, Brody and Rory on her heels. "Watch this." She went to the corner hearth, lifted her finger, and flicked the switch on the wall. "See?"

He laughed. "A woman of many talents." He took a seat, Rory jumping into his lap. "I have a question. Why did your grandmother say the cavalry had arrived when I showed up at your door?"

She heaved a sigh and sat down next to him, her elbow resting on the cushion. "I was hoping you didn't hear that. Think I was just being paranoid. How about we take a walk? I have to take the dog out, and we can talk on the way to the park."

A blast of frigid air met them as they opened the door after putting on their coats. Brody zipped up his jacket. "Brr. It's going to be a cold walk to the hotel." He glanced at her. "But I'm glad to do it."

She pulled the hood over her head and tied the strings tight. "It's not always like this; it's usually quite nice." They headed to the corner, turned right, and climbed the block to the park. "This is Lindenhof. Back during Julius Caesar's time, the Roman army had a fort up here to keep watch on the city. Let's go over to the wall." She gently pulled on the leash to lead Rory away from a small bush.

He whistled. "Oh, wow. That's beautiful. No wonder the Roman army posted themselves up here. You can see the whole town."

She pointed across the river. "See that church with a blue steeple on the other side of the Limmat River? That's

Fraumünster Cathedral. Would you like to go to church with me tomorrow night?"

His arm went around her shoulder and pulled her close. "I can't think of anywhere I'd rather be than by your side at that very old-looking church."

An unfamiliar but welcome warmth filled her despite the cold temperature, and she didn't pull away as she normally would have. They stood without speaking, staring out at the flickering Christmas lights that adorned every street and alley. Finally, he broke the silence. "You were going to tell me about what your grandmother meant by the cavalry?"

She stopped blowing on her mittened hands. "As I said, it was probably my imagination. Earlier this evening, right before I was to leave for the concert, I brought Rory here to do her thrice daily, and there was a man standing over there by that fountain who seemed to be staring at me, so I freaked and took Rory back to Gran's a different way, and I slipped on the pavement and fell on my knee. Rory bolted, which scared me to death because that dog can run when she wants to. Anyway, the same guy showed up behind me and offered me a hand up."

"Whoa. That must have sent your heart a'thumping."

"It did. The guy was tall and thin, just like the guy who broke into my place. My mind spun. Did he follow me here to Zürich, and if so, what did that mean for me staying here?" A chill—one borne out of fear rather than the cold—zipped down her. Her teeth started chattering. "We should go back to the house. You need to head to the hotel and get some sleep."

He pulled her close. "Jet lag has set in, but I don't want you to be afraid. It's normal to see a guy that reminds you of such a traumatic event. I can't imagine what that must have been like to see him standing right behind you."

"Yes, but now the cavalry has arrived at least for a few days." She pointed across the river to the right. "Do you see where that tram just stopped? There's a Levi store on the corner. Your hotel is a block up from the store." They headed back to the house, and he walked her to the door.

"How would you like to spend the day showing me around?" he said, opening the door for her and Rory. "I haven't heard a lot of English, and my German is limited to lederhosen and sauerkraut."

"It would be my pleasure. I need to pick up a few last-minute things for Christmas, if that's all right."

He leaned over and kissed her on the cheek, then backed up as her gloved fingers reached up to touch the spot where he'd kissed her. "Until tomorrow."

~

I've been sitting in the office too much, or maybe it's the altitude. Yeah, that must be it. Brody stopped to take a surreptitious breath while Maddie was gazing at a display in a shop window.

"Look at those Messer knives. Can we go inside? I'd like to buy a set of eight for Gran. There's a paper store across the street where I can get it wrapped."

Her expectant eyes reminded him of the excitement he felt as a child on many a Christmas morning. "Whatever you want." His hand felt the small box in his pocket. Did he dare give it to her tonight as they walked back to her place after church? All he knew was his self-confidence would suffer a crushing blow if she said no, but he felt compelled to ask her anyway. Lord, I'm not good at timing, and sometimes I run ahead of your advice like a bull in a shop like this one. Direct me.

He followed her around as she chose one set of knives, then saw another one she liked better. By the time they left the store, his arms were laden with bags of gifts she'd bought. After another stop at a quaint shop that specialized in stationery, cards, and gift wrap, he could barely see his feet.

Maddie, her arms also full of bags, laughed as they navigated up the hill past the Grossmünster church, its two towers casting late-afternoon shadows over their path. "I can't believe I bought all this stuff, but I owe my gran so much for letting me stay with her."

His breath was coming in spurts. "I can't believe how steep the roads are here. Think I need to start playing hockey instead of yelling at kids to skate faster." He cast a sideways glance at her. "You're not even breathing hard, and you're breathing for two."

She shrugged. "It's the daily trips up the hill to Gran's. I'm amazed that she does it every day, and she's in her seventies. How about we drop off the packages at your place, so we don't have to carry them around all day? Or we can take them back to Gran's right now. At least the weather is cooperating today. No freezing rain or snow."

He needed a quiet place to talk to her. Not only did he want to give her the ring in a place where she could respond in private, but he also had big news to tell her, and she deserved a place to react without spectators. He needed privacy to tell her things she didn't want to hear. "Is your grandmother home?"

"No, she's visiting friends today. One of them is in the hospital, and one's in a nursing home. Why?"

"Why don't we take everything to your place? I have some things to tell you, and I'd rather do so in private."

Her eyes remained on him for a long moment. "Okay, but I'm starved. Could we have an early dinner before we head up to Lindenhof? I was thinking of cheese fondue at that restaurant by your hotel—Swiss Chuchi. They also have great raclette. Are you hungry? Then we can dump off the packages, and if Gran's not home, I can wrap them quickly." Her eyebrows lifted, waiting for his response.

"Ah, the source of the cheese I smelled in the lobby. Sounds good. These feet need fortification before they head up to your place."

They slowly made their way up the hill, turning right, then left, then—he was lost as they cut through one narrow alley after another. But each gasse or lane held its own beauty and secrets—an outdoor dessert café, a small jazz museum, a statue in a fountain that offered fresh water to fill the empty bottle he'd taken from the minibar at the hotel. The US could learn from the Swiss hoteliers who offered free water and soft drinks to their guests every day.

Ten minutes later they reached the wide square where his hotel was located, the famous blue cow peering down at passersby from the second-floor balcony. He pointed up. "What's with the cow?"

She glanced up. "Her name is Heidi. That's all I know, but I'm sure there's a story there somewhere."

Luckily, there wasn't a line in front of the restaurant, and they were seated by the window at a small table. Over his menu, Brody studied Maddie's face, now focused on her menu. Should he tell her now? If he gave her the bad news, it would ruin what was a perfect day they'd remember forever, and it would preclude his proposal. She needed to know the truth, but what could he do? Tomorrow was Christmas. He was leaving the next day. Maybe she didn't need to know. No, she did.

While they waited for the fondue to arrive, they talked about their childhood Christmas traditions. He told her about the many times he'd played a shepherd at church in the annual Christmas program, about going caroling with his youth group, and the big goose dinner his mother prepared on Christmas day. "My favorite memory was going with my father to a discount store and buying wool socks, blankets, and sweaters, then driving around town looking for homeless people. When we saw a man or woman pushing a grocery cart down the street or sitting on a bench, Dad would pull the car over, and my brother and I would jump out to give the person a few gifts. Dad would catch up, pulling a twenty out of his pocket, and telling the person that Jesus was crazy about him or her."

Maddie spoke of lots of presents around the tree, Christmas cookies Gran baked, and The Miracle on 34th Street she and Beverly watched when her parents had gone to yet another holiday event, as they called them. What was missing was the meaning behind the gifts and the cookies and the tree. "I didn't discover the real reason behind the season until I came to Gran's here. This is where I learned that presents and Santa Claus didn't matter; in fact, they took our attention away from what was important—the Savior's birth. Still, I always loved Christmas when"—she stopped talking when the waiter approached with a basket of crusty bread pieces and a pot of bubbling cheese.

After a short prayer, they dug in, poking their fondue forks at the bread, then dipping a piece in the cheese and swirling it around.

As Brody went to put it in his mouth, she stopped him. "Be careful. You can burn your mouth on it. Let it cool on your plate before you eat it." She was right. The cheese was very hot, and the wine and garlic flavors made his eyes water, but it only took a few bites to get used to it.

He put his fork down. "You mentioned Beverly. Was she your babysitter?"

"Yes, she lived with us for a few years, then left suddenly. I think it was because my parents were getting a divorce."

Should he tell her now? "What was her last name?"

Her hand holding the fork stopped midair. "Why?"

"Was it Jordan?"

Maddie put down her fork. "How did you know?"

All the resolve he'd had to forestall this conversation disappeared. He swallowed past the lump in his throat. Was it caused by cheese or a warning to be quiet? His eyes lifted to meet hers. She didn't deserve this, but it was one of the reasons he'd come all the way over here—to tell her in person what shouldn't be told on the phone. He lowered his voice and pushed his plate away.

"Please hear me out. I called in a favor and did a private DNA test on the—" When she opened her mouth to protest, he held up a hand. "Please. It's for my eyes only, but I had to do what my conscience told me to do, and as a cop, I have an obligation to get guys like that off the streets." His lips clamped together as his eyes implored her to believe him, to see things from his point of view. He waited until her jaw unclenched, and she nodded.

"The sample showed a strong link to New Jersey, specifically to Clinton, and the main surname that showed up was Jordan."

Her eyes narrowed. "No, you're wrong. You're wrong. So wrong. You're talking about the babysitter? Beverly would never try to kill me! It was a guy, a tall guy in jeans…" her voice trailed off.

He grabbed her trembling hand. "Of course, she wouldn't, but someone with that name matched the DNA that was in the system. Somebody from her family. That picture hanging in your garage. Beverly was in it. Do you see the links that are forming here?"

She didn't remove her hand, but the tension remained in the stiffness of her fingers. "Her father had died when she was young, I think. That's why the family was so poor. They lived in a small house a few blocks away from mine. I don't know why she didn't live at home—maybe there wasn't room."

"You told me before she had an older brother and a younger one. Did you ever meet them?"

"I remember meeting her older brother, Bruce, but I don't think I ever saw her younger brother." Maddie's eyes filled with pain and jolted to meet his. "You mean, her brother might have been the one in my world lit class?" Just then she gasped so loud the next table glanced in their direction. She spewed out a breath. "It just came back to me.

I remember what he said. Something like, 'This is for my sister.'" Her hand went to cover her mouth. "But…but, what did I ever do to him that would make him do that?"

A mixture of confusion, pain, and even shame altered her features. It was Christmas Eve, and he'd ruined the day for her. "I'm sorry to drop this on you now. I should have waited until the day after Christmas right before I left, but when you said Beverly's name, the question came out. I'll work on my timing and my filter."

"No, I needed to know." She pushed her plate away. "One thing you said that has really helped me is 'take the next step,' so that's what I'll do. My next step is to find out what Beverly's brother's name is. While my nose was always sniffing out a new story to write for the paper, my friend, Tessa, was more aware of the other kids in school. She was in my world lit class, so she may remember the guy with the last name of Jordan." Her smile was weak, but at least she hadn't pushed him away.

After paying the bill, he loaded up the packages, and they headed to her grandmother's home. Brody would have liked to ask her now, but he didn't want to push things too quickly. Still, time was running out, and the jostle of the little box in his pocket reminded him that he only had a day and a half left with her.

The dog was the only one in the house when they dropped the packages on the sofa. Brody's hands had fallen asleep on the trek up the hill, and he opened and closed his fists to regain feeling in them.

Maddie began taking the packages out of the bags. "Do you have to go back to your hotel before the church service tonight?"

"No, unless these clothes are inappropriate."

"You're fine. I want to wrap these and put them under the tree before Gran comes home." She looked at her watch. "She's pretty tired from all the Advent concerts she participated in, so she may just go to an earlier service at her church, then come home. Do you want to help me wrap presents? We can put on a Christmas movie. What's your favorite film?"

"Elf? A Christmas Story?"

"I'm not sure Gran would have those in her cabinet. We might have to settle for White Christmas. How about you turn on the fire, and I'll go collect tape and scissors, so we can make quick work of these gifts?"

As they worked, Christmas carols playing in the background since Maddie couldn't find her grandmother's DVD collection, an idea began to take shape in his head. If he couldn't convince her to marry him for love, maybe she'd agree to marry him for appearance's sake. Maybe he had enough love for both of them, and if he were a lucky man, she'd grow to love him in time. Did he dare say anything after the bomb he'd already landed on her? Maddie's voice interrupted his train of thought. "I'm sorry. What did you say?"

She put down the scissors she was using to make a bow out of a ribbon. "Would you like something to drink? Coffee, eggnog, a Coke?"

"No thanks…I mean, yes, a Coke would be great."

"As soon as I'm done wrapping this gift, I'll go, but I need your finger."

His eyes flew up. "What? Why?"

Picking up the gift-wrapped box, she crawled over to him on her knees. "Put your finger on the ribbon, so I can get it on tight. I'll tell you when to pull your finger out."

"Okay?" He laughed at the hold she had on him.

"There," she said as she wrapped the ribbon around the package. "Now, pull your finger out." She taped the bow she'd made on top.

He winced at the package he'd wrapped. "There's a decided difference between your wrapping and mine." He held up the lumpy, much-taped package he'd just finished.

"It looks great. Gran won't mind." Maddie pushed to her

feet. "I'll be right back."

"Take your time." Once she was out of the room, he rushed to the coatrack and fumbled through his pockets for the box, then hurried back. The noise of ice cubes dropping in a glass came from the kitchen. He hurried to cut out a piece of silver wrapping paper and practically rolled the box in it in case she came in. Using way too much tape, he managed to stuff the box in his pocket just as she walked in the room.

"Here you go," she said, handing him a tall glass of soda with a festive red napkin.

He took it and gulped half of it down. Wiping his mouth, he apologized. "Guess I was thirstier than I thought."

"No need to apologize," she said, her smile still weak. "We walked a lot today. Thank you for being my valet—carrying so many packages you couldn't see your own feet."

Was that all he was for her—a valet? Lord, please help her see beyond this stubbly mug of mine to the love I have for her. Wasn't that what love was all about—carrying packages for her, protecting her, holding her when her life was falling apart? That's the love his parents shared until the day they died on that slippery road right before Christmas three years ago. Finishing each other's sentences, laughing or rolling their eyes at some joke or memory they shared. That's why he volunteered to work every Christmas. Even coming here to Zürich. He saw love at work every day growing up, and the standard was high. He'd settle for no less.

Without permission, his palm went up to caress Maddie's cheek as she finished creating the last bow for a present. She let him, which was a step forward. After stacking the newly wrapped gifts, she stood and offered a hand to pull him up. "Let's put the gifts under the tree and clean up this place before the giftee arrives home." She swiped one hand against the other. "Gran's going to come back to a home ready for Christmas."

They made quick work of the leftover paper and ribbon on the floor, then Maddie looked at her watch. "Nine o'clock. Two hours before church begins. How about I take the dog out, and then we'll leave and take our time walking to the Frau."

"I'll come with you." In truth, he didn't want her to be alone in that park. He grabbed their coats from the rack, helped her into hers, then put on his own.

As soon as they left the house, Maddie linked an arm around his elbow, which pleased him. Any little crumb she threw him was an early Christmas gift. The air was chillier now, but it fit the season.

"It's six in the morning in Vancouver where Tessa lives. When we return from church, I'll call her to see if she remembers Beverly's brother. Maybe she can find him in the yearbook if he was in my class. I call her every Christmas."

"Sounds like a step. I have another suggestion." The park was empty except for an old man huddled on a bench near the wall overlooking the city. Memories of other Christmases came to mind. "Hold that thought. I'll be right back." Somehow, he knew by the man's posture that this wasn't a tourist or a local resident. Fishing in his coat pocket, he extracted all the Swiss francs he'd withdrawn from an ATM machine at the train station. It wasn't much, but it was enough for a meal and a hotel room. "Merry Christmas, sir." Rats, he didn't know how to say it in German.

The man's eyes widened as did his mouth. "Danke viel."

"Bitte." Oh no, that meant please. "You're welcome, herr." Brody offered his hand, then saw the man had no gloves. He took his own off and handed them to him. "Here, Merry Christmas."

The man's eyes struggled to his feet and lowered his head. "Frohlichi Wiehnachte." Even in the dark, Brody could see the frayed spots in the man's coat. There wasn't a lot of need for a winter coat in Central Florida. Before he talked himself out of it, he shrugged out of the coat, making sure the pockets were empty. "Here. You need this more than I do. Für mein Papa. Good night." He slipped his hands in his pant pockets just to be sure the little box was still there. Then he left the man. For you, Dad, Brody whispered as he returned to where Maddie sat on a swing.

"Where's your coat?"

He waved a dismissive hand. "What use is a coat like that in Orlando?"

She peered toward the bench where he'd just been standing. "And your gloves?"

"It's for my dad. Ready?" He gestured with his head to the road. It was getting brisk, and he didn't want to think about the walk to the church and back.

She stared at him, her eyebrows forming that expression that said, "What were you thinking?" but she didn't say anything. Once inside, he slipped out of his boots and hastened to the fireplace to warm his hands, but electric fireplaces were more for looks than function. When he turned, Maddie was leaning against the wall, her arms folded across her chest, a smirk playing on her lips.

"You're really something. I'll go see what I can find in the closet that might fit you." She heaved a casual shrug. "It might be a little tight. Who knows what I'll find."

Brody took a seat on the couch, resisting the urge to wrap the afghan that lay over the back of the couch around him. If he had one vice, it was impatience. Police work had taught him to think on his feet, sometimes making decisions before he'd thought them through, but that was the nature of the job. The box in his pocket wasn't exactly burning a hole in it because it was too cold for that, but he felt its presence. Was now the time—before her grandmother returned? It might be the only time they'd be alone until he left.

Maddie returned carrying two sweaters, that smirk still there. "Here's what I found." She held up a sweater featuring a row of large candy canes. "This one is an XL, so it might be a bit tight. But this one is a bit bigger." She held up a bright red sweater with Rudolph staring back at him. "If I can find a triple-A battery, the nose lights up." The smile on her face held pure delight.

He grabbed Rudolph and struggled into it. "Forget the battery; there's not an inch of room for it. I have a jean jacket back at the hotel, you know."

Her head tilted to the side. "Oh, here are some mittens to keep your hands warm." She held up two of the furriest mittens he'd ever seen.

He ripped them out of her hand. "You're enjoying this, aren't you? Thank you very much, I think. At least nobody knows me here."

She held up her phone. "Put them on. Christmas memories."

With a roll of his eyes, Brody obliged her and did a slow turn around. "How do I look?"

"Like a big Christmas present." She clapped gleefully.

"Just what I dream of being." Brody pointed at the couch. "I know we have to leave, but I'd like to give you my present first." He took a deep breath, as if it could give him an extra charge of bravery. She hopped onto the couch, clearly basking in her joke on him. He hoped what he said next wouldn't ruin her fun at his expense.

"Why don't you wait until after church?" she said.

"You'll understand in a moment." He glanced down at Rudolph and shook his head. "I had another reason for coming to Zürich, and I want you to keep an open mind." The only thing sillier than a man his size in a Rudolph sweater was a kneeling man his size in a Rudolph sweater. Nevertheless, he knelt. He could tell by the confused furrow of her brows she didn't get it. "From the second day I met you—" Why did he say that? "I can't get you out of my thoughts." This wasn't going well. "What I'm failing miserably at saying is—I love you, and I would be so honored if you would agree to be my wife, to have and to hold and to laugh with—" Now he was on a roll. "And be a daddy to that baby—to love her as my own." The ring. He fished through both pockets and couldn't find the box at first. When he did, he thrust it at her, almost afraid to look into her eyes.

When he deigned to look up, he couldn't believe it. The confusion on her face was gone, replaced by a beatific smile. Now he was the confused one. "I have a plan B option if you don't like my first one."

She wrapped her arms around his neck, drawing him so quickly toward her that he almost toppled over on her. "Just for fun, what is option B?"

"Do I have to? I was kind of hoping you'd agree to option A." He righted himself and waggled the box in his hand.

She leaned forward and took it from him. "Humor me."

Sitting on the floor facing her, he took the ring, set it next to her on the couch, and took her hands. "Option A is real. I love you, and I want to marry you. Option B is for your protection if you decline my other offer. We can announce that we're married for the sole purpose of preventing your other guy from pursuing you or the baby. I'm not one who approves of lying even to criminals, but if it will keep you safe, it will be worth it." He peered at the ring and guided it with his finger toward her.

Of all things, she started laughing. Great. The sweater, the feeble proposal—and now laughter. His ego couldn't take much more pummeling.

She picked up the box and opened it, and her hand went to her chest. The ring had been his mother's—one of the few things he'd kept of hers. He hoped it fit.

Her voice came out breathy. "It's lovely. I've never seen one like it." She held it up to the light. "Is it an antique?"

"It belonged to my mother, and it might have been passed down from my grandmother. I'm not sure." Now she was toying with him. "Well? You're trying my patience, girl."

She enveloped him in a hug. "Yes."

"To what?"

"Yes, to option A. When you gave that man your coat, you sealed the deal. It would be my honor to marry you for real."

He pulled her toward him and kissed her with all the adoration and gratitude and passion and relief he'd been holding back for months now. With that single word, she'd made him whole, something he hadn't felt since his parents died. Tears were coming uninvited, but there was no keeping them back. God had answered His prayers in the most comical way. This sweater would become part of their story, told and retold.

As their foreheads touched, their eyes melding together, he could do nothing more than whisper at such a moment. "I can't believe you said yes. At the very least, I thought I'd have to put up a good fight for even the second option." Her eyes sparkled before she answered. He'd have to remember that—to read her eyes before her words.

"To be honest, you've been on my mind a lot over the last few weeks. Whenever I saw something magnificent like the perfect view of Old Town, I'd think to myself, I wish Brody were here to see this with me. In the past months, you've been the only bright star. So, if this is love, then I'm in it."

He'd have to be happy with ifs. She was a complicated woman, and there were secrets she didn't even know about in her past. He pulled her onto his lap, her arms remaining around his neck. "When is the big day?"

"Good question. I'm not one for big events, since I've been to enough of them in the last year with Gregory. Guess I should tell him, although I haven't heard from him since I told him I was attacked. Too heavy of a trophy on his arm, I suspect. But I don't want to think about that right now. Not on Christmas." She gasped. "Do you realize we became engaged on Christmas Eve? How cool is that?"

"The best gift ever for me." He held up his palm. "Not that you have to give me one. But let's not just get married at city hall or whatever they call it here. I only plan on getting married once, so let's do something special, something intimate and memorable. Any ideas?"

Just then the door opened, and Gran entered before they could detach from one another. The sight of them on the couch stopped her in her tracks. "Oh, well. Merry Christmas, and—" She spun around to leave.

"Gran, look what I got for Christmas." She held up her hand, then maneuvered her legs from his lap, and they both pushed to their feet. "He asked me to marry him, and I said yes. Can you believe it?"

Gran's hands went to her lips. "I couldn't be happier for you two." In a few steps, she'd enveloped her granddaughter in a swift hug, then included him in it. "Lord, you answered my prayer. What perfect timing." She backed up and placed her hand on Brody's cheek. "I could tell the moment I saw you yesterday, you were the one. That was a God thing. When is the big day?"

They both laughed. "We were just having that conversation when you walked in," Brody said. "My plane leaves on the 26th, so I can either cancel the flight and we can get married right away, or I can come back for it." He peered at his new fiancée. "You're the bride, so you choose, but I'd rather it be sooner than later."

Maddie linked arms with him. "I want something small, but Brody wants something big and memorable."

"I didn't say big; I said I wanted something that we would never forget, and neither of us knows anyone in Zürich—" A sideways glance at her showed teasing eyes. "Okay, I get it."

Gran peered at the clock. "Isn't it time for you two to go to church? It's going to start in twenty—" She glanced at his sweater and burst out laughing. "The last time I saw that was at a white-elephant Christmas party at work. I'm glad somebody's getting some use out of it."

"Gran, do you have a parka Brody could wear? He doesn't have a coat."

A pert smile grew on her face. "I have just the thing." She hustled out of the room.

Brody cast a sideways glance at Maddie. "The chestnut doesn't fall too far from the tree. You're getting a lot of joy out of this."

She nodded. "Christmas cheer and all."

Gran returned carrying a green letter jacket. "This was my husband's from his college days. It's a little dated and perhaps a bit dusty, but at least it's green." She helped him into it, yanking the sleeves over his sweatshirt. "There, now you two scoot."

The evening night had cooled, and Brody blew out breaths just to see the cloud of white, an uncommon sight in Florida. At the bottom of the hill, the Christmas lights filled him with a delight that he hadn't felt in a long time. In the distance, Christmas carols broke the silence, adding to the clip of their footsteps on the cobblestones. For the first time in months, he felt an uncommon peace, although everything was moving at a rapid pace. Brody still couldn't believe she'd agreed to marry him. What changed her mind so quickly? Had the geographical distance made their hearts grow warm instead of cold? Analyzing it wouldn't make it clearer. He ventured a question. "Any thoughts on when and where for the wedding?"

She sighed and closed her eyes, holding tight to the jacket he wore. "I like your idea of planning something special and intimate rather than a quicky ceremony at City Hall. And by the way—" She pointed at an old regal building that seemed to project over the river. "That is City Hall." They walked another block before she spoke again. "You've probably already guessed it, but I've never wanted anyone to know about my private life."

"Why does that bother you so much?"

"It started when I was a teenager—something to do with my father, and after my parents divorced and married others, I just felt like a fifth wheel—third wheel. After I graduated, I couldn't wait to leave home and move out of state. I figured my work would speak for itself, and the fewer people who knew about me the better. But when the viewers see my baby bump, they'll draw the wrong conclusions about you and me, so part of me wants to get married right away here, so no one will know. The longer we wait, the rounder I'll be." She peered up at him. "You sure you want to marry someone as screwed-up as me?"

He kissed her temple. "You bet, with all your perfectionist tendencies. Are you sure you want to marry an un-perfectionist like me? I mean, you can still back out. It's a big decision."

The lights of the church they approached radiated sparkles in her eyes. "Yes, I do, but I don't want to put you in danger. Who knows how Beverly Jordan's brother will react? He may see you as an obstacle to his plans for me and come after you."

"While you were talking to your grandmother, I did a quick search of your babysitter's whereabouts and found her name listed in an obituary—" When she gasped, he lifted a mittened hand. "No, not hers; it was her mother who died. Beverly lives in Tampa. I have her number. Maybe you could call her tomorrow on Christmas and ask about her family."

Her brow furrowed. "I wouldn't want to ruin her day."

"You wouldn't, and it's normal to ask about one's family."

They entered the church, which was full of parishioners who were listening to the pastor's sermon in German. They stood in the back, and since Brody didn't understand a word, his eyes took in the majestic architecture and stained-glass windows.

"Isn't it beautiful? The church was built as an abbey in

the 1200s. Marc Chagall designed those windows," Maddie whispered.

Brody blew out a quiet breath. "There's nothing like this in America. We're like… teenagers compared to this." A group of boys dressed in choir garb sang "Silent Night," their angelic voices echoing off the tall, stone walls. Then the ushers lit the candles of those sitting closest to the aisles, as he and Maddie listened to the German version of "O Holy Night." Even though he didn't understand the words, the music stirred him as if heaven met earth in this cathedral. He would never forget this.

As they walked home, her gloved hand in his mittened one, her question brought him back to earth.

"Wouldn't Beverly wonder how I got her phone number?"

Good question. "Tell her about the picture on the garage wall. Ask her if she has any idea why that would be on your wall. It's the truth."

The next day, a blanket of white sparkled in the morning sunshine as he joined Maddie and her grandmother for the day. Since nothing was open, he'd bought a box of Läderach pralines at the hotel to thank her grandmother for inviting him to share the day, and he made sure to wear his jacket and return the sweater and varsity jacket they'd lent him.

After opening gifts, they enjoyed a late breakfast of eggs, bacon, and rösti which reminded him of hashed browns, and they discussed wedding plans.

Gran sipped her tea, then put her cup down. "I'm pretty sure I can reserve one of the rooms on the fourth floor of the Opern. It's absolutely beautiful and the perfect place for a small wedding. You've been in there before, Maddie. It's the room where we performed the African jazz concert."

Her eyes lit up. "It is a lovely room. Yes. That would be perfect." She turned to him. "What do you think about early January? Could you come back so soon?"

"For my wedding? I'm sure they'd let me take some

time off for that." This was really happening. He just hoped she wouldn't regret her decision. For the rest of the day, they talked about what would happen after they were married. He'd just assumed she'd want to move back.

She tilted her head when he asked her why she want to stay in Switzerland. "Don't you see? I don't want anyone to know I'm pregnant. I can't. People will talk and wonder. I couldn't bear that."

He rubbed the five o'clock shadow on his cheek, beating the clock by three hours. "We'll be married, but as much as I'd like to stay here, I have to go back to work. I'm hoping that once Beverly's brother knows you're married, it should be enough to keep him away from you, if we haven't caught him by then. When are you going to call Beverly?"

She massaged her temples. "We'll wait another hour or so, since we're six hours ahead. I'll call my parents. They're not going to believe it."

"Why would you say that?"

"Highly driven daughters don't date much. I'm sure they gave up on me a long time ago after I refused to join Junior League." She massaged her temples.

He lifted a shoulder. "Whatever that is. If your head is hurting, lie down on my lap and close your eyes. I'll wake you up when it's time to call." He could tell she wasn't used to such a thing, so he gently pulled her toward him. "I won't bite. Too full." She complied, and soon they were both sleeping. Her phone went off jarring them awake.

Maddie bolted up and grabbed it. "Hi, Mom. Merry Christmas... Yes, I'm in Zürich with Gran." She told them about the weather and Gran's concert. "I have some news," she finally said. "Guess what? You're going to be a mother-in-law... What? No, I don't even know who he is. Ew. Brody Messner—" She looked at him with wide eyes and shrugged. "He's a police officer. Yes, he's kind of a nice man. You'll like him. I promise. He's here right now, but he has to go back to Orlando in two days. We'll probably get married next month. Gran's trying to work out something at the opera. No, no…It's going to be very, very small…Yes, you can come. Would you tell Dad for me? He can come too…Yeah, I know. Do you want to talk to Gran? ... Oh, okay, I'll give her your warm wishes. Love you." She blew out a breath. "One down. What's Beverly's number?"

He pulled out his phone and scrolled through the notes. "How did your mother take the news?" From what he'd heard about her parents, he didn't expect a joyful response.

"Mom sounded surprised more than anything, but she's never been one to show her emotions. 'Proper ladies always leave one guessing,' she told me more than once."

After he gave her the number, she dialed it, but stopped before pressing the green button. "Can we pray? I'm nervous. I just feel like such a fake calling her on Christmas of all days to find out about her brother."

He took her hand. "If you found her number any other way, would you call her on Christmas?"

"Absolutely, I'd love to talk to her. I just don't want to be duplicitous."

He peered up. "Big word."

She shrugged. "Could we pray that God gives me the words? If I were investigating a rapist, an abuser, I wouldn't have any problem getting the answers any way I could, but Beverly's part of my family—at least she was for a while until she left."

"Let's pray then." His words stumbled to begin with, then came together. It was as if God gave him the words to pray back to Him.

When he said Amen, she opened her eyes and whispered, "Thanks. I'll put the phone on speaker." She pressed the call button, counting each ring. Maybe she could just leave a voicemail with her name and phone number, so Beverly could call her back after Christmas on a more appropriate day.

"Hello?" a young girl's voice said. "Who's this?"

"Lindsey, hand me my phone. Merry Christmas."

Maddie cleared her throat. "Beverly? This is Maddie Caldecott. Do you remember me?"

A momentary pause ensued. "Little Maddie? Of course, I remember you. How are you? I can't believe it. How did you find—Just a minute." Maddie heard her whispering to the child to go play with her new puppy. "I can't believe it's you."

"I hope I didn't call at a bad time. If I did, I can call you back when it's more convenient for you."

"No, we just finished with dinner. My brother Bruce is here with his family. Are you calling from New Jersey?"

"No, I'm at Gr—" He tapped her arm and shook his head. If the brother was there, he didn't need to know that Maddie was calling. Brody hadn't anticipated this, but he should have. It was Christmas after all. "Where are you, Beverly? Your area code is from Florida. Is that where you live?"

"Yes, I'm in Tampa. My cousin, Colleen, lives here, so I moved down to help her with her kids while she works."

"I live in Orlando, an hour away. Maybe we could get together for lunch. How have you been? I've thought of you so often. Everything changed so fast after my parents split up and you left. I hope you've had a good life."

She didn't answer right away. "God is good. I have a daughter, April. What about you?" They talked about how they came to live in Florida, and Maddie told her she was engaged to a police officer.

Beverly congratulated her. "My brother, Chandler, do you remember him? He was about your age. After he finished his time with the marines, he applied to become a police officer, but it didn't work out."

Maddie's eyes were saucers. "Is that the brother who's at your place?"

"My older brother, Bruce, is here with his wife and two kids. They live in Ohio but came down for Christmas. It's great seeing them. I haven't been up north in I don't know how long. Enough about me. When are you getting married?"

"Soon," Maddie said, "but we haven't finalized a date yet. Your brother Chandler, what's he doing now? Where does he live?"

"Oh, that boy. He's a bit of a drifter. We go months without talking, but he calls from time to time. He's a good kid, but he has his problems. Last I heard he was into body building."

She'd asked enough. "It's good to hear your voice, Beverly. How about when I return from Gran's, I'll call you, and we can have lunch. I'd love to hear what you've been doing all these years. I should let you get back to your family. Merry Christmas."

After she disconnected, she sat there staring at the phone, then looked up. "Sorry. I didn't think it right to pummel her with questions. Not today."

"We have our guy. Let's put it behind us for now and enjoy the rest of the day. It's already starting to get dark outside. Do you want to take a walk? We can take the dog. My flight's at noon tomorrow, so I'll have to head to the airport at nine. Let's redeem the time we have left."

"Good idea. I'm going a little stir-crazy being inside all day." After she leashed the dog, they donned their jackets and headed out, the fresh breeze invigorating him immediately. "My head's already clearing. How about we stroll down to one of the markets for an afternoon snack?"

"Sounds good." For the first time, the seed of excitement began to sprout. She'd said yes. It still seemed too good to be true, and he prayed that she wouldn't have second thoughts. They were going to be married, and he'd have the chance to be the kind of father to their child that his own father had been. No longer would he go through each day feeling he was only half a person. He'd do everything in his power to make up for the pain she'd endured with her broken family.

They reached the bottom of the hill to the melodies of Christmas carols and lights just starting to twinkle in the descending darkness. Throngs of browsers chattered at various booths, some pulling sleds with children bedecked in snowsuits. It brought back memories of his own childhood in the Midwest where his dad and mom took him tobogganing or ice skating after Mom's big dinner.

"If we have a boy, you wouldn't be averse to me teaching him to play hockey, would you?" He cast a playful eye at her. "Or ringette if it's a girl?"

She exaggerated rolling her eyes. "Firstly, I've never heard of ringette, but it sounds painful, and do you really want our child to lose her front teeth to an errant puck? And secondly, we live in Florida."

"There are plenty of indoor skating rinks in Orlando, and now that I know about this awesome city, we just have to come back."

She linked her arm around his. "I'm happier than I've been in a long time, and I'm delighted you like Zürich."

"I like Zürich, and your grandmother, and I kind of like you too." He kissed her temple.

They stopped at a sausage stand and bought a sandwich and hot chocolate, then found a bench overlooking the lake. She pointed at the last remains of the sunset, the lights creating a halo of light, a phenomenon he'd never witnessed before.

"Knowing Gran, she'll invite all her church friends and orchestra members to the wedding. Are you okay sharing our day with strangers?"

He wrapped his arm around her shoulder and pulled her close. "I'm marrying you, Maddie Caldecott, so I won't even be aware of anyone else on that day. She can invite the whole city if she wants."

She nodded. "I feel the same way. My parents will come, and Tessa. I'll ask her to be my maid of honor. What about you? Do you have a best man in mind?"

He hadn't thought about that. "Don't know. Buddy, my best friend from high school. He's a pilot based in Chicago. I haven't talked to him in a while, but I'll give him a call when I return. He's a bit of a joker, but you'll like him."

She finished her sandwich, gathered their wrappers, and threw them in the receptacle next to their bench. "Rory's getting a little restless. Ready to head back up the hill?"

"Sure." It saddened him their time together was drawing to a close. "It's going to be hard to leave you here. Please don't change your mind."

"How could I do that? You're sacrificing everything for me."

"Don't say that. If all this hadn't happened, I still would've begged you to marry me. It doesn't matter. I love you, and I hope you'll grow to love me."

Maddie reached up and drew him into a tender embrace. "Don't you know I don't give my heart to just anyone? You, Brody Messner, have my love. It's not just gratitude. You've been on my mind ever since I met you. I just didn't understand it all because of everything that was happening."

They returned up the hill without speaking, but what else was there to say? Anything else would ruin the sacred bond they'd formed. When they turned left at her grandmother's lane, the dog pulled on the leash to reach the door.

"Guess she's had enough of a walk," Maddie said, giggling. When they reached the condo, an envelope leaned against the door. "A Christmas card from one of Gran's neighbors. They usually put them in the mailbox. Here, take the leash." She reached down to pick it up, then pushed the door open. "Gran, we're back. You have a—" Turning to him, her eyes grew wide.

"It's not written to Gran; it has my name on it."

He took it, recognizing the scrawl of her first name. A pall of dread covered him. His eyes met hers. "May I open it?"

Her lips taut, she nodded.

Still standing in the foyer, he tore open the envelope and scanned it, then he closed his eyes and dropped his head. "I can't leave now."

"What does it say?"

"It's from Absalom. Merry Christmas, my love. You've given me the gift of all gifts. A child borne of our love. Now the world will know that you're mine and mine alone. Don't run away from me again. Remember, a kiss from a rose."

Chapter Seventeen

"A secret is powerful when it is empty."
~ Umberto Eco, The Paris Review (2008)

Maddie wilted to her knees, her hands trembling. "He wins. I can't get away from him."

Brody knelt and pulled her toward him. "I'm here. He has to go through me first." He framed her face in his hands. "I'll cancel my flight, and we'll get married as soon as we can. Tomorrow or the next day."

She shook her head, her eyes evading his. "I can't put my grandmother in danger. As long as I'm here, she's—"

He tipped her chin up. "We'll move up our plans, and if you want, we'll fly back to Orlando together. Then he has no reason to stay in Zürich."

Her eyebrows furrowed. "I don't understand why getting married right away will keep him away. This is a guy who broke into my house and raped me, and now he knows I'm pregnant. How is our marriage going to stop him, especially since I'm carrying his baby?"

He caught a teardrop with his thumb. The intimate act made her feel safe for a moment. She wasn't alone in this, but the moment passed too quickly.

"We know who the guy is. He'll follow us when we return to the States, but you won't be alone. If the police or the FBI can't stop the guy when he enters the US, I'll be with you to keep you safe until we catch him."

"Oh, you're back." Gran entered carrying a dishrag. "I bet the markets were busy. Did you get something to eat?" Her smile disappeared when she saw their faces. "What happened? What's that in your hand?"

How much to tell her? Gran didn't deserve this, but she needed to know. "It's another note from the guy." She took the envelope from Brody and held it up, then dropped it on the floor. "No stamp. He's here."

Brody picked it up. "We know who he is, and that will help us catch him. He's probably in the system. Maddie, you might as well tell her what we've learned."

She pushed to her feet, took off her coat, and hung it on the coatrack. "Let's go into the living room and sit. Then we can make a new plan." She picked up Rory and stroked her head, finding comfort in the familiar scent of her fur. Once Gran had settled into her chair and Brody sat next to Maddie on the couch, resting his arm around her shoulder, she began. "Gran, do you remember Beverly Jordan, the girl who moved in with us and lived in our basement for a time?"

"Of course. She lived with you after your mom went back to work. She wasn't much older than you."

"Yeah, four or five years. She had a younger brother named Chandler, who we think is the one doing this." She cast a sideways glance at Brody, who nodded for her to continue. "Remember I told you about the picture from my photo album that he hung in my garage? In the picture were four people—Mom, Dad, me—I was about fourteen at that time—and Beverly. We all looked unhappy to be there. Dad's face was stormy, Mom and I looked like we'd been through a battle and lost, and Beverly was looking away. Yesterday it came back to me. Something he'd said when he attacked me. He said, 'This is for my sister.'"

Gran took off her glasses and leaned forward. "I don't know what that means. Unless he's exacting some kind of sick revenge for something you did to Beverly, but that can't be. It must be something your dad did. Do you think he did something to her?"

Maddie squeezed her eyes shut and lowered her head, forcing the images out of her mind.

Brody tightened his grip around her shoulder. "We don't know. It could be something Chandler Jordan imagined. The guy's nuts."

Gran sat back, turning her head from side to side. "That must have been about the time your mom started divorce proceedings. If I remember right, Beverly left several months later. Your mother didn't want my advice, so I kept my distance. That's why I moved here."

Maddie huffed. "You see what I mean, Gran? Bad blood leads to bad things. The man who ruined Beverly—his blood's in me. The guy who attacked me—his blood's in my child. What does that mean for her future?"

Gran's head tilted to the side. "You don't give God credit."

She frowned. "What does that mean?"

"That means you and your baby are God's children first and foremost. Physical blood means nothing unless you give it power."

Maddie turned that over in her mind for a long moment until it sank in. "I think I understand. Thanks, Gran. In many ways, you've become my family, especially after my parents started new ones. I was just baggage to them—extraneous."

Brody whispered in her ear, "Another big word, but you're not extraneous."

She had to laugh, which disrupted her self-pity.

Brody spoke up. "Since we don't want to bring trouble to you, we want to be married right away and then return to the States. Is there any way we can speed up things? We'll forgo the ceremony for now and just get married at the city hall here—" He must have heard her sigh because he took her hand. "We'll come back and do it right when this is all over."

Gran leaned forward. "Maddie, is this what you want?"

It caught her off guard. Was any of this what she wanted? Even though everything seemed to be out of control, she wanted to marry Brody. "Yes, this is what I want."

Gran stood, always one to take charge. "Let's get to work. Tomorrow, if the city hall is open, go there and apply for a marriage license. It might take a few days, but we'll get it done. I'll call the pastor and see if he can officiate. We can do it here. He'll probably want to meet with you beforehand. I can be a witness, and I'm sure one of my colleagues can stand in as the other witness."

The flurry of activities fell into place over the next few days. By paying extra, they procured a marriage license in twenty-four hours after getting blood tests. After they met with Gran's pastor in his office, he agreed to do the ceremony in a small chapel in the church.

There wasn't time to ponder if she was making a hasty decision. One thing niggled at her, but she didn't have time to figure out what it was. In the last light of the day before their wedding appointment—that's what it felt like—as Rory pulled on the leash to reach the nearest tree, Maddie half-listened to Brody describe his conversation with his boss at the police department.

"They did a search for the Chandler Jordan, but he's not in the system. He may have changed his ID. I sent them a picture of the Christmas card he left at the door. They're going to make it a top priority to find him, although they don't have much to go on."

So much for ease of mind. "One thing bothers me. How did the guy know I was pregnant? It's not as if I'm showing yet, although my jeans are a bit tight. The only one I told was my boss, so how could the guy know? I can't even say his name. It's too hard."

"Call your boss. You also told Gregory and your mother."

"I didn't tell Gregory I was…with child, just that I'd been assaulted. My mother knows the whole truth, and she probably told my dad."

"Not too many sources then. See? That narrows down our perp's location. All we have to do is call your boss and your parents and find out who they told and when they told them." He took out his phone. "Let's go sit over on that bench. I want to try something."

She followed, gently tugging Rory, who wanted to stay where she was. "You have me intrigued. What's up?"

After pulling up something on his phone, Brody shifted to face her, his lips tight. "One of the clues we haven't followed up on is that line that's repeated in each note—'A Kiss from a Rose.' It's that song I played for you. Could I play it for you now? Maybe it will evoke some memory that will help us advance this case. Please?" He laced his fingers.

Why now? She sighed. "Okay, go for it if it will help." He tapped play, and the familiar madrigal of strings began, followed by a man's haunting but beautiful voice in a minor key. Immediately, she fought the strong urge to turn it off as the image of a public restroom stirred her senses. "I can't— I can't listen. A bathroom. Turn it off. Now!"

"No, we need more information."

She squeezed her eyes tight to erase the image. A dirty bathroom. A guy laughing. She tried to get away, but he grabbed her arm, forcing her to stay. She grappled to free herself. He was talking, saying things she didn't want to hear. Two girls carrying books walked in, gasped, then giggled when they saw the guy. Maddie used the moment to jerk free and run for the door. The song mercifully ended, and Brody clicked off the phone with his thumb.

"Let's go." She was already halfway through the park before he caught up.

"I'm no shrink, but I think we made some progress," he said.

Her teeth hurt from clenching them. "What progress?"

she enunciated.

"What happened in that bathroom. It could be the key to what you're blocking."

She described the images the song evoked. Quick strides took them to Gran's house.

"That's why you left school that day. Chandler Jordan accosted you in the school bathroom. He told you something you didn't want to hear. That's why you didn't want to go back to school."

Maddie opened the door and hurried in. "If the girls hadn't entered, who knows what would have happened? But Why does that song trigger such bad memories?"

"I'm just a cop. The fact that he ends each note with its title means he knows something we don't. Yet. We're getting closer." He tried to pull her into a hug, but Maddie backed up.

Her lips pursed of their own accord. "Not now. Everything is moving too fast. I don't like being out of control, and I certainly don't like being a specimen to be observed and poked at." She could feel her neck warm, which meant she was losing control again. "Let's just get through the next couple days with some kind of dignity." Brody looked like he'd been slapped. She pressed a hand against his cheek. "I didn't mean that the way it sounded. I'm overwhelmed is all." She kept her hand on his cheek until he offered a weak smile.

"Sorry I pushed so hard. I'll leave now. Lock the door behind me. I'll see you tomorrow at the chapel." He kissed her on the cheek, then went to the door but turned. "You can still back out."

~

He hoped she wouldn't back out. Brody nodded toward the hotel manager as he waited for the elevator to take him to the third floor. He would have liked to bring Maddie here for their first night together as man and wife. It wasn't the Ritz, but it had a certain historic charm. Unlike the service of some hotels, the staff at the Adler cleaned the room daily and left little treats like a box of small jars of Swiss jams or a ribboned plastic bag of homemade cookies.

He trudged to his room, opened the door, and flipped on the light. Even with the light on, the room looked as dark as his spirits. On this eve of his wedding, he should be euphoric—that was a Maddie-sized word. She was rubbing off on him. Instead of moping, he did what he always did when examining a crime scene. He tucked his heart away so he could investigate without becoming involved in it, so it wouldn't tear his heart open. Maddie was pulling away; he'd pushed too hard.

The same message he'd told her when they'd first met— take the next step—came to mind. That's all he could do tonight—prepare for his wedding day tomorrow afternoon and be ready if she didn't show. The first step—turn on the shower to steam the wrinkles out of the long-sleeved shirt and pair of decent pants he'd stuffed in his bags. His eyes landed on the Rudolph sweater. He should wear it. Maddie would laugh—if she showed up.

As he rifled through the bag for clean socks, his hand landed on his gun. If there was ever a time to have it at the ready, it was tomorrow. It was good that he'd been prepared. His captain had read him the riot act when Brody had asked him to approve the permit for international travel, but since he was officially working on Maddie's case, the captain begrudgingly relented. That meant he had to check two bags, one with the weapon, the other with the ammo, and he'd alerted TSA that he'd packed a weapon. He dug the ammo out of his sneaker and loaded up.

An hour later, he did a quick survey of the hotel room and bathroom, stuffing everything he could in his suitcase. Maddie's level of tidiness was miles higher than his. He threw away the half-drunk bottle of Coke and packed the pile of papers in his carry-on. With hours left before he'd likely fall asleep, he thought about heading down to the restaurant, but his appetite had vanished—a first. Either tomorrow would be the best day of his life or the worst.

He picked up his well-worn Bible, not having the energy to open it. Advice and encouragement were in there somewhere, but he didn't have room in his grieving heart for any words of comfort. He tossed it on the bed and sat with a plunk, turned on the television, and searched for an English station, finally landing on a sports channel. What he needed was a good hockey fight to erase the drearies, but he'd have to settle for soccer.

During a commercial, his eyes wandered to the Bible and remained there. Absalom came to mind. He leafed through II Samuel with an eye for any hint as to why Chandler had chosen that name. His finger stopped at a chapter with Absalom in the title, and Brody began to read. The third son of David and Maacah, Absalom had been a handsome dude. Brody rubbed a hand over the scruffy stubble on his face. What was the benefit of good looks if it didn't go any deeper? Absalom had a daughter named Tamar. Wait, what? A daughter? Wasn't Tamar his sister? This was part of the story he'd forgotten. He read on.

The oldest son of David, Amnon, became infatuated—"lustuated" was more like it—and he raped Tamar, his half-sister. Then Amnon hated her after he'd taken her virginity, and she moved to Absalom's house to live out her life as damaged goods. King David, Tamar's own father, didn't do a thing to punish Amnon, so no wonder Absalom sought to avenge his sister, but he bided his time. Brody could find nothing wrong with Absalom so far. As a cop, he sought justice every day, which on the face of it might look like revenge—an eye for an eye.

Brody skimmed through the six chapters on Absalom's life and death then sat back staring at the ceiling chandelier. The thing he'd overlooked about Absalom was the long period of time that he'd stewed and schemed to exact revenge. It took two years before he put his plan into play, inviting all his brothers to a party, then killing Amnon. For six years he conspired to kill his father, King David. Why would Chandler Jordan go after Maddie instead of going after her father if he indeed was the one who had assaulted Chandler's sister? Maybe because he had a thing for Maddie and was more like Amnon than Absalom, or maybe he was a mixture of both.

The Sins of the Father. The words pelted him. His mind reeled with the answer. Jordan's need for revenge for what had happened to his sister, Beverly, had smoldered over the years into obsession, and like Amnon, he loved Maddie, and he hated her. At the same time, Chandler Jordan saw himself as the great avenger of his sister's honor. It didn't matter that Brody and Maddie were marrying; Chandler Jordan wouldn't quit until he killed her.

Chapter Eighteen

"Do nothing secretly; for Time sees and hears all things,
and discloses all."
~ Sophocles

Jolted from sleep, Brody sprang off the bed at the earnest rapping at the door. "Coming." It was dark in the room except for the cricket game on television. What time was it? He ran fingers through his unruly hair and padded to the door, peering through the peephole. Maddie? He swung open the door. "What's going on?" Even in the dark, he could tell she was upset.

"Can I come in?"

He pulled her into the room. "What's wrong?"

She held onto his arms. "I couldn't go to bed knowing things weren't right between us, especially on this night of all nights. Could you just…hold me?"

"Gladly." They remained by the door for a long time. Then he pulled away and tipped up her chin. "Now what's really going on?"

Her eyes were swollen and red. "Let's never go to bed angry. Ever. My parents went to bed mad all the time. I don't want to be like them."

"'Don't let the sun go down on your wrath.' I totally agree." He led her by the hand into his room, sat in the only chair, and pulled her onto his lap. "Is the wedding still on?"

She merely nodded, her lower lip trembling.

He leaned back. Relief flooded him, and his eyes closed.

"Thank you, God." He opened them. "I thought you had changed your mind."

"Of course not." Maddie framed his face with her palms. "I did a lot of thinking after you left. What's always been important to me is independence—making it on my own. But I don't want to do life alone. I want to do life with you."

Yes! He mentally fist-pumped the air. "We could make a great team—you and I."

"That we could," she said, brushing at her eye.

"While I'm glad you're here, you took a big risk walking all this way in the dark, especially with—."

Her bottom lip quivered. "I thought about calling you, but I wanted to see you face-to-face. I needed to." She looked around the room. "This is charming."

He shrugged. "It's not a honeymoon suite, but if you want, we can stay here tomorrow night. They even take dogs."

"Rory is staying with Gran. I want you all to myself." She kissed him on the nose, on each cheek, then her lips met his with a force that surprised him. Then she pulled away. "This is what I want every night."

"Me too," he whispered, then sat up. "It's going to be a big day tomorrow, so as much as I'd like you to stay, I'm going to stand up, grab my keys, and walk you home."

On the way back to her grandmother's house, Brody told Maddie of his 'aha moment' when he'd read the whole story of the historical Absalom. "As we both know, Chandler Jordan is one crazy dude. He sees himself as the righteous avenger of his sister, just as Absalom avenged the rape of his sister, Tamar, by his half-brother. My guess? Jordan let his high-school infatuation with you turn into bitterness when you didn't return his feelings."

She stuffed her hands in her pockets. "I didn't even know who he was."

"There lies the problem, but you did nothing wrong. As I said, he's one crazy dude."

They'd reached the middle of the walk up to her grandmother's place when Maddie stopped in her tracks. "Brody, I've come to a decision. I am so sick of playing the victim, and you know what? It's going to end right now." She took out her phone. "I have to do this before I chicken out. Right here. Right in this place. Take my phone, please."

He took her phone. "What in the world are you talking about?"

Removing the hood of her ski jacket, Maddie ran a gloved hand through her hair. "I'm probably a mess, but if I don't do this right now, I never will." She pointed at the nearest streetlight at the entrance to Lindenhof Park. "There. What I want you to do is record me."

He felt his face scrunch up. "You want me to record your last night as a single person?"

She unzipped her jacket. "Not exactly. I want you to record me as a pregnant person. I'm tired of keeping secrets and hiding, so I'm going to tell the truth. Ready?"

This girl was a bag of surprises, but there was something going on in her he'd never seen before. The lift of her chin, the determined look in her eyes, her erect posture—all revealed the assertive woman who did what it took to get a story. The woman who'd risen to the top of her career all on her own. He still didn't understand, but it was enough that she did. "I'm ready." He tried to keep his hand steady as he pressed record.

"Good evening, Orlando. This is Maddie Caldecott coming to you from Zürich, Switzerland. Tomorrow is my wedding day. Yes, I'm marrying the man I love, Detective Brody Messner, also from Orlando, but that's not why I'm in Zürich. I'm here because I was raped. Yes, I was raped by an intruder who broke into my house and assaulted me. I won't divulge his name. That's up to the police department. So, why am I sharing this information with you? I've always been painfully disinclined to share my private life with anyone other than a handful of people; therefore, my immediate reaction to discovering I was pregnant was to run away and hide." She stopped, her eyes blinking, then that chin of hers lifted again. "I have decided after much thought and prayer to keep the baby and bring her up to the best of my ability. It's not her fault. I also don't want her to live a life of feeling inferior because of the violent way she was conceived. I want the rapist to know he has no power over me, and I will not hide anymore." She nodded for him to stop recording.

Now his lips were quivering. "I have never been so proud of anyone as I am right now."

She ran over to him. "Did I look okay? Did I say the right things?"

"Girl, you done good." He held up the first frame that showed her standing next to the ancient stone fence that lined Lindenhof park, her chin resolute, her countenance bathed by the glow of the streetlamp above her.

Maddie took the phone from him. "Ew. I don't care what it looks like. I'm sending this to my station manager before I lose my nerve." She typed a few words then read them aloud. "Use this any way you wish. If you want to add it to the lineup, I'm okay with that." Squeezing her eyes shut, she pressed the send button.

He wrapped her in a tight hug. "What you just did, overcoming your greatest fear…did you see what you just did?"

Maddie blew out a breath. "I can't take it back. That's why I had to do it before tomorrow afternoon. I don't want you to be married to a victim. He can't hurt me by threatening to tell everyone I'm pregnant because I just did. Now I need to get some sleep." She waved him away, then turned to leave. He followed his warrior princess and watched from the corner until she was safely in the house, although she most certainly could take care of herself.

Chapter Nineteen

"Camouflage is a game we all like to play, but our secrets
are as surely revealed by what we want to seem to be as by
what we want to conceal."
~ Russell Lynes

Gran had done a beautiful job of decorating the small
chapel, although there wouldn't be anyone to enjoy it except
the three of them, a violinist who worked with Gran, Mel
Steinman, and Gran's pastor. Lovely vines draped the
lectern, flanked by vases of moonlight white roses on each
side with another arrangement of red roses in front. Maddie
flinched at the first sight of them, but it didn't matter now.
Soft stringed music played in the background. Elegant but
understated, the room was perfect.

The crème-colored off-shoulder sheath she'd borrowed
from Gran was a bit longer than she usually wore, but it was
roomy in all the right places. Gran was conferring with the
pastor, so Maddie took the opportunity for one last trip to the
restroom to check her hair, which she wore in an updo.
Brody hadn't arrived yet. Had he changed his mind? Of
course not. That fleeting thought was just a product of
wedding jitters.

A small lounge with a loveseat opened to a second room
with two stalls and a small oval mirror over a single sink. A
vase of plastic flowers sat next to a stack of paper towels.
One stall was locked. Maddie looked underneath. No feet, so
she entered the other one for one last chance to relieve

herself, something that occurred more and more each day. It seemed the first thing she looked for was the nearest restroom whenever she entered a new establishment.

After she flushed the toilet, she pulled up the shoulder straps and smoothed the dress, so it hung neatly around her middle section. A check of her makeup and hair and a fresh application of lipstick and she'd be on her way to await Brody.

As Maddie took her lipstick from the small clutch she'd brought, the chords of a familiar song played from somewhere in the room. Her breath hitched. Wedding jitters must be working overtime in her. She rushed toward the door, but a man stepped out from behind the wall of the anteroom blocking her path.

"Hi, Princess. Surprise!"

She gasped at the tall man she worked with. "Chip? You came to my wedding? I can't believe—What are you—Oh." She backed up three steps, almost tripping over her heeled sandals as he walked toward her with confident, slow steps. The pieces fell into place. Chip, the security guard at work—Chandler.

A smile that didn't reach his eyes played across his lips. "You never recognized me, did you? I didn't expect you to. Your mind was always so full of rooting out evil even in high school you didn't see what was right around you. Like your own father." He took another step toward her. "I sat right next to you for a whole semester. You saw me every day at the studio. Not the best investigative reporter, are you?"

Her eyes darted around the room for a means of escape. She would die in this bathroom, and her child would die with her. Her mind jolted with the memories of another restroom, larger, more stalls and sinks, utilitarian and old. "It was you in that bathroom way back then, but you were different."

He chuckled. "Yeah, a pock-marked face and as thin as a rail. I had to wear my brother's hand-me-downs. Since then, I've added a bit of muscle. My sister—you remember

Bev—got to wear your mother's handoffs."

Maddie backed up to the sink, her eyes searching for anything that could be used as a weapon. Paper towels and lipstick. Her only friend was time and the fact that Gran or Brody would come looking for her. "You told me something that day in high school, but whatever you said I've blocked. Tell me now."

His eyes held a hatred she hadn't seen before. "You're so naïve. Exposing people just to get ratings when you shielded what your father did to my sister. He molested her. Because of your father, my sister lost her future. She wanted to go to nursing school, but she lost her way after what your father did. Now you gotta pay up."

"I don't remember anything. You must have told me in that bathroom, but it was so terrible I blocked it. But you're wrong about one thing. I would have never condoned or hidden what my father did if I'd known."

He took another step toward her. "Pathetic. Did you see the picture I hung of you and your happy, rich family? Did you notice my sister's face? No, you're not much of an investigative reporter. 'An eye for an eye.' You must pay for the sins of your father."

She jumped back as he lunged at her, the heel of her sandal breaking from her weight. She stumbled back and fell to the hard floor. Her head swam, and dizziness assailed her. Dread filled her as her eyes squeezed shut.

A loud thump, and a weight fell on her legs. Not again. Not in here. Her eyes squinted open to see the top of Chip's head on her knees. She tried to scurry back, then something stopped her. Her eyes travelled up. Brody. A gun. The room spun. Black spots coalesced into a sheet of darkness…

"Maddie, are you okay? Maddie, wake up." Gran's voice.

She felt herself being propped up into a sitting position. "What happened?"

"You fainted." Her gran was blotting her forehead with a cold cloth. "Everything's all right now."

Memories came back in quick succession, but they didn't make sense. The bathroom. Chip. The fall. Brody with a gun. "How long have I been out?"

"Twenty minutes? Your fiancé is waiting for the police to take your stalker away. They should be here any second. Then you two can get married. Do you feel up to it?"

She squinted to see where she was. Still in the bathroom. "I'm dizzy is all. Did he shoot Chip? How did Brody even know I was in here?"

"I don't know all the details yet, but I do know he hit the guy on the back of the head with his gun and knocked him out."

Maddie pushed to her stockinged feet, plodded to the sink, and splashed water on her face. Her hair was a mess, Gran's dress was a mass of wrinkles, and her eyes looked like a raccoon's. Despite the vertigo, the events were starting to coalesce. Chandler was Chip, and Brody had fulfilled his promise to stop him. No longer would she have to look over her shoulder. No longer would she have to check the rear-view mirror.

Gran joined her, peering at her with a smug look on her face. "You'll never forget your wedding day. Nor will I."

She laughed. "No, I don't suppose I will. Did you know Chip worked with me every day at the station? He was one of our security guards. That's how he knew so much about me." Her eyes widened. "He probably stole my keys and made a copy. That's how he entered the house. So much makes sense now, but so much doesn't." She turned to face her grandmother. "You know what he said? He said I was clueless about what was going on around me, and he mentioned Dad. You were right about him and Beverly. Guess it will all come out in the courtroom." She grabbed a paper towel, moistened it, and wiped the counter. Her worst fear—exposure of all her deep, blocked secrets would all come out. Untimely tears threatened to sprout. Not now.

Gran pressed her cheek against hers. "It will be all right, sweetie. Don't you see this whole thing has little to do with you? This is between your father, Beverly, and her brother. Through no fault of your own, Beverly's brother took it out on you."

She shook her head. "I am so sick of hiding secrets, Gran. Did you know last night I made a recording for my boss telling the world I was pregnant due to being raped? It was my feeble attempt to stop hiding. I thought that was enough. Now there will be a whole lot of publicity—"

Gran huffed. "Enough pouting. Put everything behind you. There's a man out there who came all the way to Switzerland to rescue you. Don't let Chip win by ruining your wedding day." She planted a kiss on her cheek. "Will you do that for me and Brody?"

"You're right." Carpe diem. Fortunately, she'd brought sensible flats, which she changed into. Maddie didn't want to spend another minute in this room, but she sent Gran out first to see if the coast was clear. The last person she wanted to see was Chandler Jordan. Maddie cringed at the way 'Chip' always sat on the corner of her desk, making snide remarks about Gregory, his face so close to hers that she could smell the mint gum in his mouth. Enough thoughts about Chip. He would not seize her day.

"Coast is clear. The police took him away. Brody's waiting. My pastor is looking at his watch."

"I'm coming." With one more look in the mirror and a glance at the floor where she'd fallen, she left, never intending to return. Everyone was sitting in the first pew when Maddie entered the chapel. They rose in unison as she approached. "I'm so sorry."

Brody stood and joined her. "Don't you be sorry," he whispered. "Let's do this."

She had so many questions, but she'd save them for later. "Right now, before something else happens."

It was a simple ceremony that lasted ten minutes at the most, but it was enough. Flanked by the two people who meant the most to her, she said, "I do" with such vigor that the pastor burst out laughing.

Gran treated them to dinner at Bernadette's, a beautiful restaurant next to the opera that overlooked Lake Zürich. Brody and she feasted on veal in a cream sauce and rösti, while her more-adventurous grandmother and Mel Steinman chose wild boar. She offered them each a bite, which they declined. "Don't worry about calling your parents with the news. I'll call them. How many days until you fly back?"

Brody put down his fork. "We leave the day after tomorrow at noon." He looked almost sad. Maddie understood why.

She took a sip of her water. "You're okay with watching Rory until I pick her up early in the morning before our flight?"

"Of course, sweetheart. You two deserve some worry-free fun."

As Maddie savored a teaspoon of a berry-marscapone truffle, she finally addressed the subject they'd tacitly agreed not to mention. "Brody, how did you know?"

"Know what?" He stirred his coffee so quickly it spilled onto the white tablecloth. "What's with these child-sized spoons?" He took a sip.

"How did you know that he'd come in the bathroom?"

Brody trailed his finger around the rim of the demitasse. "Because of the song. He was going to recreate the scene from your high school, and I figured the last thing he wanted was for you to get married. Ergo, the chapel bathroom. I hid in one of the stalls and recorded the whole thing."

Maddie rested her head against his shoulder, wishing that someone in the restaurant would tap their teacup so she could kiss him. "Thank you for being so smart."

He grimaced. "Smart but out of shape. My leg cramped

from crouching on the toilet seat. I didn't want Jordan to know he had company."

"And when you heard me fall, you came charging out with your gun ready to save me?"

"More like hobbling out, but I figured hitting him was better than shooting him, especially at church. He'll probably sue me for aggravated assault."

She wrapped her arms around him. "I love you, cramps and all."

Chapter Twenty

"Do not tell secrets to those whose faith and silence you
have not already tested."
~ Queen Elizabeth I

It felt good and bad to be back in Orlando. The weather
was better, although Maddie much preferred walking the
streets and hills of Zürich to driving on Orlando's busy
highways and toll roads. Since she'd sublet her condo until
June, she and her new husband moved into his condo.

Brody had promised to hire a cleaning crew when he
opened the door, insisting on carrying her over the threshold.
She'd laughed and said it wasn't necessary to hire cleaners,
but it didn't take long for her to have second thoughts. To
his credit, Brody hadn't known he'd be bringing home a
bride a mere week after his surprise trip to Zürich.

Maddie would do what she always did when a daunting
task confronted her. She'd break the job into small pieces,
starting at one corner of the bathroom and working her away
around the walls of the whole place. Her first task, though,
was to do what was necessary—she'd call Beverly Jordan. It
was unlikely she'd know about her brother's arrest, and
Maddie wasn't looking forward to telling her, but she needed
the answers that only Beverly could fill in.

Beverly seemed less surprised to hear from Maddie than
she had on Christmas day, and she agreed to meet her for
lunch at a restaurant in a small town near Tampa. As Maddie
reached the restaurant's door, she almost missed the demure,

slight woman who stood by the entrance, but when Beverly stepped forward to greet Maddie, the smile on her face was undeniable.

"Beverly." She enveloped her in a long hug, Maddie's eyes misting at this woman whom she hadn't seen since everything went wrong in her family. She seemed so much smaller than she remembered her. "You're so petite."

"And you're so tall." Beverly chuckled. They entered the restaurant and were seated right away in a booth by the window, their server leaving after taking their drink orders.

Maddie handed her one of the menus. "By the time I was eighteen, I'd shot up to five foot seven. Both my parents were tall, but you know that."

Beverly nodded and stared out the window.

"Tell me everything about your life since you left," Maddie said after the server delivered their iced teas.

The server had to come back three times to take their food orders. Maddie learned that Beverly had moved to Ohio to live with her cousin. A few months later, Beverly had married a man from her church, and they'd had two children—a girl named April, and then a boy who had died of SIDS.

"The marriage didn't last long after Scotty died. Franky started drinking—his way of mourning. He was a good man but had a weakness for the drink. Then it got him in its hold, and he left never to be seen again." She sighed and shook her head. "April was three at the time. I packed up our tiny apartment's furniture in a U-Haul, and we moved to Tampa. My cousin had moved there, so we could stay with her until I could make my own way."

Their salads came. "Did you get a divorce?" Maddie winced. "I'm sorry. That was rude."

Beverly trailed her fork around the edge of the salad plate. "It's okay. As far as I know, I'm still married. I loved him. Who knows? Maybe he'll return someday to see his daughter."

Maddie took a bite of a tomato, her appetite waning. "What do you do for a living?"

"I work at a rehab center as a healthcare worker. Mostly elderly patients, but I love them." A smile spread across her face. "And what about you? Did you become a lawyer like your parents?"

She took a sip of her tea. "Not a chance. I'm a news reporter, but I took a leave of absence because—" Was now the time? How could she burden Beverly with the truth? Maybe she should just keep it to herself, but Beverly needed to know the truth. Maddie said a quick prayer for wise, kind words, then pushed her dish away and leaned forward on her elbows. "I have to tell you something that's not going to be easy to take, and I'm sorry, but you'll find out sooner or later, so I'd rather it come from me."

Beverly's eyes opened wide, then she put down her own fork. "What is it?"

God, give me the words. "I wasn't the brightest teenager. Your brother, Chandler, was in my English class, and I didn't even know it because I was so busy with the newspaper and video news, I didn't notice anyone. Another thing I didn't notice was that your younger brother works as a security guard at my news station. He goes by Chip. I didn't recognize him. In fact, I'm pretty sure I never met him, although I met your older brother."

She frowned. "You're kidding. That's a coincidence he'd end up working at the same place you did. Chandler had a thing for you in school. I was already in Ohio by that time, but he talked about you when he called. How smart and pretty you were, but that you didn't give him a second glance."

"As I said, I was pretty much clueless. Still am, I guess." She took in a fortifying breath. "There's more. A few months ago, I received a note and some flowers at work. The note was signed by Absalom." She shrugged when Beverly's eyebrows rose. "Then there were more notes, and then this

Absalom broke into my house and hung a picture that was taken in my backyard. You, my parents, and I were in the picture."

Beverly straightened in her seat, and her lips pursed. Maddie could tell she was trying to make sense of it all. "What does this have to do with my brother Chandler?"

Blowing out a breath, Maddie told her the rest of the story, ending with what happened at the wedding chapel. "They arrested Chandler. I'm so sorry." She reached for Beverly's trembling hand. "I have more to tell you, but first, would you explain why you moved out of our house so quickly?" When Beverly lowered her head and didn't answer, she tried again. "Did my father do something to you? Is that why you left?"

Beverly's eyes slowly rose to meet hers, two distinct lines forming between her brows. "What do you mean—do something to me?"

Maddie searched for the right words. "Did my father…make you feel uncomfortable?... Do I have to spell it out?"

Her eyes widened. "No, of course not. He wasn't the warmest person in the world, but he never did anything to me." She looked away again.

Maddie grabbed her hand. "It's okay. Please tell me the truth."

A long moment passed as Beverly circled her straw around the rim of the glass. "I put all this behind me. Why do you want me to dredge it all up now?"

"It's important. You'll understand in a minute."

Beverly's eyes closed, and her head tilted to the side as if the weight of it was too heavy to lift. "The truth is I was envious of your life—of your clothes, your bedroom, your dance lessons, your vacations. I wanted your father to be my father. I'd never met a successful man before, and he was so smart, so well-dressed, so everything. Of course, I kept my feelings to myself, but I knew they were wrong, so I had to get out of there quick. That's why I left—it was stupid envy."

Maddie let out a whoosh. "I didn't see that coming at all." When she noticed Beverly's crestfallen face, she held up a palm. "That's good. You did the right thing. I'm just glad to know my father didn't hurt you."

Beverly swiped at a tear from her face. "It was wrong of me. I'm so sorry."

Maddie patted her hand. "It's okay. You were a teenager. I'm just glad my worst fears about my dad are wrong. But why would Chandler do all that to me if my father hadn't hurt you?"

Beverly hesitated, stared out of the window, then shook her head. "He was a troubled kid. Smart as a whip too, but he was ashamed of our family. We didn't have a lot of money. My mother did the best she could raising our brood after my dad died." Then she met Maddie's eyes. "We lived three blocks from the big houses like yours. It didn't help that I'd come home describing some special meal your maid, Virginia, prepared or some beautiful gown your mother wore to a ball. Is Virginia still with you?"

"No, she left after you did."

"My brother probably heard me go on and on about how great your father was—about his fancy car and the places he flew off to. Envy of the rich neighborhood just blocks from our shack must have led him to draw the wrong conclusion when I moved away without any explanation. I couldn't tell my family I was leaving because of my own envy. It's all my fault."

Maddie patted her hand. "No, neither you nor I can blame ourselves for what Chandler thought or did."

Beverly covered her meal with a napkin. "I don't know where he went wrong, where he became so bitter and twisted, but if he tried to attack you in the school bathroom, it probably started after I left your place and moved to Ohio. I am so, so sorry."

Maddie sat back. "You did nothing wrong. In fact, you did what was best for you at that time, but know that despite our 'riches,' our house was not a happy place. Beverly, let's not take the blame for what Chandler did. This little baby inside me did nothing wrong, and I will not raise her to be ashamed." Maddie gasped. "Do you realize you're the aunt of this baby?"

Immediately, Beverly's face turned red, and she started coughing. When Maddie offered her a napkin, she waved it away. "I'll be all right…just give me a moment."

The absurdity of the situation dawned on Maddie, and her giggles turned to laughter, then the hiccups started. "I'm sorry. It's just so…convoluted. It's not like I want to throw a family reunion or anything yet, but—" She lowered her eyes when the server and the people at the adjoining table turned to stare at her.

Beverly had recovered, and she shrugged. "Families are messy, aren't they? If you'd let me, I'd be honored to be an aunty to your little one. I could babysit just like I took care of you, 'cept I won't let her cop an attitude like you did."

They held each other's hands after the server removed the dishes and left the bill. "This one's on me," Maddie said. "I was a spoiled brat. You were the one who taught me about God—you and my grandmother. I remember a Bible story you told me about Joseph after he met his brothers who'd kidnapped him and left him for dead. He said to them, 'you meant evil against me; but God meant it for good.' Chandler meant evil against me, but look what God brought out of it? You and I have reconnected, and my baby is going to have an aunt who doesn't live too far away. In a way, if it wasn't for Chandler, I never would have met my husband. That's something to celebrate."

Chapter Twenty-one

"If you want to keep a secret, you must also hide it from yourself."

~ George Orwell, 1984

"You already cleaned out that closet."

Maddie spun around as best she could from her place on the floor. "What are you doing home from work?"

Brody stood just outside the closet door, his arms crossed, an imperious look on his face. "Just came home to tell you something." He stepped around her to get into the closet. "Where'd you put my hockey jerseys? You didn't—"

"Of course, I didn't throw them away. I'm just trying to create more room. We're going to need space for the baby's things. If you go out in the garage, you'll see the new clothes rod I installed yesterday. All your gear's out there."

He huffed something about mildew, side-stepped her, and plopped on the bed. "Now I'm being relegated to the garage."

She pushed to her feet, a bit more cumbersome now that she was halfway through gestation. "You are not being relegated anywhere. It's just we need space for a bassinet and a dresser. I can't exactly take the baby out in the garage to change her diaper."

He patted the place on the bed next to him, which she gladly took. "Here's the thing…no, two things. The condo is spotless. There's nothing more to clean. Do you hear what I'm saying?"

She nodded. "It's just I don't know what to do with myself. All this waiting—" This waiting to go back to work, waiting for the baby to come, waiting for the interns to move out of her condo, but she and Brody hadn't really discussed what they were going to do with the condo or what she was going to do about work.

His smile grew into a laugh. "You're as tightly wound as a spinning top. Why don't you call your boss and ask if you can go back to work? This place isn't used to so much Lysol."

Maddie's hand went to her growing belly. "Really? But I don't have any clothes that fit."

He raised a shoulder. "Go buy some then. If you don't want to buy maternity clothes, just buy a bigger size. Nobody's going to notice anyway." He kissed her temple. "You look simply mahvelous."

She shifted to face him. "Would you be okay with me going back to work? At least I don't have to worry about Chip being there, right?" Brody's smile faded. "What's wrong?"

"That's what I came home to tell you. Charges against Chandler Jordan have been dropped. Switzerland doesn't have any anti-stalking laws, so the court indicted him on assault charges, and he pled down to time served and a fine." His lips tightened.

"Oh," she breathed out, "So Chip will come back here, if he hasn't already." Suddenly, the room looked darker.

He put an arm around her and kissed her temple. "I know this isn't good news, but hear me out. If we brought charges of the rape, breaking and entering, and stalking against him, we could either arrest him here, or we could extradite him to the US to stand trial here—"

Maddie slapped the bedspread between them. "I really wish I hadn't been so worried about what other people thought. What a mess my pride has caused." She could feel her shoulders deflate. No, she wouldn't become a victim again. Maddie straightened and turned to face her husband. "Is it too late to bring charges against him?"

He shook his head. "Would you be up to all the public scrutiny? It won't be easy."

She stared at her stockinged feet. Reindeer socks. "It's the battle of pride versus justice. Chip needs to be put away. He needs to pay for his crime. Plus, I wouldn't have to worry about him stalking me or this child anymore." She patted his hand. "Have at it, Detective Brody."

"Are you sure?" When she nodded, he wrapped her in a sideways hug. "I've never been prouder of you."

It occurred to her in the following week that what had motivated her to clean and scrub every inch of Brody's condo was the fear of the unknown. What would happen when Chip came back? Would he stalk her? Would he abduct the baby? Although Maddie still didn't have answers, at least she could do something to stop him, even if it just meant getting a restraining order against him. That's what a victim needed—power. With that realization, she put the cleaning rags away.

After buying a few maternity tops and a dress, she called her boss, Morgan. It had been a while since she'd applied for a job. Would he be able to fit her into the schedule as a reporter? At this point, she'd take anything he offered. It was better to keep her mind busy than to sit at home and think. She pressed the call button.

"Maddie? How are you?"

Morgan's voice immediately calmed her. "I'm great. Fat and sassy, as they say. How are you?"

"I'm a happy man now that I'm talking to you. Where are you? Did you get married? Are you back in town?"

"I'm back in Orlando, an old married lady with a baby

on the way." She chuckled. "I guess that isn't the best way to ask if you have a job for me, is it?"

"Why don't you come in tomorrow morning at eleven, and we'll have a chat about it."

"I'll be there." That was easy. More than two months had passed since she'd last stepped foot in the studio. That wouldn't be so easy.

Nerves woke her up earlier than normal. The telephone call with Morgan was so short she didn't have the chance to ask if he'd received the video she'd sent him from Zürich. He hadn't mentioned it. Did that mean it was too controversial to broadcast on the news? Now that she thought about it, if she were a viewer watching it, it would make her feel a bit uncomfortable. Maybe she shouldn't have sent it to him. Now it would be awkward to meet with Morgan. She wouldn't bring up the video unless he did. With that decision made, she drove to the studio.

Not wanting to draw attention to her midsection, she wore a sweater over the dress she'd chosen. Hopefully, the interview would be short, and she'd be in and out. Morgan wasn't one for long conversations, but she did have to warn him about Chip. What excuse had he given Morgan for leaving so quickly? Had he taken a leave of absence or just quit?

The secret of her pregnancy had kept her from saying goodbye to the staff at work. They had to have wondered why she'd left without a word. Chagrin weighed heavy on her shoulders as she got out of the car and headed into the studio. She nodded at Dana, who was on the phone when she passed by. Dana's mouth and eyes opened wide, and she waved. One down, many to go.

Morgan's office door was slightly ajar. She knocked twice.

"C'mon in," came from the other side.

With a deep swallow, she entered, as nervous as she'd been for her first job interview after graduating. Morgan hadn't changed a bit, while everything had changed for her.

When he glanced up from his computer screen, he stood, rounded the desk, and enveloped her in a warm hug. "You look magnificent. One-hundred-percent better than the last time I saw you." He backed up to survey her. "Motherhood agrees with you."

Any fear she'd felt disappeared with his hug. He motioned to the chair by his desk and brought another one over to sit next to her. Morgan held her hand as the whole story spewed out.

He blew out a long breath. "That explains a lot. Chip left shortly after you did. Said there was a death in his family, and he didn't know how long he'd be gone. So, Chip was the guy who—"

"Yes. Apparently, he sat next to me in my English class in high school, but I didn't recognize him when he worked here. Guess that was a long time ago."

Morgan took her hands. "Well, I'm just glad you're back with us, safe and sound." He pointed toward her stomach. "Are you feeling well?"

"Very. I've cleaned every nook and cranny of Brody's condo, so I'd like to come back to work, if you have anything available."

"I didn't think you could stay away for six months, so I had the other anchors cover for you. They'll be very happy to have you back as the weekend anchor. Will you be able to handle it for the next few months?"

"Yes, work will really help."

"Good. Can you start next Saturday?" He rose from his chair and led her to the door.

"I sure can. Can't wait." It felt good to be back. She said goodbye at the door, and turned to leave when he took her by the elbow.

"Before you leave, there are a few people who want to say hello to you."

What? Morgan rarely left his office. Everyone at the

studio figured he had a secret door to the parking lot. Instead of turning left, which led to the reception area, he turned right, which led to the common area and her old office.

The moment they rounded the corner, Morgan raised his voice, "Everyone, look who's come back to us."

In unison, the dozen or so editors and reporters stood to their feet and started clapping and singing, "For She's a Jolly Good Fellow." Even Blythe, Page, and the two anchors appeared and joined in.

Maddie glanced sideways at her boss. "What does all this mean?"

He shrugged. "I guess they miss you."

When the singing stopped, Sydney joined Maddie and wrapped an arm around her waist. "We just want you to know how proud we are for what you did. Recording that video for the viewers to see took a whole lot of courage. We all know how much privacy matters, so we salute you for your bravery. For refusing to be a victim. For caring enough about others to sacrifice your privacy. Congratulations, Maddie. Not only that, but also the ratings skyrocketed when we showed it. They've never been higher. Welcome back, Maddie."

Maddie didn't see any of this coming. Ratings? At any other time, ratings would have been important, but not now. What mattered was the support of these people, and Brody and Gran. She and her child would need their support in the months to come.

The End

Author's Notes

(Spoiler Alert: Don't read until you've finished reading the book)

It's often said that authors write about what they know; therefore, there's a little bit of the author in their books. That certainly is true of my novels, and it's true of this one. No, I wasn't a news anchor; nor did I have a stalker who broke into my house. Like Maddie, I'm a list maker and don't allow myself to go to bed until I've checked off every item, but unlike Maddie, I'm certainly not averse to a misplaced book or an untidy desk. However, I do have my OCD proclivities. I confess that I rarely cook the same thing twice because I derive great pleasure from working my way through a cookbook, always making the next page's recipe.

What parts of the book are based on my own experiences? Well, I have a shih tzu, I live in the Orlando area, and I loved spending time with my grandmother when she was alive. As was true of Maddie's early life, my pre-teen years were shaken to the core when my parents divorced. At the same time, my father, a physician, was regularly in the local news for his connection to Roe v. Wade.

Like Maddie's father, mine was named father-of-the-year in the local paper, and I remember the photographer coming to our house to take a picture of our happy family out on our lawn, when in reality, it was anything but. Also, we had a babysitter who lived in our basement who was only a few years older than I was, but that's where the similarities with Maddie's babysitter ended. Lydia (not her real name) was wonderful, as was the rest of her family, including her brothers.

However, the most disturbing thing that was true of my life as was true of Maddie's life was the fact that we both blocked some experience that happened when we were in high school. I still can't remember what happened, but my mother told me I came home from school one Friday and said I would never go back to that school again. Within three days, I was living with my grandparents in a different town.

The idea for this book came to me decades ago, years before I wrote my first book. I remember sitting in a hotel room in Phoenix, where my husband was attending a conference, and for the very first time, I spewed out a synopsis of a story on my laptop. All I knew was at some time in the future, I had to write this book. About the same time, Francine Rivers wrote a similar novel, The Atonement Child, so I put the book idea on the back burner for twenty-seven years.

So, the time has come to write it. With regard to the "attack," I used the experiences of two close friends, both of whom were raped—one, like Maddie, hovered over herself as an observer when it actually happened. The other friend drove around all day long after the attack, not wanting to go home. Another close person in my life was raped as a teenager, and it changed the trajectory of her life until it ended. That's why I wrote this book.

I certainly hope I don't come across as preachy, but my purpose for this book is to reflect in a small way what a victim has to go through in the days and weeks and months to follow. Harder still is to tell the story in a romantic suspense novel, where action and pace take precedence.

I love research, so for this novel, we traveled to Zürich, stayed at the Adler Hotel, where Brody stayed, attended the opera, walked the streets of Old Town, enjoyed fondue and

Rösti at the restaurants —it's a hard life. I interviewed a former news anchor with the ABC affiliate in Orlando, Jamie Holmes. I thank him for his information about daily work in a newsroom. I also thank my son Joshua for filming selected places in Zürich and his help with designing the book cover. I thank beta-readers Julie Russell and Brenda Cox for their great suggestions and corrections, Diane Tatum for her excellent editing of the book, and Cynthia Hickey, my publisher who does such good work.

I have a feeling that you, the reader, will either love this book or hate it. The subject area is uncomfortable for those readers who read for escape, and I do that. The issue of abortion divides people, but hopefully you'll keep an open mind and understand this is one person's journey and choice.

You notice that I left some details hanging for a possible sequel if there's interest. Let me know your thoughts in an honest review on Amazon or contact me via a message on Facebook or my website. www.stewartwriting.com

Sherri Stewart

Sherri Stewart is a woman of faith who loves all things foreign and different—whether it's food, culture, or language. A former French teacher, principal, attorney, and flight attendant, her passion is traveling to the settings of her books, sampling the food, and visiting the sites. She savored boterkoeken in Amsterdam for A Song for Her Enemies, and crème brûlée in Paris for its sequel, What Hides beyond the Walls, and raclette in Zürich for Secrets Dark and Deep. A widow, Sherri lives in the Orlando area with her dog, Lily, and her son, Joshua, who always has to fix her computer. As an author, editor, blogger, speaker, and Bible teacher, she hopes her books will entertain and challenge readers to live large and connect with their Savior. Join, chat, and share with her on social media. Newsletter Facebook Twitter Instagram Website